CYBER GENIUS

THE FAMILY GENIUS MYSTERIES

Patricia Rice

Other Book View Café books by Patricia Rice

Mysteries:

EVIL GENIUS, *A Family Genius Mystery*, Book 1
UNDERCOVER GENIUS, *A Family Genius Mystery*, Book 2

Historical Romance:

WICKED WYCKERLY, *The Rebellious Sons*, Book 1
DEVILISH MONTAGUE, *The Rebellious Sons*, Book 2
NOTORIOUS ATHERTON, *The Rebellious Sons*, Book 3
FORMIDABLE LORD QUENTIN, *The Rebellious Sons*, Book 4
THE MARQUESS, *Regency Nobles*, Volume 1
ENGLISH HEIRESS, *Regency Nobles*, Volume 2
IRISH DUCHESS, *Regency Nobles*, Volume 3

Paranormal Romance:

TROUBLE WITH AIR AND MAGIC, *The California Malcolms*
THE RISK OF LOVE AND MAGIC, *The California Malcolms*

CYBER GENIUS

Patricia Rice

Published by Rice Enterprises, Dana Point, CA, an affiliate of Book View Café Publishing Cooperative

Formatter: Vonda N. McIntyre

Cover design: Mandala

Book View Café Publishing Cooperative

P.O. Box 1624, Cedar Crest, NM 87008-1624

http://bookviewcafe.com

ISBN 978-1-61138-5403 ebook

ISBN 978-1-61138-5403 print

One

"THE WORLD IS FULL OF EVIL, and tablet computers are the right hand of the devil," I warned, tugging EG—Elizabeth Georgiana, although Evil Genius works too—away from her admiration of a businessman's expensive new device. "That one tracks your every move. You might as well have a drone hovering over your head 24/7 and hand out tickets to your bank account."

I checked the airport's overhead signs for international arrivals and picked up speed.

"Why is it bad if some stupid computer company tracks my every move? They really want to know I'm in my bedroom? And I don't have a bank account." Fascinated by new tech, EG dragged her feet and strained to see what the guy was doing. "If we had a system like that, you could use it to find me."

I continued marching past Dulles baggage claim belts, forcing her to run to keep up. "You want me to *hack* MacroWare to find out where you are?" I asked, performing my best incredulous act. "You think I have nothing better to do?"

With no apparent doubt that I could perform miracles, EG shrugged. "You'd have more fun doing that than sending Mallard to look for me. Intercoms are so last century."

"My baby sister, the techno-fashionista." I knuckled EG's shiny black hair and changed the subject. "Are you going to tell me what inspired Tudor's visit? Last I heard, he was neck deep in some hacker competition and couldn't even meet Magda for dinner when she was in London."

Magda being the so-called Hungarian princess who had birthed me and my roving half-siblings—incredibly long story. As an example, I'm Anastasia Devlin, my next sibling is Nicholas Maximillian. The first names continue in royal arrogance while the last names change with regularity. Our mother's non-maternal instincts would be the reason Tudor was heading this direction and not toward her.

I wanted to resent that Tudor had sent his itinerary to a nine-year-old and not to me, but unfortunately, I understood. I'd spent years raising my younger half-siblings, then years hiding from them.

Sixteen-year-old boys were easily confused. My little brother hadn't known if I'd tell him to jump off a cliff or go home where he belonged—not that he actually had a home other than his boarding school.

Despite his apparent confusion over my frame of mind, Tudor had bought the tickets and sent EG the info, knowing she couldn't do anything to stop him. This rated pretty high on my Here-Comes-Trouble meter.

EG shrugged again. "It was the middle of the night when he emailed me, and I doubt he had your phone number."

Which made me even less comfortable—Tudor was our family communication central. If he wanted to find my number, he'd find it. After all, he'd been the one to locate my hiding place in Atlanta so EG could visit me earlier this year. *Best scenario*—he just didn't want to talk to me.

I feared otherwise. As a family, we had essentially been raised to flee in the middle of the night at a moment's notice. I feared teenage rebellion was too easy an excuse for Tudor's arrival, and buying last minute plane tickets was a dead give-away. Tudor was on the run.

My phone pinged a text warning. Popping it from the case on my belt, I scanned Nick's message and frowned. "Nick says watch CNN. Think Patra is on the news?"

Our twenty-something half-sister had only recently moved to Atlanta to take a job with the news station. She was a pretty—emphasis on pretty—junior reporter. A live shot seemed unlikely, unless she was in trouble—far more probable given our history.

"We've got time," EG said eagerly, turning around to find a newsstand with a television.

I'm not tall and willowy like Patra, but I'm well-muscled. I can move fast. I passed EG, and she had to run to catch up. To see what had set off usually blasé Nick, I pushed my way through the crowd that had formed around a TV monitor.

"In breaking news, Stephen Stiles and four of MacroWare's top executives have been hospitalized for possible food poisoning after Wednesday's conference dinner at a D.C. hotel. MacroWare stock prices are plummeting over worries that their new product release will be delayed."

I frowned in puzzlement. Patra wasn't making the announcement. Now that we had a nest egg to invest, I'd socked it away in mutual funds, not something as risky as MacroWare stock. I saw no relevance to our lives in a bunch of over-fed execs pigging out and getting sick. I'd had enough food poisoning experience in my childhood to know the routine. They'd spend the day on the Royal Flush and someone on the catering staff would get fired.

I was about to turn away when I caught the file clip of VIP attendees at the conference. I froze and gawked. Sauntering into the hotel wearing a sleek Italian business suit, with his hand in one pocket and looking bored was our landlord, Amadeus Graham, hermit extraordinaire.

What on earth? He couldn't condescend to leave his lair to have dinner with us, but he could go to a public dinner with Stephen Stiles and a thousand computer geeks? This was not normal by any standard I'd learned these last months of living under Graham's roof.

Amadeus Graham had been an ascending political god until his life had gone up in flames with the Pentagon in 9/11. His wife had died in the tragedy, and he'd emerged from the fire badly scarred in more ways than one. He'd deliberately incinerated his political career with his crusade against powerful figures influencing the president—a crusade he carried on to this day. Only these days he did it in private. He'd painstakingly eradicated his existence, leaving the world to think him dead.

Appearing in public was very much not Graham's style.

The clip was only a brief glimpse. I couldn't be *positive* that was our reclusive spy in the attic striding into the hotel as if he owned it.

Who was I kidding? We'd sucked each other's faces not that long ago. He was the irritant under my skin, the hindrance to my every desire—except lust—and just watching him cross a TV screen escalated my pulse rate.

Graham was so bloody reclusive that I was pretty certain Nick had never seen him. In his position at the Brit embassy, our budding diplomat brother must have heard more pertinent news than I was seeing. I texted him a YEAH, AND?

What had been so important that Graham had come out of hiding to attend a geek business conference—one in which five extremely important, powerful men had turned up sick? Men who could affect stock markets!

My gut roiled as if I'd been the one poisoned. No good came of surprises like this. Or maybe it was just worry over Tudor that had my paranoia alarm turned on.

The news moved on to the latest yawn about a crooked mortgage lender and a banking oversight committee's ruling. I tugged EG back toward baggage claim.

"We must have missed the story Nick wanted us to see," EG said in disappointment. "If I had one of those new tablets, I could go online and look for it."

"Only if I had a hot spot on my phone or you pay for the public Wi-Fi here and risk getting all your game coins sucked out." Her school tablet didn't have accessible Wi-Fi, thank all the heavens. But I lied about the hot spot. I didn't go anywhere without access to the internet—which was why I knew how dangerous it would be in EG's hands. "And I'm not footing the bill for either. I keep telling you, MacroHell wants to drain every penny from your pocket."

Which had me wondering if they really were run by demons, and the heavens had struck the demons down with diarrhea. Justice would be served.

"We have money now," EG protested, still on the tablet kick. "You shouldn't be so tight-fisted."

Old argument, not one I intended to indulge as I hunted the dumping ground for international passengers coming through customs. The area was a colorful bazaar swarming with chatter, luggage, and exotic garb. Given my world-traveling youth, I felt right at home.

"There he is," EG shouted excitedly.

She was running before I could see what she'd seen. I took time to scan faces. I almost missed Tudor's.

He'd probably been ten the last time I'd seen him. Once I quit the thankless job of being my mother's doormat, I'd left my half-siblings in the care of their parents, where they should have been all along. Tudor's Aussie father had deposited Tudor in an English boarding school for tech geniuses—a far better choice than my care.

Judging by the grungy clothes on the tall, lanky kid EG was chattering to, geniuses didn't do laundry. His wavy red hair hadn't been cut in months, so I didn't have high expectations for his personal hygiene either. But behind the teenage lankiness I could still see the red-headed tot who used to cling to my leg and beg for ice cream.

We didn't hug. Our family is high on drama, pretty stingy on affection. He'd be shocked if I hugged him, especially since he was now almost six inches taller than me, drat him—but I took the handle of his heavy wheeled bag. He almost managed a smile in return, revealing his crooked tooth. No braces for our boy, no sir. Even his thick black-rimmed glasses looked nerd-stylish.

Our glamorous mother had left her mark on all of us, sometimes in very strange ways. In Tudor's case, rebellion against perfection was the result.

"Sleep any?" I asked as I steered him toward public transportation.

"Not much," he admitted wearily. "Look Ana, I'm sorry for popping in on you like this—"

I cut him off as I aimed for the bus counter. "Let's save it until we're home. It's good to see you. Next time, call, okay?" That was as close to affection as I dared offer.

He seemed to melt with relief and actually nodded. "Okay." That lasted until he saw my goal. "Bus, Ana? We've got all this money now and you still take the bus?"

"I'm not wasting what could be college funds on taxis. The bus will take us to the Metro," I explained. "We live way downtown."

He didn't say anything, and he didn't move. The grinding in my stomach grew sharper. He examined the transportation signs, then wordlessly took back his suitcase, and made a beeline for the taxi stand.

He opened the door of a cab at the end of the line.

My fear kicked up another notch. Magda had taught us how to avoid long taxi lines if we were on the run. EG and I looked at each other, then dashed after him.

While the taxi stand supervisor jogged over and tried to explain that we were breaking the rules, we performed Magda's Dumb and Dumber act. Gabbling in French, Russian, and Tagalog, we played ignorant tourist and piled into the back seat. Ultimately, both driver and authority surrendered and let us go on our way.

I gave the address for the train station. Tudor didn't blink. Well trained in caution by our international journalist/spy mother, we didn't speak until the cab let us out at the Metro.

I marched them both down the platform on the line that would take us to our neighborhood and EG to her school.

She gave me the evil eye. "I shouldn't have to go to school today," she informed me.

"I'll give you a note excusing you for being late. Tudor needs sleep. You'll be home by the time he's awake."

"How long will this take?" Tudor asked anxiously, scanning arrival screens as if he had a clue as to which line was which.

"No longer than a taxi, given the traffic in the area at this hour, and anonymity is safer. I take back what I said earlier about waiting until we're home. At what point do we get explanations?" I demanded as the train rolled in.

"I just don't want anyone to know where I am for a few days," he said with a frightening air of exhaustion. "It's been a bad week."

I knew he would be safe when I got him home. This was the reason I put up with Graham—he owned the fortress I needed to protect my perpetually troublesome family. That fortress had belonged to our grandfather and ought to be *ours*. I had calculated that, several lawsuits down the line, it would be ours—one of the many reasons I was hanging on to the few dollars we'd salvaged from the theft of the inheritance our grandfather had left us. But until we proved our ownership, we lived on Graham's grace and my ability to act as his virtual assistant.

"The house belongs to all of us," I said reassuringly. "You're welcome to stay as long as you need, or until your father drags you home."

"He won't even know I'm gone," Tudor admitted, as the train pulled out of the station.

"Give her a week and Magda will," I warned. Our mother might not be maternal, but she always knew where all her chicks were and hunted them down if they weren't where they should be.

Tudor closed his eyes and just leaned against the pole that was holding him up.

Yeah, I kind of had that reaction to our exhausting parent too. I'm thirty, so I know Magda is pushing fifty, but she has the stamina of a toddler and the morals of a meth dealer. I'd rather not have her bearing down on us any time soon.

WE GOT OFF AT THE STATION near EG's private school and left her, still protesting, at the school office where she could be escorted back to her classroom.

"The house is half an hour away by foot," I told Tudor. "Walk or Metro?"

He was wearing a heavy backpack and had reclaimed his rolling suitcase. He gazed at the busy traffic and the less-crowded sidewalk. "You're going to interrogate me anyway. It might as well be where no one else can hear."

"That bad, is it?" I took back the rolling bag.

"Worse," he admitted. "I may have just sabotaged the entire internet."

Ouch. Tudor has a clockwork mind. He wasn't given to self-aggrandizement or exaggeration, so the grinding in my gut escalated to a buzz saw. He was perfectly capable of having wiped the internet off the face of universe.

"I'll be out of a job," I said selfishly, grappling with the impossible vision of a world without instant research.

He snorted at my paltry assessment. "Chaos, anarchy, total economic destruction," he predicted gloomily.

Yeah, that pretty much nailed it, if he knew what he was talking about. "Any evidence to support this theory of your omnipotence?"

"The cookie-blocker I've been working on?" He raised a questioning eyebrow to see if I was familiar with his project.

I nodded. By "cookies" he meant the internet hooks that many websites planted in a computer. Some were nasty little devils that broadcast our searches to companies that used the information to bombard us with ads.

Cookies didn't bother me much because Graham's master network used a non-commercial operating system and had an impenetrable firewall that crumbled the hooks like... cookies.

But the huge commercial operating systems sold by corporations like MacroWare encouraged cookies in the interest of efficiency and—most importantly—selling more stuff. Most people liked the results and allowed cookies, not understanding how dangerous those little devils could be in the wrong hands.

In the commercial world, cookies were a legitimate form of hacking. Leave it to my genius hacker brother to try to block himself.

"Cookie blocking is pretty standard," he continued. "To win the competition, I had to do something *different*, like expand the program to worm my personal information out of selected websites and crunch it. If the website's software is operating according to protocol, it's not anything really radical and should only target specific files with my ISP signature. I tested it on a bunch of commercial sites and it worked perfectly. Then I accidentally left my program on when I accessed a government website."

Tudor stayed silent another half block while formulating his explanation—leaving me way too much time to imagine what would come next.

"Instead of just crawling into the website's internet files and grabbing my data the way it normally does," he finally continued, "my worm kept going. It disappeared down some kind of *cyberhole*. It didn't even need handshake protocol to fall directly into their server. When I noticed the signal I'd set to show the program was activated, I opened it up to turn it off, and all kinds of code scrawled by that shouldn't have been there."

I'm tech savvy enough to know that a worm is a small program that works its way through software to spy on other servers and sometimes commit acts of sabotage. I wasn't seeing how eating or blocking cookies was the end of the world, but a *worm*, that could be problematic. I waited without comment.

Tudor gritted his teeth and continued. "My cookie monster started eating *through all data files*, not just my website information. There should have been an impenetrable firewall between that website program and their servers!"

Eating files? Eating, as in destroying entire computer files? I couldn't even understand how that was possible with a worm. Hacking for information, I understood. Destruction...? Automatic destruction—as in a giant delete button? Had it eaten through the website program itself? That would certainly destroy the internet.

"What website?" I asked, trying to ground my spinning thoughts.

"I got accepted to MIT and Stanford. I was just checking to see what kind of visas I needed," he said gloomily.

Talk about being torn! I needed to smack him over the head—what visa website?—but I was refraining from screeching in joy and hugging him in the middle of the street. To me, a college education was the epitome of success.

"MIT? *Stanford?*" I cried in such excitement that heads turned around us. Attending college had long been a wish of mine, one I wasn't much likely to attain given my GED and lack of funds. But scoring the cream of the college crop? I was in awe. "You didn't shout it to the world?"

Tudor shrugged again. "I just got the letters. I was kind of excited. That's why I didn't think to turn off the cookie monster program when I went to the visa website. I shut down as soon as I saw what was happening, but the site crashed while I watched. The whole site was still down yesterday. If my worm is no longer performing search and destroy on just *my* ISP signature and isn't blocked by firewalls, it can conceivably creep through every network connected to the server."

If this had been our half-brother Nick, I'd call him an arrogant idiot for thinking he'd personally destroyed the internet with one website crash. But this was Tudor. He hadn't told me the worst.

"Okay, I'm back off cloud nine now," I said in resignation. "What did you do, decide to experiment more with Scotland Yard's operating system?"

"No, I was simply accessing the U.S. Department of State," he said with a sigh. "My monster went on a search-and-destroy mission for ISPs and wiped out entire government data files before I could break the connection. That's when I bought the plane tickets."

Two

I SHIVERED IN THE COLD NOVEMBER WIND as Tudor and I strolled toward the Victorian-era neighborhood that I called home. Towering painted ladies and enormous brick edifices lined narrow residential streets, now occupied mostly by embassies and foreign ambassadors instead of families.

Our grandfather's house was substantial, taking up almost the entire footprint of a large lot. An antique wrought iron fence lined the front walk. A foot of green grass separated fence and foundation. It would be warmer inside, out of the wind.

We did not turn in that direction.

With the buzz saw of fear whirring in my gut, I steered Tudor around the block and down a less fancy street of deteriorating old homes. Tudor glanced at me worriedly, especially when I trespassed on the broken concrete parking lot of an enormous abandoned building that looked part church, part warehouse.

"We don't live here, do we?" He studied the high block walls and eccentric mansard roofline.

"I have it pegged as someone's half-remodeled carriage house," I said as I trotted across the parking lot to a gate hidden among the brambles along the property line. "Let's not lead anyone tracking you straight to the front door."

I didn't know if the State Department was capable of tracing incredible inedible worms back to Tudor, but I was betting infuriated roars had federal techies around the world scrambling to find the creator of destruction. And I didn't like any of the possibilities of what they would do to Tudor when they found him.

Tudor's eyes widened in surprise as I opened the rusty gate to reveal a fantasy land of vined arbors, herb and rose gardens, complete with haunted house. Accustomed to the damp cold, he halted to gawk at the gables and towers of our newly acquired sort-of home.

"What did you do after you ate the state department?" I prompted before we went any further.

"I shut down my computer as soon as my alerts flashed, but it's not my fault that there's a *hole* in their security," he said defensively. "We really live here?" he asked in awe, averting the painful subject. "Is there a dungeon?"

"Yeah, and the dungeon's mine." I let him get away with the diversion while I explained the lay of the land. "Our landlord has spyholes all over the house, apparently left over from our grandfather's regime. How much of your problem do you want known?"

"None, if possible." He looked like a little lost boy.

"Tell me how bad this hole is in the firewall," I demanded, lingering by the gate. "Will a patch fix it?"

He hesitated and looked longingly at the tower. But Tudor had known he'd have to pay the price of my curiosity if he showed up here.

"The website's program was stored in a MacroWare operating system. I tore apart the MacroWare code on my computer," he said, "and I couldn't find the source for a security breach. I thought maybe the flaw was in the firewall of the website. But that doesn't explain how my worm was able to get past the website program and continue destroying files in a government server."

I had only learned enough code for basic hacking. I lacked Tudor's expertise and grappled for terms I could comprehend. "You're saying there's a spyhole—a backdoor—in the state department's computer, possibly in their *operating* system—not their website program—that isn't in a normal computer?"

He nodded miserably. "That's what it looks like without more experimentation. MacroWare operating systems are used by most government and commercial organizations because they work with the majority of computers. Most cookie blockers work with them, so I designed my software like a virus that went one step further. It's supposed to eat through dangerous cookies and any data containing my ID. It works perfectly even on Chinese and Russian websites."

I tried not to roll my eyes. "In other words, you created illegal malware that infects websites."

"It might be *technically* illegal, but it was never designed to act as a Trojan horse to open doors directly into computers—that's way over the top dangerous and requires that someone on the other side let it in. I didn't program limits into my software for going beyond its intended target, because I never expected it to go any farther. For all I know, it somehow got corrupted and started multiplying and hunting ISPs one digit different from mine, then two digits... But unless there was an open back door, my worm shouldn't go further than the website address directory. It shouldn't have been a problem."

"Evil minions," I muttered, thinking aloud. "In your scenario, wouldn't the hole have to have been built into the State Department's MacroWare system? If MacroWare can plant spyholes in one government computer, how many others can they be spying on?"

Tudor glared at me. "Stephen Stiles wouldn't do anything like that. He's a genius who doesn't need to spy to get rich. He's a hero who gives fortunes to the poor and to medical research. He wouldn't deliberately plant holes in a system that practically runs the world."

"Don't be naïve," I said scornfully. "For all you know, that's how he gets government contracts, by knowing what his competitors bid."

Tudor looked me fearlessly in the eye. "He's not that kind of creep. I sent him and his top staff a message warning of the problem before I left, and they acknowledged it immediately. You'll see, they'll fix it. I just need to wait it out."

"Which is why you ran like hell, got it," I said, proceeding toward the house, trying not to reveal that the buzz saw in my stomach had been joined by a jackhammer at this latest news. *Tudor had notified Stiles of the flaw? The* Stephen Stiles who was just hospitalized for poisoning?

I feared I would pass out at any moment as numbers added up in my head. Coincidence didn't happen in my world. "When did you send the message?"

"Tuesday evening, my time. Guess that's Tuesday morning, your time. I'm wiped. Can we talk about this later?"

I led him to the kitchen entrance, but I was already formulating the timeline—Stephen Stiles and company went to the dinner on Wednesday night, a day and a half *after* Tudor had sent his frantic e-mail warning. If whoever had received that email—and Tudor was crafty enough to have private corporate email addresses—gone directly to Stiles, there had been time before the dinner for a whole lot of techies to get their panties in a twist.

Another scenario—I didn't know how likely— was that someone at the State Department had been smart enough to blame disappearing data on an operating system malfunction and not an attack from North Korea. They would have come down hard on Stiles.

Either way, I didn't like the coincidence of MacroWare learning of a huge security breach a day and a half before five of its executives were poisoned—but *food* poisoning? That didn't even begin to make sense. Stiles and company would be up and whupping ass in twenty-four hours.

So someone wanted them out of the way for a day?

My mind kept replaying the image of Graham entering the building where Stiles and company had been poisoned. That had been Wednesday. Today was Friday. I had no idea what he was doing at any given time, so I couldn't say where he'd been that day.

I wanted to trust a man who had helped rescue my sisters. But I knew our mysterious landlord was nose-deep in political guano that was well over my head. I was almost afraid to show Tudor to a room in the mansion. Maybe I should have hidden him in a hotel.

But Tudor was clearly exhausted, and I didn't know any cheap hotels. I dumped him in one of the spare second floor bedrooms, then headed to the backyard to call my brother Nick, out of range of Graham's hearing. I needed to know what Nick had wanted me to see on the news.

I hoped Graham hadn't bugged the arbor. It was danged cold with the wind tossing the gnarled vines, but I didn't trust my basement office to be unbugged. There had been a time when I'd mistakenly thought Graham was a cripple who couldn't infiltrate my private space. I'd been wrong too often about that man to take any chances.

Nick answered at once. "Was that him?" he asked without preamble.

I closed my eyes and counted to ten. "Was what whom?" I asked, stalling. I knew what he was asking.

"Graham!" he said impatiently. "You've seen him. I haven't. We're monitoring the Stiles situation. The ambassador's security staff swears that was Amadeus Graham entering the building on Wednesday, the day of the conference. Was it?"

"What difference does it make?" Since I promise my clients

privacy, I couldn't tell Nick anything until Graham gave the go-ahead. "I'm pretty certain he didn't cook their food! What's this really about?" I started running my hands over the arbor posts, looking for anything that might be picking up my voice or my cell signal.

"The ambassador thinks Graham's been running a secret security operation for years, spying on the embassy and who knows who else. They want proof that he's not only alive, despite reports otherwise, but that he's not the broken cripple everyone else assumes."

I snorted. At least I wasn't the only one he'd hoodwinked. Amadeus Graham had deceived the entire world, including top notch, high-tech security staff of powerful governments, into thinking he'd died or retired after he was injured during 9/11. No wonder I sometimes liked the alpha jerk, or at least respected his hermit tendencies.

"Why ask me? I am not proof that Graham exists," I retorted. "Are they trying to prove he's incompetent at safeguarding his clients?" And since Tudor had only just told me about his faux pas, I assumed the Brit embassy knew nothing about MacroWare's possible software problem. It was the food poisoning they were focused on—why? I really shouldn't have the suspicions I did, so I added jokingly, "Was Graham supposed to be a taste tester?"

Nick sighed in exasperation. "Do you want me to advance in my job or not? Inside info is my reason for existence."

I knew that. I adored Nick. He was the closest sibling to me in age, and we'd grown up together in the rough streets of a dozen foreign slums. He'd survived, gone on to Brit public schools with his dual citizenship, and wasted his education gambling for a living while chasing male tail. But now that we had a place to stay, of sorts, and EG to look after, he was settling down. He had a good job as an aide in the British embassy and had just leased a new apartment so he could take his boyfriends home.

I owed Graham some loyalty. I owed Nick more. "You don't really think the ambassador hired you because you were living in Graham's house, do you?" I asked. Nick has a few self-esteem problems to sort out.

"Yeah, I really think that's part of the equation," he agreed sullenly.

"Then they're full of crap and you deserve better. If I tell you it looked like Graham, and I have no idea where he was on Wednesday, what happens?" I'd have to look at my computer to remember where *I'd* been two days ago.

"Nothing happens at this point, except speculation on what MacroWare will do now that its entire executive staff is dead or incapacitated. The market is likely to follow MacroWare down soon unless the company shows someone powerful—or someone with powerful connections—is in charge. According to the staff, Graham was once considered a world-class technical and security wonk with massive political clout. If it can be verified that he is actually alive and possibly taking over the company, the whole world would sit up and take notice. There isn't any chance that he might be in line for an executive position, is there? He wouldn't break secrecy for anything less, would he?"

In panic, I pushed aside the hilarious scenario of reclusive Graham leading a public corporation and focused on what mattered most. "Dead?" I asked. "Of *food* poisoning? I thought all they needed was their stomachs pumped."

I clung to an arbor post and tried not to let my suspicious mind take over, but I'd seen too much in too few years. What would be the point of killing execs over a stupid software problem? CEOs couldn't solve anything.

The food poisoning had to be accidental. The faulty operating system and Tudor's warning... totally coincidental. Unfortunately, my spy mother had taught me how the bad guys made things look coincidental.

"Stiles and one of the other execs is dead," Nick said. "Three are in comas, on life support after they quit breathing. The dead pair apparently ate more of the *fugu chiri* than the others. Theirs was the only table that requested the soup, probably the only table that was granted special requests. The chef is being interrogated, but puffer fish is inherently poisonous. If the chef wasn't trained in preparing it—" He let the sentence trail off with a shrug I could almost hear.

Remembering Tudor's idolization of Stiles, I grimaced and rubbed my temple. A philanthropist and geek genius deserved better than puffer fish poisoning, although if his goal had been to get high on the toxins, maybe he deserved to be slowly paralyzed from the feet up for consuming one of the most lethal poisons in nature. But well-prepared puffer fish was a perfectly safe gourmet delicacy.

With a sigh, I gave Nick as much as I honestly could. "As far as I'm aware, Graham has been in his office all week, but he comes and goes as he pleases without telling me. It looked like Graham in the video, but I was in a hurry and only caught a glimpse. We were at the airport picking up Tudor. We have more problems than Graham. We need a family confab somewhere safe."

Nick practically growled in irritation. He knew I wouldn't call a meeting unless it was important. "Patra won't have time to make it," was all he said.

"We'll leave it to you to pass on the info to her. I just need to talk somewhere safe, which isn't here. Tudor has major news, not all of it good, and some of it possibly related to Stiles." That was an understatement, but I wasn't trusting cell phone waves.

"Okay, tonight, about seven." He named a restaurant half way between our places.

I didn't want to drag EG into this, but it was Friday, she didn't have school tomorrow, and she'd want to be part of any family gathering. I was rapidly learning the problems my mother faced when raising a herd of small children while spying on enemies. I didn't have a mini-me to leave EG with, as my mother had, and even at nine EG was too smart to be fobbed off for long. She'd just investigate on her own if we didn't tell her what was happening. I had been just like her at that age.

I agreed on the restaurant and clicked off, then stared up at the towering fortress I wanted for my own more than I wanted anything else in the world. I hadn't been entirely truthful about saving our funds for college. I was hoping we could buy our house back from Graham if the lawsuits didn't work.

I had never owned more than my computer. I despised our nomadic life while growing up. I longed for a solid foundation for EG to thrive on.

I was terrified that my mother was right, and we needed to keep moving to be safe. The world is not kind to people who are different, and my family of weird prodigies couldn't get any more different. We couldn't cook or clean but we all excelled in trouble.

CHILLED TO THE BONE and shivering after talking with Nick, I crept down the stairs into the warm cellar where Mallard, Graham's butler/spy, resided. Heavenly smells drifted from the kitchen. For all I knew, he was cooking puffer fish soup.

That Graham had the ability to serve poison soup, I had no doubt. I wanted to believe he wouldn't do it unless the victims were intent on *violent* world domination. MacroWare had already managed commercial domination, so that horse was done gone, as my pappy never said.

Besides, it still wasn't proven that the poisoning hadn't been anything except pointlessly accidental.

I hurried down the tiled corridor to my office on the front side of the basement. We'd moved here in the heat of summer. At the time, my office had stayed blessedly cool. I liked rooms insulated by earth.

But I needed a space heater to get warm today. I turned it on and rubbed my hands together, trying to warm them up enough to tackle my keyboard.

"Upstairs, *now*," the intercom on my desk gargled abruptly.

Now that Nick had made me think about it, Graham had been sending me documents to work on these last few days—so he'd been in his office—but we hadn't really talked.

Was it my imagination, or did he sound... weary?

Graham was grouchy 24/7.

I sat up and punched the intercom button. EG was right. Intercoms were so yesterday. "Do I bring my sword or a king's ransom?" I asked, just because I hated being bossed around.

Graham *never* verbally invited me to his lair. Something was very wrong.

"I'll have Mallard hogtie you and haul you up," he threatened, but it was half-hearted and not up to his usual standard of intimidation.

Realizing this day wasn't getting any better, I made my own amusement. I popped an antihistamine—Graham had a cat and I'm allergic. Then I scooted a chair beneath the trap door in my ceiling.

A few weeks ago, I'd discovered Graham's treachery in installing this secret passage. Now I used it to annoy him—and because it was faster than following the elaborate winding public staircases to the third floor.

Using muscles I'd worked on for years, I pulled myself through my office ceiling into the closet of my grandfather's master suite on the first floor. Inside the closet were the hidden stairs that led directly up to Graham's office. An elevator would be more practical, but oh well—I needed the exercise. I trotted up.

Graham's office is a dark lair lined with computer monitors that at any given time could be covering a war in the Mideast or an ice cream truck in San Diego. Today, several screens showed the hospital where presumably the Macro execs were being treated, plus newscasters commenting on the economic effect of Stiles' death. They were freaking out.

"Personally, I'd snap off the talking heads," I said as I studied the screens. "Are we wallowing in muck today?"

"We live in muck. The death of Stephen Stiles has sent the markets plummeting. They'll recover once the new product is released on schedule," he said angrily, punching his keyboard to bring up the stock market reports. "They won't recover so fast if they discover Stiles was murdered."

There it was, the hammer I'd been waiting to fall.

Three

TOTALLY KNACKERED BUT DETERMINED, Tudor dug through his backpack for the used tablet computer he'd purchased from one of the profs. He'd had to sell all his powerful equipment and empty his savings for the plane ticket when everything went pear-shaped. The tablet had taken his last shilling. He was stranded here at Ana's mercy.

He'd been nervous about his reception but pretty certain she would take him in. Beneath the tough exterior, his half-sister was a marshmallow—she'd do anything for family. Unfortunately, that worked both ways. If his cock-up threatened EG, Ana might take *him* down instead.

There were bound to be nasty repercussions if he'd fragged the internet and Interpol showed up. His fingers shook so badly that he had to try twice to hit settings and disconnect all the tracking devices on the tablet.

He had to know how much damage he'd caused. His cookie monster program was dodgy, but so was hacking. It wasn't as if he'd *intended* to sell the program to anyone but MacroWare as a cautionary security plug. Or maybe to an anti-virus programmer if MacroWare wasn't interested.

If he was really, really lucky, more experienced people had patched the State Department's operating system shambles before his worm crawled deeper. He held his breath as he tested for nearby Wi-Fi connections and located a strong one.

The beastly tablet operated on a Peanut system, not MacroWare. He wasn't as familiar with Peanut's programming, but the basics weren't too different. The strong signal was password protected, of course. That would be here in the house. He bit his lip and anxiously tried a few basic passwords.

He didn't have a hacker program that worked with the tablet. He couldn't crack the code. If Ana had set it, his software probably couldn't hack it either. She didn't know programming, but she was devious. She had the smarts to take the basic hacking knowledge he'd given her and run with it.

He ran down the list of available networks until he found someone's laptop that was unprotected. Pathetic wankers.

The signal was weak. He sat on the window and moved the tablet around until the signal strengthened. Would Ana give him access to her network later? He couldn't do much at this speed, but he had to know how big a shambles he'd made.

Fingers trembling, he tuned in to the tablet's search engine. It came up as always—the internet hadn't totally collapsed then. Maybe that gave him a little time.

He checked MacroWare's site to see if they'd announced an emergency security update.

Instead, he read the headline about the death of Stephen Stiles. *Gahhhh, nooooo!!!!!!*

Paralyzed in shock, he simply stared for a full stomach-churning minute. The geek king was *dead*? How was that possible? Stiles should be invincible, like Superman.

But *fish* poisoning? That was so cocked up!

Selfishly, his next thought was to wonder if there'd been time for anyone to consult with Stiles about Tudor's message. Had he set his programmers to fix the hole in the O/S? *Oh blimey bloomin' hell...* what if he hadn't?

Desperately, Tudor searched for news of crashing websites, a dangerous worm eating government data, or a security update.

He found nothing.

Rocking back and forth and moaning, realizing he was not only up a creek without an oar, but sitting on the bleeding Titanic, he wondered what in the name of Ramses he did now.

Ana lingers in Graham's lair

I SHOVED MY HANDS INTO THE POCKETS of the old corduroys I'd worn to the airport and stared at the back of Graham's head. "Murdered?" I inquired innocently, as if I hadn't been sitting on fear all morning.

His black cat leapt from his lap, circled my ankles in disdain, and escaped through the door I'd left open. I sneezed, which added to my irritation.

Having my paranoid conspiracy fantasies confirmed wasn't supposed to happen. "Food poisoning hardly qualifies as murder."

"Puffer fish numbs the mouth. Anything else in the food wouldn't be detected." He brought up a health department warning of symptoms on one screen, then what appeared to be a hospital medical record on another. "Knowing puffer fish had been served, doctors had no reason to look further than the toxicology reports showing toxic levels of tetrodotoxin in the blood stream. The symptoms and evidence are correlated to the fish."

If I hadn't known about Tudor's little problem, I would have shrugged and said *food poisoning, got it,* just like everyone else. But food poisoning of execs sitting on a potentially major operational failure that could cause stockholders gazillions... that had my suspicious mind on edge.

Graham had said murder. Why?

"And?" was the only reply I could summon.

"The symptoms disguised massive botulism poisoning." He crossed his arms over his chest and glared at a new screen he'd keyed up.

Even sitting, Graham was a big man, with wide shoulders, broad chest, and powerful arms. It was warm up here in the windowless attic, so instead of the heavy sweaters the rest of us wore, he was wearing a long-sleeved T-shirt that clung lovingly to pectorals and biceps. I wanted to swat him upside his thick head of ebony hair just for existing, which admittedly made me surly.

"Not making sense yet," I warned. "Botulism is still food poisoning, not murder."

"Botulism is overkill. I doubt the doctors looked for it. I had to confiscate a blood sample and have it tested." He grunted and wielded his keyboard to open a few more screens of talking heads.

Graham said outrageous things like that all the time without apology or explanation. Nick's employers had a right to be suspicious about him.

"Why?" I demanded, knowing I had to drag every grain of information out of the tight-lipped rat. "Why would you test a sample when the doctors are satisfied with puffer fish?"

"Stiles kept a pretty close monitor on his food, hiring special chefs. He wouldn't hire an incompetent *fugu* chef," he said, fine tuning a camera showing a hospital entrance. "I get paid to know things like that. I am not idly living off Max's millions."

Wow, a personal admission, two, actually. A new first.

"I never thought you stole our inheritance. I thought our grandfather's lawyer smoked all the money," I said angrily. "Did you think I'd live in the house of a callous crook who would rob little children?"

I was stunned that he thought I'd considered him a thief. A lying, conniving, creepy spider in the attic who had misappropriated our house by legal means, yes, but a common thief, never. He was a brilliant man who'd been on a high-speed destiny path and had worked with the president of the United States, for pity's sake. He probably still worked for the CIA or worse—that had always been my vision of him.

So, he wasn't a philanthropist but a paid security something or other. Big freakin' deal.

This was probably the longest and most revealing conversation we'd ever had. Usually, we flung a few insults, played competitive head games, and got back to work. I had to wonder where this was going—and worry.

"Max was ill, not stupid." Graham opened a document on screen showing a bank transfer receipt with a whole lot of zeroes on it. "He started moving funds before he died. That could have precipitated his death."

My grandfather's coke-sniffing renegade lawyer had robbed, then poisoned him, but that ship had long sailed. The lawyer was dead now and couldn't be our current culprit.

I stared at my grandfather's name on the bank receipt and got wobble-kneed. Our inheritance might still be out there? That realization had me hunting for a place to sit before my legs collapsed under me.

Unable to find a chair in the dark, I folded up and took the floor. "Why didn't you tell me this sooner?" I wanted to shout and kick and throw a tantrum, but that wouldn't impress Graham. "That's *our* money!"

Money that might buy back this house. Or put the remaining four of my younger half-siblings through college. Probably not both house and college, especially if MIT was their goal, and all the others demanded an equal share.

"I don't have the code to access the funds or the time to figure it out," Graham admitted. "Swiss banks will sit on assets until the end of creation before they'll release accounts, unless you can find the access code. I'm simply telling you that I earn my money the same way you do." He clicked a switch and the receipt was replaced by a lab report.

"Like heck you do," I muttered. I knew how to swear in twenty languages. I'd trained myself not to for the sake of my younger siblings, but sometimes... I needed to kick something—like Graham. "I'd have to work fifty hour days to afford this set up."

"People pay for my knowledge and contacts. You don't have anything worth that kind of dough," he said.

Before I could smack him upside the head for the insult, he turned around and dropped the shock bomb. "I'll give you all the information I possess on your grandfather's accounts if you'll work this case for me."

My jaw dropped but no sound passed my lips. The explosion in my head was so huge that it took a few moments to process all the ramifications of his declaration. All the normal questions like "Why now? Why me?"—and the fury that he'd been concealing Max's accounts—coalesced into one loaded shell of sarcasm.

"Giving me the information on Max's money amounts to paying me with my own coin! Why can't big bad you do it yourself?" I said.

He didn't even shrug. "Because once the cops get smart and realize Stiles was murdered, they'll be coming after me next. I have both motive and opportunity. The murderer couldn't have set me up better if I'd planned it." He slumped wearily in his high-backed desk chair.

His computer screens didn't provide adequate illumination to read his expression, but I could read his body language. He was tense and desperate.

"What motive?" I demanded, because that sounded really bad.

He hesitated. Obviously, he wasn't interested in coming clean across the board. I refused to budge until he answered.

"Let's just say that Stiles had a few close... associates... who took a different career path. I don't want to bias you with those reports. I'd prefer you look at everyone, but several people on the managerial level were about to be fired. At least one of the ill executives argued against the firing and others accused Stiles of letting me run the company. They've started internal rumors of my replacing the board. After the murder charge is placed, they will report all this to the police. Once the police realize I do exist, they will happily believe I'm capable of corporate takeover by puffer fish, especially since I was in the hotel that night. It will be incredibly difficult to find the real murderer if I'm behind bars."

I knew Graham was secretive about his identity. Amadeus Graham, hermit extraordinaire, would not normally walk into a major company like MacroWare as himself. He would have used an alias. What identity the board feared wouldn't matter once the real Graham's existence was confirmed.

"If those associates are the prime suspects, would they really kill off Stiles to get at you?"

"It's possible that they're stupid," he grumbled. "But there are other elements involved. I don't want to taint your investigations by listing my enemies when the motive could possibly be elsewhere."

"I'm not a detective," I reminded him. "I can't even read that lab report that seems to have set you off. If the police are satisfied with food poisoning as an explanation, I can't even see why you're worried."

"Puffer fish poisoning isn't always deadly. A lot of it depends on how much is consumed and the physical condition of the person eating it." He brought up another medical screen with a list of botulism symptoms. "But it will lower the immune system sufficiently for another poison to complete the damage. I called for the blood work because they didn't have enough fish poison to die."

I skimmed the article and slammed into the remedies. Botulism could be cured! "If you're saying they had botulism as well as fish poisoning," I nearly shouted in shock, *"have you called the hospital?"*

"Why the hell do you think I'm worrying?" he shouted back, proving he was unusually unnerved.

Normally, we'd both be taking out our panic by kicking and beating bags in the gym, but we didn't have time for that.

"I sent an anonymous warning," he said wearily. "They should be treating the surviving three for botulism now. Once they recover, they'll start talking, and that's when the cops will start looking for me."

I finished reading the article. This was all quite fascinating, but

I wasn't seeing direct connections to Graham or Tudor, my main concerns. "They were eating badly canned veggies?" I asked, grimacing. "That does not compute."

"Of course it doesn't. That's how I know it's murder. Someone deliberately added tainted food to their entree. It takes hours for the symptoms to appear, so the kitchen was already clean before anyone became sick. The rules of puffer fish preparation require complete removal of all remains immediately. The health department searched Thursday, after Stiles was hospitalized and the diagnosis of fish poisoning was made, but any trace of the meal was long gone. The killer knew what he was doing."

"The killer must have had motive and opportunity too," I protested. "If you were there, did you see who was with them?" I loved a good puzzle. I wasn't loving this one.

"Are you saying you'll work with me?" he asked.

As much as I liked having him by the short hairs for a change, I resented the insult. "What, you think I'll let them hang you and let a killer go free?"

He didn't so much as blink an eyelash but continued as if I'd said *yes*. "I'm on retainer to hunt security breaches in MacroWare's software as well as their internal network. Stiles recently alerted me to a national security breach and demanded that we meet in person."

Uh oh. Here it was. Even knowing heads were about to roll, I couldn't resist curiosity. "You'd never met? He paid a fortune to an invisible spy in my attic?"

He swiveled his chair enough to give me a gimlet glare. Beneath thick lashes Graham has deep dark eyes that could skewer with just a look.

"They *pay* for invisibility. You do the same, so quit gloating, or you'll be arrested for harboring a criminal when I go down."

I could just move out, but I wouldn't, and he knew it. That's what happened when I let people into my life. They owned me.

"Ok, fine." I waved a dismissive hand as if I was handed national security assignments every day. "Did you meet Stiles?"

"Only briefly. He wanted me to join them at dinner. I told him that was a ridiculously reckless idea. I arranged a suite to meet in privacy and had the place swept for bugs while they ate. Only Stiles and Bates, his right hand man, came up to the room. This was several hours after dinner and speeches, and they weren't feeling well. They pointed me at a security breach, and I called a doctor for them. I left them with staff, but if a whiff of murder comes out, it won't be difficult for the police to trace my presence."

"You don't see any connection between a security breach and poison?" I asked, not so innocently. "Did you look for the breach?"

He sighed and managed to look conflicted. "This is to go no further than this room, but the operating system breach is in their brand new, unreleased beta software that's only recently been given to designated government and commercial organizations for testing."

Graham called up programming code and scrolled through it, highlighting lines of jargon. If he expected me to follow what he was doing, he overrated my abilities. "The breach appears to be limited to the beta program. It will take time to uncover the extent of damage. If that's Tudor you've stored downstairs, I could put him to work, too."

I would let Tudor sleep a while before pounding his head into a pillow and telling him he wasn't responsible for crippling the internet—MacroWare was. Or that was my assumption, anyway. MacroWare had far more power than my baby brother, even though it was hard to imagine the State Department testing beta software.

Instead of complaining about Graham's spying on my guests, I diverted the subject. "I'm a research assistant, nothing more. I have no idea what that code says or what it does. What can I do about someone who apparently breaches computer security and poisons CEOs? You need an army just to protect the guys in the hospital."

"The list of designated agencies testing the beta program is not reliable. I'm copying you on my research into which websites and agencies have been breached so far. We'll need to drill down, find the related servers, computers, and technicians. Maybe we'll find a pattern."

Yeah, and maybe someday I'd walk the moon.

I pried myself from the floor, trying to calculate how I could untie this mighty knot of secrecy. He needed to know about Tudor's monster and that he'd been the one to warn Stiles, and Tudor needed to know about the beta program and his hero's murder, but the knowledge was too explosive to share without permission. "Did it ever occur to you that you might need a team of experts for jobs of this scope?"

"About as often as it occurs to you to cut your hair," he said, going back to flicking through a dozen screens at once. "Samson complex?"

My hair is black, but thicker and straighter than my Irish father's curls. I usually wear it in a long unfashionable braid down my back.

"If I cut it, then how would you recognize me?" I retorted. Not giving him time to answer, I stalked back down the stairs to my office.

I'd never indulged in girlfriend games, but my reaction to this relatively—emphasis on relative—intimate conversation came dangerously close.

I was running the show now, I chanted as I dove into my work. Graham needed *me*, instead of the other way around.

Four

WITH MY FEAR FOR TUDOR'S FATE, I was having a lot of difficulty concentrating on the information Graham sent me on Stephen Stiles, the founder and CEO of MacroWare.

Tudor had the potential to be another Stiles if properly channeled.

Unfortunately, our family does not channel well. We're too independent-minded to play well with others, and profit is seldom our primary motive.

I still wanted Tudor to have choices. I wanted him at MIT. I didn't want his future destroyed by accidental wormholes in faulty operating systems.

My focus was shot. Besides fretting over Tudor, I had to worry about Graham... *Crap.*

I should just bash my head against the desk. That would be about as productive as worrying over Graham.

I ran searches on *tetrodotoxin*, the puffer fish poison, learning how it worked. The bunny trails were fascinating—powdered, the poison was said to create zombies in Haitian voodoo. The tales had been discredited, but my imagination raced picturing Zombie MacroWare execs attacking Wall Street.

EG ran down the basement stairs as soon as she arrived home from school, interrupting my fantasies.

She dropped her books on a chair and practically bounced. "What did Tudor say? Is he staying? Can I wake him now, please? I want him to install that war game he told me about."

Six short months ago, she'd been a cynical, pessimistic nine-year-old version of me. Now that she'd finally found a school of similar minds and had a home that didn't involve trains, planes, and buses, she was almost normal. Again—normal being relative. She'd at least lightened up on making dangerously accurate predictions of doom.

Giving my siblings the normal life I never had was the reason I put up with Graham and hoarded cash like a dragon sitting on gold.

"We're meeting Nick for dinner," I told her. "Let Tudor sleep until it's time to dress. And no, you're not installing war games. Do your homework now so you have all weekend to torment Tudor."

I wasn't in a hurry to wake the kid. I didn't know how I'd break the news that his hero was dead. Leave a newspaper at his door?

"He's going to visit MIT, isn't he?" EG crowed. "He said he applied. Can we go with him to see the campus?"

Nice excuse for the kid's presence here, should anyone learn about it. I liked that. I wasn't ready to tell her how much trouble he was in. "We'll see. He may not want us tagging along. And he got accepted by Stanford too. That's across the country and too expensive for all of us to visit."

She pouted but grabbed her backpack and dashed upstairs.

Restlessly, I looked up the visa website Tudor had mentioned, but I didn't see any screaming news about massive cyber-attacks. Websites crashed for all sorts of reasons, and no official would admit to the media that their site had been hacked—especially if they traced it to a sixteen-year-old.

I sorted through Graham's folder of notes from Stiles on offices testing the beta software and chose an innocuous one. I followed his pathway through the breach and unimaginatively drilled down through layers of computers on a government financial committee working on banking laws. I yawned. Who would spy on red tape like this?

Oh, yeah, right, crooked mortgage lenders and megabanks who were being hauled over the coals might want to know what regulations committees were pondering. Charming. But people into selling and trading didn't know how operating systems were made, they just expected their computers to work.

The committee's website looked fine to me, and when I used Graham's information to access their files, they looked complete. Maybe the kid had panicked over nothing.

Not likely unless he was doing drugs. Tudor had not inherited any drama queen tendencies from our mother. Had I been the one to wreck a government website, I'd be envisioning collapsing dominoes, one country accusing another of cyber-war, and nuclear warheads. But that's just my experience talking.

My expertise is in detailed research. By the time I heard excited chatter upstairs, I had the names of people who used the banking committee's website, locations of their computers, and utterly no idea what to do with the information.

Living in a constant state of danger while growing up, I overdosed on caution. Fearing police would carry Graham off while we were out to dinner, I backed up all my drives on an external disk that fit into my overlarge purse and sent a duplicate into our cloud server. As an extra precaution, I unscrewed the cases and detached the hard drives. Those, I stored above the trap door in the secret closet. That would puzzle anyone who dared impound my precious Whiz.

Tudor had showered and changed while I was dismantling the equipment. EG had evidently told him of our dinner plans. I waved at them in the parlor on my way upstairs, and he glanced up at me warily before returning to trouncing EG at video games—on a tablet computer.

Criminey, *Tudor had access to the internet.* EG was only allowed to use the internet on my computer, under my supervision, but she possessed the family genius for knowing too much for her own good. She would know where to find our network password and pass it on if asked.

If I knew my brother—and I did, we had similar stealthy habits—he'd already been rummaging around online. I no longer had to wonder how to tell Tudor about Stiles. How would a parent comfort their kid after such a devastating blow?

I halted in the doorway. "You saw the news?"

Tudor glared. His eyes were suspiciously red. "It doesn't make sense," he said.

Despite his lack of words, I knew what he meant. Why would anyone murder a CEO? Once someone was elevated to that status, their productive days were over, in my opinion. While alive, Stiles had been little more than a salesman in these last years. He had minions to build code these days.

I couldn't tell from Tudor's reaction if he'd put two and two together, but once his head cleared, he would.

"I'm sorry," I said. "Give me a minute to change, and we'll talk about it over dinner."

For our family, that was a meaningful exchange. I knew Tudor was upset about the death of his hero, but unlike some of us, he wouldn't display it by an emotional outburst. Tudor was a mean gamer with an adolescent ability to make illogical connections with reality. My fear was that he'd go rogue on the internet, and rip it apart in search of any real or imagined villains if we didn't give him some meaningful work to do.

Wondering how I could keep both Tudor's and Graham's secrets without cutting out my tongue, I dressed in leggings, knee-high boots, and a black sweater that hung almost as long as my black wool skirt. I'd learned the wonders of consignment store shopping and had stocked up on warm. To keep Nick from harping at me, I wore a boring black wool coat instead of my army jacket.

Tudor and EG griped when I made them dress warmly and head down the basement stairs instead of using the front door.

"I know we have money now," Tudor insisted belligerently. "A taxi won't break us."

"That money is tied up in mutual funds. Besides, survival is for the fittest. The restaurant is only half a mile away." Ignoring his snit, I tugged his scarf tighter.

I'd grown up living with both wealth and desperate food-stealing poverty. I didn't want my siblings to know hunger, but I didn't want them to turn into privileged snots either.

"You want to be like the rest of the rich and weak?" I asked. "Besides, if you go to MIT, you'll need money. How much of a scholarship can you expect? One that covers room and board?"

That shut him up. I'm betting he hadn't told his father about his grandiose expectations.

"How much school are you missing?" I asked on the way down the stairs.

Tudor shrugged grumpily. "It's our quarter break next week. Everyone skips these last few days."

"Yeah, right, and you have no finals?" But I knew he could ace the tests once the teachers were persuaded this was a family emergency. Solving his problem in time to get him back into class so he could keep his MIT future was the real trick.

"Why this way?" EG asked suspiciously as we traipsed across the backyard.

"Because officially, we have no idea where Tudor is," I admitted with a sigh. "Let's not reveal his presence until we know what happens next."

Tudor sent me a grateful glance and quit complaining about the walk.

EG took the news that Tudor was hiding completely in stride, checking out the back gate to be certain we weren't watched, tugging Tudor's knit hat down so no trace of his copper hair could be seen.

Sneakiness is apparently genetic.

The restaurant Nick had chosen was dimly lit, crowded, and noisy. With Tudor and EG to consider, he'd gone for an all-American beef-and-potatoes kind of place, except it was well known for its fabulous soups and salads. Nick and I had been spoiled by Mallard's gourmet meals.

I insisted on a booth in a dark corner behind a large post. The hostess looked us over, decided we weren't important enough to put on display, and hid us as requested, much to Nick's disappointment.

As usual, our glamorous brother was decked out in an elegantly tailored suit with just the right suave open collar and loosened tie to set off his carefully styled golden hair. Nick was the fashionista Magda should have had for a daughter.

"What's wrong now?" Nick demanded as soon as a server took our drink orders.

I glared at Tudor. "We work together. Tell Nick."

"And EG?" he asked warily.

"EG, either plug your ears or learn to keep quiet," I told her.

She stuck her tongue out at me. Since we both knew she would sneak until she found out what was going on, I didn't argue with that.

I pinched the bridge of my nose and forced myself to admit my dilemma. "I hate to tell you this, folks, but I think this one has to go to Graham, too, if he doesn't already know. I'm not sure how long we can sit on Tudor's little difficulty."

The kid slid down in his chair. "I'm going to jail."

"You create illegal software. You hack websites," Nick pointed out. "Sooner or later, jail's a given."

"Not if Graham gets involved," I asserted. With luck, if I could persuade Tudor to give up his secret, I could trade it for revealing Graham's. I was still angry about our landlord knowing where Max's money was all these months, so I wasn't giving away anything for free.

The missing millions were *not* a topic for tonight or nothing would get done. I wanted more certainty that the money existed before mentioning it to my family.

Tudor looked wary about my suggestion but didn't throw a tantrum. He gave a general explanation of what he'd done, then concluded, "If Stiles died before a patch was ordered, my worm could be anywhere, doing anything. My e-mail could be sitting in a dead person's box. For all I know, I've unleashed a *real* monster."

"Or it could have died on impact. I've spent the day looking and have seen no evidence of serious destruction from your worm," I told him. "If MacroWare has a security breach, it's a bigger potential problem than your baby cookie monster. China and Russia could be sucking data out of classified databases right now. We could have a world war on our hands, international bankruptcy, economic chaos."

Tudor rubbed the bridge of his nose but nodded to show he was processing what I was telling him.

"You can work with Graham to analyze the extent of the damages," I continued, "but more importantly, the two of you can start searching the affected computers for signs of intruders." I didn't want to give away Graham's secrets, so I had to be deliberately vague. "It's just a matter of time until he finds your program tramping around in files, so you might as well help him."

"Work *with* him?" Tudor's eyebrows soared, as did Nick's and EG's.

"His suggestion," I said triumphantly. "He needs our help anyway."

I had them there. Their curiosity about our spy in the attic would tilt their nosiness-meters into red alert territory. The rest of the evening was spent answering questions and debating possibilities, probabilities, and other futilities.

By the time we finished our meal—I'd gone for the chunky minestrone and Nick, the lobster salad—we'd all agreed that Tudor had to give up his secret and work with Graham. Nick insisted on walking us home. D.C. streets after dark aren't the safest place, but I was as adept at beating off thugs as Nick. Still, it was good to have adult company. Not until I thought that did I realize I was back to mothering my younger siblings again.

It had taken me years to escape my doormat role in my mother's life, but this time, I'd done it to myself.

Strangely, I was good with that.

On the way home, I instructed Tudor to stay off our computer network and lay low with all his friends. He assured me he'd be discreet. But he was sixteen. That wasn't much better than telling EG to cut out her tongue.

I didn't have the stamina to tackle Graham in his lair once we got home. I sent Nick off and the kids to bed and ran down to my office comfort zone.

I texted Graham that Tudor had info on the MacroWare breech, but I couldn't reveal it until Graham allowed me to tell Tudor what he knew about Stephen Stiles and the poisoned execs. I shut down my phone before he could respond.

Let him stew in his own juices a while longer. I didn't intend to forgive him for trying to trade what was rightfully ours for his own benefit. That placed him way below an alligator's belly in my book.

I returned my Whiz to working order. From the volume of mail and documents that instantly downloaded, I knew he was still up there in his attic.

The top story he dumped on me—the three surviving MacroWare execs were being treated for botulism and the cops were parked at their hospital doors.

Ana's Saturday morning

I TRIED NOT TO READ NEWSPAPERS if I could avoid it. I had good friends and acquaintances in half the places that were currently being bombed. I didn't want to imagine the bakery where they made my favorite *kulche* reduced to rubble or envision the sweet little cottage in Kenya burned to ashes.

National news wasn't any happier. I hated thinking that the American public was too stupid or ignorant to see through political greed agendas. Loosening Wall Street and banking regulations would improve the economy, really? Whose economy, theirs or mine? I was thinking if politicians had to operate on *my* economy, loosening mortgage regulations would be the last thing they'd be concerned about.

But having a landlord involved in the latest headline scandal forced me to read the miserable front page on Saturday morning.

Stiles Murdered? was the least of it. After that, objectivity went all to heck.

I set my cell phone on the breakfast table as I consumed my fresh-squeezed orange juice and eggs benedict. Tudor was still sleeping—or hiding in his room. EG was reading her school tablet computer. She'd probably had Tudor spend the night installing prohibited internet access. I'd check later.

Right now, I waited to see which of our family journalists annoyed me by calling first for the story behind the story.

On the dot of seven-thirty—sister Patra won the prize. It was a weekend. She should be sleeping in. I let my phone buzz and indulged in a cup of hot tea. The house phone rang. Somewhere in the bowels of the Victorian, Mallard answered it.

He'd given up hunting us down for phone calls months ago. He texted me now that Patra was trying to reach me. I hit "k" so he'd know I'd seen his message.

The next call was from Sean O'Herlihy. He was a real journalist, not a Patra newbie. But he and Patra had connected professionally—and personally—so I wasn't feeding him information yet either. I let it go to voice mail.

By this time, EG was casting curious glances my way. I really hadn't reached anywhere close to my most maddening behavior yet. A few weeks ago I'd smashed an entire street full of news vehicles when talking heads had gone out of bounds. I was hoping that had taught the media to be a little more discreet this time. That it was only Patra and Sean calling —people who knew us—meant word on the street hadn't touched on Graham. *Yet.* The rest of the world didn't know Graham the way Patra and Sean did.

But if I fed any information to Patra and Sean, the media would be back on our doorstep in minutes. Graham was worse than me. He would most likely stealth bomb the street. By allowing us into his hermitage, Graham had opened himself up to invasion.

I knew what it was like to have my privacy invaded. I wouldn't force that violation on a man who—despite his rudeness—had helped my family when they needed it. But this time, *he* had disturbed the hornets.

Messages would be flooding my email box by now, I calculated. Graham could see everything in the computer he'd provided for me. He would recognize Patra and Sean's addresses. I debated turning on my phone's irritating ring and sitting it next to the candelabra in the center of the table where his intercom would pick it up, but in sympathy for his predicament, I figured I'd start out polite and crank the amps later.

EG finished her breakfast and sat playing with her tablet, waiting expectantly.

Finally, the candelabra shouted, "Ana, get your ass up here now!"

"How many million are you paying me for working on Saturdays?" I asked innocently.

Once upon a time, he'd threatened to heave us out of the house if I didn't toe his line. Revenge was sweet, and turnabout, fair play.

Five

THE CANDELABRA'S CURSES SHUT OFF ABRUPTLY. Once upon a time, I'd shoved the nosy silver into the sideboard. Now, I simply enjoyed my morning tea.

Let it be known here and now that I may be an introvert who prefers my own company, but I am *not* shy. I am well aware of my worth, I'm assertive, and unfortunately, I possess my Irish terrorist father's temper.

I do not take well to being shouted at in foul language over the breakfast table.

I leisurely finished my tea while waiting for Graham to digest my rebellion. He'd had the upper hand for too long. Role reversal soothed my angry beast.

"Does this mean we can go to the Smithsonian today?" EG asked deviously.

My little sister knew the candelabra was listening as well as I did.

"I have other clients who need my time," I said airily. Although, in reality, I'd been cutting back my client list. Family and Graham's demands took a substantial chunk of my once carefree workaholic's hours. "Maybe tomorrow."

I imagined Graham writhing in wrath at the possibility of my taking two whole days off from addressing his concerns. The man seriously needed an attitude adjustment.

"Does this mean you're not taking me up on my offer?" the silver candelabra asked in a menacing tone.

"It means I consider your offer of payment *insulting*. I expect the banking information you're withholding to be downloaded immediately in a gesture of respect, at which point you may ask me politely to visit your office when it's convenient for me." I kept my voice neutral. My father's fiery oratory had got him killed. Mine could still get us booted from paradise. I'd learned caution—but sometimes offense is better than defense.

"Ana..." Graham said in a deep voice that could be dangerously seductive, or just plain dangerous.

I opened my phone's mailbox app and watched a large file from his office hit the screen. It was too large to open on my phone, but I was wagering Graham wasn't playing games when his cojones were on the chopping block. That should be his file on my grandfather's Swiss accounts.

"Nice," I said, sticking the phone in my pocket. "If you have a few minutes to spare, I'll be up in ten. Clear your cat out."

The silver remained blessedly silent. One could hope I'd taught the devil a lesson in respect.

No one had defied Graham quite so blatantly in these last months of walking on eggshells. EG stared at me in awe for good reason. "I'll go finish my homework now. Should I wake Tudor?"

Since I was currently Ruler of the World, and Tudor was part of my evil plot, I nodded. "Good idea. Tell him to eat quickly before the silver turns mean."

Graham used to have a sense of humor, but I heard no sarcastic chuckle now. I could see where he might be a bit off his feed with a murder rap on his horizon. So I politely ran down to my office and checked his folder to be certain that bank receipt with all the zeroes was in it. I didn't have time to salivate over all the possibilities of recovering my grandfather's wealth. I had to beard the lion in his den.

I took my time using the main stairs since EG and Tudor were expecting to see me. They didn't need to know about the secret passage. Passing by them on the second floor landing, I could see that Tudor looked unkempt and tired. I waved and continued up to Graham's level.

Graham probably looked worse than Tudor, but with no window and no lights, it was hard to tell. Judging by his silhouette against the light of a dozen monitors, his hair seemed rumpled. He impatiently shoved aside a thick hank falling into his face. I was pretty certain those were the same jeans and long-sleeved shirt he'd worn yesterday. The sophisticated, tuxedoed, diamond-cufflink man who vividly haunted my memory was visible only in his supple movement as he adjusted various monitors for my perusal.

I sneezed. He opened a drawer and handed me an antihistamine. Rolling my eyes, I choked it down dry.

"Here is the list of the dinner's attendees." He scrolled down a list of hundreds on the first screen. "Here are photographs and films taken during the meal." Images of linen-covered hotel tables with a variety of nerds trying to look professional flipped silently on another screen. "We need to verify faces against names."

"That will only take a hundred years." I boldly reached over his shoulder and zoomed in on the head table with Stiles and cohorts. "Who served the Last Supper?" I asked irreverently. The image on the screen showed utensils untouched and napkins still folded.

He snorted and started flashing through images. "Not Judas."

Instead of showing me the servers, as I'd requested, he zoomed in on Stiles, then went around the table, naming the occupants.

"Henry Bates," Graham said, identifying the other dead man. Henry wore black-framed nerd glasses like Tudor's, but his starched collar and glossy tie were meticulous and probably expensive. "Stiles' right hand man. Bates helped Stiles develop MacroWare's programs. He was the best candidate for gathering a team to repair any security breaches."

"If Bates was a programmer, he knew who had the chops to add spyware, if that's what we're dealing with," I added. "A good reason to want him dead."

Graham nodded reluctant agreement. He moved the screen to a youngish man with a full head of blond hair and an ad exec's smile. "Adam Herkness, VP of Public Relations. He would know nothing about security, but a breach in the new system would be a PR nightmare."

The monitor changed to focus on a short, rotund, balding man. "Bob Stark, VP of Finance." The fifth and last man was a middle-aged Latino with a mustache. "Enrique Gomez, VP of Security."

"Any good reason they'd tell a financial guy about any security breach?" I asked as Graham opened more video images and zoomed up on the executive table at the front of the room.

"Bob Stark helped fund Stiles when they started out. They were friends. And reports of a breach could be disastrous to stock prices and the bottom line. He had to be prepared for a shit storm."

I didn't often respect rich people—money creates illusions of superiority and I'd been around too many wealthy tyrants growing up—but I could respect friendship and honesty. "So we have five people here who feared the new software had a problem and weren't worried enough not to feed their faces. Doesn't sound as if the breach was big enough to murder for."

The last murder case I got stuck investigating had snowballed—or fireballed—into murder and mayhem endangering my family and friends. I was not eager to get involved in anything similar.

But Graham had helped us. In no universe could I reject his request for aid now. The problem was obviously larger than the local police department, who had no good reason to call in the feds, yet. The local cops didn't know about the hole in the State Department website firewall. They probably didn't even know about the beta program.

Graham opened a screen showing my bulging mailbox. "I've sent you all the material I uncovered last night. As far as I've been able to ascertain, even if the flaw is only in the few distributed to government testers, it has the potential of breaching national security on every level from the NSA to the laptops of Senate committees. If the flaw is in every program..." He didn't have to explain. The nightmare was universe-size.

"Stiles may not have known the extent of the breach that night," Graham continued, "but he recognized enough of the possible disastrous repercussions to call me in. He didn't have time to send all his files before he was hospitalized, so I don't know what kind of actions—if any—have been taken already. And under the circumstances, I'm wary of hacking MacroWare right now or revealing information he gave me in confidence."

"So far as we know, none of this actually affects the internet, right?" I asked, voicing Tudor's terror. "The web remains up and running?"

He shot me a puzzled look over his shoulder. "The internet does not run on MacroWare."

A fat lot he knew if he didn't realize Tudor's monster could chomp into website servers through that damned hole. But he didn't know about that... yet.

Graham halted one of the dinner videos and backed up. A plump waitress in a discreet black pant suit was slipping entree dishes onto the table while the men laughed and ignored her. She was white, not young, not pretty, just efficient.

Graham took a screen shot and sent it to my mailbox. "Start there when you research the list of kitchen staff I sent you."

"She didn't cook the soup, and I'm not seeing her shooting up the veggies," I protested, reverse bigotry in full sail. I wanted the old white dudes to be guilty.

"Chain of command. Who assigned her to that table? Who handed her the tray? I need you to ask the questions. I cannot be found and drawn in for questioning—I know too much about subjects that are irrelevant to murder."

I assumed his paranoia had a substantial basis given his checkered career. And knowing the underbelly of governments, I didn't argue his point. Given his level of knowledge, Graham was a ticking time bomb a lot of agencies would like to get their hands on.

"I may have to disappear until this case is solved, so I'm leaving a lot in your hands," Graham reminded me in a grim voice.

"Not the cat, I hope," I said facetiously, but he had opened the subject uppermost on my mind. "Tudor can help you. He knows more about the breach than anyone. He's willing to tell you what he knows, but I'm not willing to get him involved in murder unless I know we've employed all possible caution. I need to work with *all* my family on a job this large."

He quit clicking his keyboard, sat back, and actually looked at me. That didn't happen often. I straightened, crossed my arms, and waited. His dark eyes, razor-sharp cheekbones, and square jaw could be intimidating, but physical appearance didn't daunt me as much as brains. Graham possessed more than should be humanly possible.

"How much family and how involved?" he asked, sensibly. He understood Tudor's talents and would question him in geek-speak later. The rest of my family, on the other hand, were capable of starting nuclear wars if called upon.

"Not Magda," I assured him, "unless one of her boyfriends is involved. But Tudor knows programming and hacking. Patra can ferret info out of media files. Nick has Brit intelligence resources at his fingertips. Relying on each other is how we work."

He glowered, then returned to the videos. "My business relies on secrecy. It's much easier for me to operate if no one but my clients know I exist or how to find me. Patra is building a career on revealing information I'd prefer was kept private. The media are obsolete and no longer the protector of our constitutional rights."

"Blah, blah, blah," I retorted, intelligently. "Media are gossips, voters are uneducated idiots, the government is corrupt, and what exactly has changed in centuries? You use the tools you're given. We need information. I obtain it through connections, not cameras on every corner. Obviously, your methods are different. We either combine forces or I go back to my clients and translating letters from Thailand."

As a virtual assistant with international contacts, I often juggled translations, scientific research, and communication for a variety of scholarly clients. Graham had taken advantage of my skills and contacts more than once. He had to trust my knowledge or we couldn't do this.

"You've never had to keep this level of confidentiality," he argued.

"I was Magda's right hand man for twenty years," I responded in a voice heavily laden with sarcasm. "My grandfather was her tutor as well as yours. Do you really think I led a charmed life while you were dining with presidents?"

"I don't like it," he said flatly.

"You should have thought of that before you took an ego trip to meet Stiles in person instead of Skyping. Get over it. Find a new business model, whatever. You were the last person to see Stiles before the ambulance carried him off. Half MacroWare's board is ready to pin motive on you, the interloper, a man with the ability to *cause* the breach. Your neck is on the line and our priority is to save it. Deal with fall-out later."

Prioritizing, I excelled at. Choosing between going hungry and running for my life—piece of cake. Graham was dithering over the method of his downfall. "You're getting soft," I taunted.

"I could just disappear again," he retorted angrily, stopping the video at the speech-making part of the dinner.

"Or you could clear your name, move on, get a life, get help for agoraphobia, any of the above. Anything I can do, you can do better."

"That's not how the song goes," he said wearily. "And *you* are still hiding in the basement."

"I'll happily move into your attic. Look, stop the footage, go back." I pointed at the screen where Stiles was at the podium, gesticulating. "There, stop there."

In the background, the same waitress was quietly clearing the head table. None of the execs looked green yet, although they'd obviously finished their dinner.

"Herkness scraped off his salsa and he lived," Graham said, focusing his formidable attention on the scene.

"Did all five test for botulism?" I watched as the blond VP of PR waved away his plate while seemingly fascinated by his boss's boring speech.

"He might just not like salsa," Graham warned. "This does not make him a suspect. We don't even know the salsa was the source of the botulism."

"But from the medical reports, Herkness is far more likely to recover than the other two—which certainly points fingers at the salsa. You'd better get security on him, whatever the case. And now will you admit that I'm not an idiot, and I know how much to tell my family and when?"

"I know you're not an idiot, although spotting salsa isn't proof. It's Nick and Patra I don't trust. I don't like wildcards. Tudor better know enough to make my agreement worth it."

"Tudor is the one who warned MacroWare about the spyhole." I stood back and waited for that to sink in. "He has some illusion that he notified Stiles directly, although I'm not going to ask how he came up with a private email."

"Crap." Graham uttered a few more choice expletives as he ran through a screen apparently monitoring Stiles email account. So much for not hacking.

"Search on Kinghenry with a UK address," I told him.

Tudor's email appeared in seconds.

"He should learn to spell," Graham said dryly, reading the cryptic text that was more a Twitter hash fest than anything legible.

"He buried the info in tweets," I ventured. "Follow the MacroWare hashtag and his signature on Twitter."

"I hate working with amateurs," he growled with a sigh, setting one of his monitors to Twitter.

"You hate getting old and out of touch. The kids have been using this format to get around Magda's nosiness for years. Or think they're getting around it. Who knows if Stiles followed it, but someone might have."

He returned to surly mode and ran a search on hashtags to show he wasn't out of touch, but I could tell I'd hit a sore spot. As

Tudor's panicked message emerged amid myriad other MW hashtag messages, he growled in disgust.

The once very public Amadeus Graham thought he was his own CIA. He was pretty darned good at it. But as I'd learned to my displeasure, sometimes, one had to live life to learn new things.

Graham apparently thought he only needed computers. I had made it my goal in life to disillusion him.

Six

ANA WAS A BOSSY PAIN IN THE ARSE, but Tudor was eager to meet dodgy Graham, who played the family strings like a meta-gamer. Ever since they'd learned Amadeus Graham had taken over Grandpa's mansion, Tudor had been digging into Ana's rat in the attic, but the bloke was impossible to ferret out. Graham had firewalls beyond anything the NSA had ever developed. For that reason alone, Tudor wanted to check him out.

Nick had said the house and its contents were worth millions, and Old Max had left it to all his grandkids. With his share, Tudor figured he could quit school and start his own software company. But no matter how deep he dug, he hadn't uncovered anything to get the sod thrown in jail. If Ana hadn't been able to do it... But she never told him anything, so he didn't know what she had up her sleeve except lawsuits. He'd be out of school and a corporate drone before they'd be settled.

EG had begged him to take snaps when he went to Graham's office—she had never seen their landlord and she was living here!

But standing in the doorway of Graham's creepy attic room after breakfast, Tudor was pretty shaky about even entering.

The man in the chair was big, and the office... beyond *awesome*. Tudor stared like a dork for a full minute at the bank of computer monitors. He could swear one was showing Nick entering the embassy, but it switched to a hospital too fast to be certain. How could anyone watch all those screens at once? ADD much?

And then Tudor spotted the Twitter screen following the #cookiemonster tag. His stomach sank to his shoes.

"Would you like to explain the software that allowed you to breach the government's visa website?" the hulk in the chair asked without greeting.

Tudor had the weird feeling the man had eyes in the back of his head.

"The worm was only supposed to remove my footprint," Tudor

replied defensively, glaring at the incriminating evidence on the screen. "No one has the right to keep track of all my information."

"There is no law that says they *can't* track anyone who enters their website," Graham pointed out. "Quid pro quo, you want their information, you have to give them yours. You don't want their information, stay off their website."

"I didn't *mean* to use it on the visa site," Tudor said defensively. "I just forgot to turn the program off. But the worm was programmed to only eat *my* information. It should never have gone past the data folder." Tudor took a deep breath and asked his greatest fear, "Did it gut anything vital?"

"Besides national security?" Graham asked dryly. "No, it seems to have been content with destroying only the data level where user information is stored. One hopes that was backed up elsewhere and that they shut down before the worm could attach itself to other documents. Just the fact that you breached the State Department's firewalls is chilling enough."

Thankfully, the room was too dark for anyone to tell he'd been sweating. Tudor swallowed a lump of relief. "But someone with real spyware could have gone in through that hole and stolen all the info, right? That's what I told Stiles."

Graham dialed up a screen showing Stiles' personal email account, the one Tudor had turned up from his hacker buddies. He opened up Tudor's coded email. It looked pretty pathetic up there on the wall.

"Stiles is dead," Graham said bluntly. "He died soon after he had the software tested and found the holes in the websites you told him about. He found more."

Tudor grokked that Ana thought Stiles had been *murdered* because of the spyhole. The stories he'd read had said food poisoning. He didn't think he was important enough to have been personally responsible for the death of his hero, but he would gladly take down anyone who might have done it. He asked warily, "And what do you want me to do?"

"Go to MIT, get out of our hair, don't show your face here again," Graham said. "But what I want and what I need aren't necessarily the same, as your sister has so crudely pointed out."

"Yes, sir," Tudor said with caution, not entirely understanding. "I don't have the funds to visit MIT. Does that mean it's safe for me to go home? I can ask Ana for a loan."

"No, it's *not* safe for you to go home, not with your fine hand all over that Twitter account." He gestured at the screen before working some magic with his keyboard and making all the messages disappear, leaving the Twitter screen blank.

Tudor watched in awe as Graham ran a search on the tag he'd just deleted and nothing showed up. He'd *wiped* the tag clean from the public Twitter database. How was that even possible? Well, it wasn't, entirely, but the copies would be buried so deep in such obscure places, someone would really have to know what they were doing to find them.

As if he hadn't just performed magic, Graham continued, "I would recommend eliminating all your social media accounts and lying low, preferably forever. A mind like yours is a frightening thing."

"Yes, sir." Tudor wasn't certain where this was going. His people skills often failed him. "Ana told me not to use your network, though. Should I go to a library?"

Graham kneaded his forehead before speaking. "No, you cannot leave the house until we find who killed Stiles and why. That person is ruthless, and if his motivation had anything to do with the security breach, then you're in danger. You will delete all trace of yourself using a computer not connected to this network. I will set up a new identity through a server in Uzbekistan for your use. Send me a copy of your damned monster program, and keep it out of the O/S breach this time. Once you've eliminated your social media, start tracking who has had access to the affected software."

Uzbekistan? Tudor gulped and nodded. "Yes, sir. I don't think my tablet will do the job, though."

"Unfortunately, I don't think I can let you out of my sight with anything more dangerous than a tablet. If you want a full computer, you'll have to use that one over there." Graham tilted his head toward a corner of his workspace.

Tudor widened his eyes. "Here, sir? I'll be working here?"

"Safer than a jail cell, anyway." With that, Graham returned to work.

***

Ana ponders the impossible

MY MAILBOX BOILED OVER with Patra's curses and pleas for information on whether Graham knew Stiles or anything about the murders. I figured if I left the mansion, Sean would pop out from behind light posts. Our nosy reporter wouldn't dare actually knock on the *door*. He had issues with Graham that I didn't totally grasp.

Since Graham's preference was complete silence, he wouldn't deign to speak to anyone, much less journalists. I had to be his portal and choose what information to give out, and when. Right now, all Patra and Sean were doing was grasping straws based on the CNN video, old photos of Graham, and insider knowledge of Graham's obsessions that no other reporters possessed.

Our bargain was that I fed them what I thought they could use without mayhem and destruction, and they helped me dig into files I didn't have the time or expertise to comb through. Right now, they didn't have anything I wanted.

While Graham interrogated Tudor, I dug through the files that had come in overnight. Graham either had a spy or spyware inside police headquarters, because all the police files were here along with media reports, hospital reports, and anything else Graham thought relevant.

If I was having difficulty keeping up with my last remaining on-line clients, Graham must be having a devil of a time, given the ton of information in this folder. He couldn't have slept at all.

Sifting through, I learned that the police had received the first rushed lab reports about the botulism poisoning. They now realized what we knew first—this was not a mundane case of fish poisoning. I read panic in the terse sentences.

I couldn't read the hospital reports as easily, but it seemed the three survivors were hanging on. Herkness was doing better than the others, and his lab reports tested lower on botulism, so the salsa was probably the culprit, if the dinner remains were any evidence. Stiles and Bates did not rise from the dead and walk the halls like zombies from puffer fish overdose. The botulism on top of fish poison had made certain they were good and dead.

I did not read anything I didn't already know since, until botulism came into play, the Department of Health and not the police had been doing the investigating. I needed to read the reports from the DOH. I had to think beyond what the police would do so we weren't duplicating efforts.

I wasn't held back by the regulations the police had to follow.

We might have a twenty-four hour head start until someone learned that Graham was probably the last man to talk to Stiles before the CEO was hauled off to the hospital.

The police didn't know about the security breach—yet. What I really needed was to be inside MacroWare, to see who Stiles had told about the previously unknown spyhole in their all-powerful operating system. Hackers were always finding new holes in *browsers*, but in the system itself... I thought that might be something totally new. And in undistributed beta software—almost totally impossible.

I e-mailed Graham to ask if he'd lowered himself to hacking into the company's internal network yet. I got a message back from Tudor saying he was on it. I tried not to gape in astonishment.

Fine, we were all on the same page. Next.

I went through the Department of Health reports and found the names of the kitchen staff who had been there that night.

Reading the report, I'd say if Graham hadn't intervened, the killers would have won a *Get Out of Jail Free* card. Accidental puffer fish poisoning would have gone on the autopsy report of five wealthy men.

It was Saturday. Few employees in the DOH would be working today unless they were on emergency calls. I rifled through Graham's files from the health department—rudimentary at this point. Fugu chefs are trained in excessive cleanliness. The instant the soup had been served, the pot and all utensils, including the cutting board, used for the soup had been scrubbed with special cleaning compounds.

According to the health department reports, Adolph Nasser, the head chef, asserted that the fish guts had been properly disposed of per regulations. This involved wrapping them in layers of plastic and taking them off to be destroyed by chemicals—burning doesn't kill the poison. They'd tried to question the soup chef—one Hiroko Kita—but he'd left work on the day the DOH showed up and wasn't answering the phone. I didn't see any evidence that the police were getting a warrant, so they might be in touch with him by now.

At the time of the report, the DOH hadn't known about the

botulism and hadn't tested for anything else. There wasn't much hope of finding contaminated salsa or anything else lying around days after the meal was served, although they were apparently turning over the kitchen looking for any violations. I didn't think that was a useful avenue of pursuit.

One of my specialties is tracing people through the sticky web of computers—it's paid the bills on many an occasion. I ran Hiroko Kita through the routine and discovered he'd not been with the kitchen for long.

Suspicion alerted, I ransacked the hotel's personnel files—even an amateur hacker can slide into most of those. Human Resource departments tend to be run by extroverts who like to talk, not people who care about passwords or computers. All I needed was the hotel's email address, an HR employee's name, and after a couple of tries— the password *4people*. I sighed and shook my head at the predictability.

Skimming through Hiroko Kita's slim file, I noticed he had been recommended by Tray Fontaine, a chef on the west coast. Tray didn't give an employer, so I looked him up—he ran the fancy dining room at MacroWare's corporate headquarters. Who knew nerds got their own chefs?

Having MacroWare's chef send a puffer fish cook to serve poison soup to MacroWare's execs certainly sounded... fishy... to me.

It was a wee bit early to call the coast, so I dug into Tray and Kita's backgrounds a little more. I didn't find anything that appeared potentially blackmailable on either of them. I wasn't planning on blackmailing—unless I thought it was necessary—but chances were good that whoever wanted Stiles dead might have coerced one or both of them into helping.

I can't help it. That's the way my mind works. Blackmail and money are the grease that turns the wheels of governments—why not corporations as well?

I could tell from the files falling into our shared cloud account that Graham and Tudor were tracking down hotel security staff and happily erasing Graham's existence from the meeting room. I'm more of a let's-get-the-bad-guy person. I wanted to talk to Kita before the police got there.

There was a nine-year-old fly in my ointment however.

EG would be sulking because Tudor wasn't there to play with her. Nick had taken off to have his own life and couldn't keep her entertained. She was capable of amusing herself—but a miffed EG should never be left alone.

Our grandfather's portly butler Mallard had unbent enough to accept our presence, but I couldn't continually strain his goodwill by making him babysit.

Hiding in closets and sneaking around is my preferred modus operandi. That's impossible while dragging a child around. How does one query kitchen staff about a missing worker without going undercover?

Pondering, I dug deeper into Kita, since he at least lived on this coast. The police report showed they'd looked for him at the address in the hotel's records. My eyebrows shot up when I checked my quarry's credit report and found a recent inquiry from a landlord at an address in the Adams Morgan neighborhood where Nick was currently residing. The street was slightly north of here and not exactly a cheap place to live. How much did fish chefs get paid anyway? Well, since he was called a *poissonnier*, maybe he got paid for the fishy title.

I looked up the hotel, which was toward the center of the city—not a bad commute by Metro.

I texted EG to ask if she wanted to see the National Geographic Museum, which was near the hotel.

She texted a sneering emoji. Okay, so she'd seen the museum a few times.

The zoo was on the upper end of Adams-Morgan, not precisely near Kita's address but a few stops away.

ZOO? I texted.

I got a pouting emoji in return. Tough luck, kid. It wouldn't hurt to cruise Adams-Morgan, see if Kita had moved in. He might hide from the police, but me with a kid...? Pity it wasn't Girl Scout cookie season.

I texted Nick and warned him we were headed his way. I'd told him repeatedly that I wasn't taking full responsibility for EG, that he had to shoulder his share. He'd agreed. We needed to rope Patra in, but she was just out of school and needed to try her wings. As the eldest of our tribe, Nick and I were the ones who had decided to settle down.

I sent Tudor a map of the area we were heading into and asked if he wanted to go to the zoo. His reply was explicit and impolite. Teenagers are so predictable—but he'd know where we were if we ran into trouble.

I threw a few of my favorite spy tools into a tote and went upstairs to pound on EG's door. She'd let her bangs grow out, and the purple dye had faded. She now appeared to have blue-black raven wings clipped back from her face. She had Magda's dramatic cheekbones and big green eyes that would slay dragons in a few years. Right now, they narrowed suspiciously at my tote.

"I'm not staying with Mallard," she stated flatly.

"You will if I tell you to, and if that's your attitude, that's what I'm inclined to do," I said cheerfully. "But if you'll lighten up, we'll go exploring before the zoo. Get your walking shoes."

"It's November. It's forty degrees out there. Who goes to the zoo in winter?" But she was already hunting under the bed for shoes.

"Fewer crowds, good exercise, it will toughen you up. Want me to tell you about the winter we spent in Russia where we didn't need a refrigerator, we just kept food on the windowsill?"

"Yeah and how long it takes to thaw milk. I've heard that about a thousand times. Tell me what we're really doing."

"I'll let you know when I figure it out." I watched her drag on furry boots and suffered a pang of envy.

EG had to go outside to school every day, so I'd bought her warm clothes. I'd been living in Atlanta last winter and hadn't needed boots. I never left my office here if I could avoid it, so I hadn't bought warm footgear. I glanced down at my wooly socks and sandals. "Maybe we should go shopping instead of the zoo."

"That makes sense. Let's get Nick," she agreed eagerly.

My little sister was showing dangerous signs of following in our glamorous mother's footsteps. I'd gone the opposite direction, probably because I couldn't compete with our mother's blond beauty. I'm short, my hair is inky, and I turn nasty when men stare at my boobs, so I hid them. Mostly. Today, I was wearing a man's fisherman's sweater because I couldn't find one in a woman's size at a reasonable price. With luck, I could tuck my braid in a knit hat and be androgynous.

That hope lasted until we stepped out the front door and ran into Sean O'Herlihy at the gate.

Seven

"THAT WAS GRAHAM ENTERING THE HOTEL where Stiles was killed, wasn't it?" Sean asked, joining us as we walked toward the Metro. "You do know Stiles was murdered, don't you?"

A little history—Sean's father and my father were Irish terrorists together. They died at the same time as Graham's father. Sean and Graham both had connections to my grandfather and possess a deep-seated neurosis about bringing the bad guys to justice. I've learned to trust both Graham and Sean, for different reasons.

Other than his insane obsession with digging into Graham's activities, Sean was a decent guy, and not bad looking. He had a head full of sexy black curls and big blue eyes that could float ships. I'd fancied him for a while, until I realized he was more brother than boyfriend. I think he likes Patra, but there's nearly a ten-year age gap between them, so their relationship remains long distance.

"Hello to you, too," I said, striding briskly for the Metro. EG rattled her gloved hands along the wrought iron fences and ran ahead of us. "Lovely day for the zoo."

"Dammit, Ana, I thought we were friends. Why not give me the scoop? There are already rumors flying that Graham was up for a position on the board. Until that news clip showed up, no one even knew for certain he was *alive*. If he was in that hotel that day, the police will be all over him before sundown." He paced angrily beside me.

"You want me to speed them on their way? Do you think I'm an idiot? We'd be out of a home by sundown." Knowing that Graham's story was why Patra and Sean were breathing down my neck—they not only knew he was alive but where he lived—I'd given the problem some thought. Sean had been extremely helpful in the past. I wanted him on our side. But I wouldn't screw around with Graham either. Much.

So I'd have to give them something just as ripe. Graham, the paranoid hermit, would probably bust a gasket at my revealing any info, but that was his problem.

"As usual, you're working the wrong side of the street," I told him. "I cannot confirm this—I'm not a Macro employee—but Stiles and his execs were sitting on a potential national security nightmare. Contemplate who would want that covered up."

"Everybody from the president on down!" he practically shouted. "Rumors don't cut it. I need facts."

I shrugged. I couldn't clone myself, so I needed his help as much as he needed mine. If I fed him just enough, we could work out a trade. "That takes time and work. You can tag along with me, or you can hang around the hotel restaurant and see if the missing chef's fellow workers will spill anything about him."

"The puffer fish chef is missing? How do you know that?" he asked in good journalist fashion, not giving away whether he was just curious or disbelieving.

"The same way you would if you'd bother with tedious detail instead of hanging out on street corners trying to catch Graham flying through windows. He's an agoraphobic recluse, not Dracula." Well, some days he liked to be Batman, but that was an inside joke involving EG's interest in bats and my scorn of Graham's superhero tendencies. The man *is* capable of laughing at himself.

We'd reached the Metro station. I grabbed EG before she could disappear into the crowd. "You go one way," I told Sean, "and I'll go the other. We can keep in touch," I suggested, hopefully.

He glared at the time on his phone and shrugged. "Can't hurt. I've only got two more hours to make the story my own, so find something relevant."

"Keep me informed or you get no more goodies," I warned.

He saluted and jogged off for the southern side of the track. EG and I headed north.

"Who are we spying on today?" she asked in satisfaction.

"We're just casing a neighborhood," I said airily. "We should know what's available should we ever have to move."

"You'd nail yourself to the door before you let that happen," EG said, mimicking my insouciance.

"What kind of books are you reading that such a thought would enter your head?" I asked in mock horror.

"There hasn't been anyone good since Machiavelli, but I think he was more into poison than nails. It was easier to poison people back then."

I tried so hard to keep her out of the family business... I handed her my phone. "See if you can find consignment stores nearby. Be normal for a while."

With delight, she took off her gloves and grabbed the phone. She was still punching when we arrived at the stop closest to the address I was seeking.

"There are two stores north of the Metro," she reported as we stepped into an icy wind and pulled our gloves on again. "We need to go right."

"Not yet." I'd made a mental map of street names before we'd left. In the bad old days before we carried computers in our pockets, I'd learned to memorize my surroundings. One never knew when it would be necessary to escape irate merchants or rabid camels.

Chef Kita's potential address was in an area of colorful turn-of-the-twentieth-century buildings. They weren't much more than boarding houses, but in this exclusive neighborhood, they had been upgraded in a manner no slum had ever seen.

In celebration of the rainbow nature of the community, some houses sported pink trim, others flaunted blue shutters or orange bricks, anything to brighten the boring facades. Nick had chosen to live on a more sedate street in acknowledgement of his diplomatic position, but his place wasn't too far away.

Kita's tenement was a little less spiffy than the others. The chartreuse paint was peeling around the windows. The burgundy-covered porch was streaked with what might have been mold or dried egg for all I knew. The potted geraniums were dead—not promising, although I was pretty sure geraniums didn't like November.

A FOR LEASE sign adorned the lower floor window. I'd already researched ownership and knew the landlord lived in one of the apartments. Judging by the mailboxes and doorbells, there were two tenants—only the landlord's was labeled.

"Step back and keep an eye on the windows over the porch," I told EG. She did as told—without question. Amazing.

I tried the blank bell just for the heck of it. No one looked out the empty downstairs window. I glanced at EG and she shook her head.

I tried the second bell and was rewarded with a "Who is it?" from the intercom. Nice. So Graham wasn't the only who wired old houses for sound.

"Hi, this is Patty Pasko." I'd given up my Linda Lane alias after I wore it out in my last escapade. My new ID showed Realtor on the business card, although I'd also set up other websites and mail drops with matching business cards, depending on my needs of the moment.

Apparently, introverts do better with assumed identities.

"I'm a Realtor looking for an apartment for a client," I told the intercom.

Bingo, the magic words. The landlord said he'd be right down.

Dave Scoggins could have been called the Gray Man: less than six-feet tall—which still had him towering over me—with graying hair, gray beard shadow, and sweater and slacks that could have been gray or oatmeal or dead mouse. He blinked through wire-rimmed spectacles at seeing equally mousily-dressed me. Oops. Realtors tended to be a lot spiffier.

"I was just on my way to the zoo with my niece and saw the sign." I smiled and nodded at the window. "Is the apartment empty?"

EG was playing kid, spying into the front windows.

"The last tenant never actually moved in," he said in disgust. "He skipped out on the lease. I can show you the rooms, if you'd like."

"He paid a deposit and didn't move in?" I asked in surprise. "How odd." I entered the high-ceilinged hall. An old walnut staircase—battered, never painted or refinished—led straight up along one side of the house. The first floor apartment door was on the left.

"He only paid the deposit, not the first month's rent. Asian fellow, said he'd just moved to town and had a new job. He promised to pay the rent when his furniture arrived." Dave rattled the key in the knob and opened the unpainted walnut front door. "His credit record was clean, so I gave him a key."

"Did you ever see him again?" I asked, pretending to study the spacious front room that we entered.

"I thought I heard him come and go a couple of times, but he was quiet. People like to measure windows and clean up and stuff before they move in, so I didn't think anything of it." He opened the next door and glanced in.

EG bounced in after us, poking around into cabinets and disappearing toward the back of the house. I didn't know how much she could learn, but I let her at it. I followed Scoggins to the next room. Judging by the double closet doors, it was intended to be a bedroom.

"Closets, nice," I said casually. "Not too many of these old houses have double ones." I opened a door.

A body rolled out.

Scoggins screamed. I rushed to the door and prevented EG from running in.

Thinking fast, I took another good look at the corpse—male, Asian, wearing bloody whites—then pushed EG back toward the front door. "I'm sorry, Mr. Scoggins, I can't involve my niece in this. My sister would take off my head. You'd better call the police."

I'd lived in war-torn countries. I'd seen dead bodies, some far worse than this. My stomach still churned as I pushed EG out the front door. Mr. Kita had apparently been in that closet for a while. He was no longer stiff. The blood on his chef whites had dried to an ugly brown.

Let me repeat—I am a virtual assistant, not a detective, not by a long shot. My innate and well-honed survival instinct prevented any desire to play detective. Someone else could cover the forensics. My only goal at this moment was to keep me and EG away from the cops.

"What happened?" EG asked anxiously as I nearly dragged her back toward the Metro.

"We will not be questioning Mr. Kita in this lifetime," I said as we turned into the more commercial district. "Consignment stores. Let's shop now."

"He's dead?" EG asked eagerly. "You found a body?"

"You're gruesome. Every living being deserves respect. We're not insects to be cruelly stamped out if we get in someone's way." I was working up a pretty good hate on the killer. My usual reverse bigotry, I supposed. Kita had been a cook, a worker bee. I could sympathize with him and his family far easier than with Stiles and his gazillions, and I was angry.

I yanked out my cell and texted Graham, then Sean. In the

information business, it was necessary to trade for value, so I trusted Sean to give back as good as I gave. And someone else needed to be working on this besides me.

Repeating the mantra, *I am not Magda, I will not desert my family,* I turned off the phone. I'd promised EG shopping, not murder and mayhem, and I would see that she got it—even if she behaved as much like a vulture as our mother. Kids can be cruel unless they're taught better.

Which made me wonder about my mother's upbringing.

EG was irate that I hadn't let her close to examine her very first dead body. I simply dragged her into a store and showed her purple. She was absorbed in no time.

Kids are easy. Adults—particularly the freaking weirdoes I hung out with—were a real pain.

Nick arrived before we got through the first store. Nick is blond, tall, gorgeous, and better dressed than I'll ever be. I narrowed my eyes at his approach and removed a leopard-spotted fur hat from a rack, pulling it down to my eyebrows.

"Very Russian," he concluded, producing a matching pair of fur-lined boots from the rack below. "Why is Tudor texting me and not you?"

"I told you we were headed this way." I deliberately pulled an ankle-length black wool coat off the coat rack. Women's size medium, it would cover the boots if I wore them. I would look like a demented bag lady.

"You didn't tell me you were hunting dead bodies. Did EG see it?" He didn't have to stand on his toes as I did to find EG scouting the kid clothes.

"No, she did not, although the little shark keeps begging to go back and look." I didn't argue when Nick dragged the ugly coat off of me and stuck it back on the rack. He left me wearing the Russian leopard hat. "Did the landlord call it in to the police?" I asked.

"He did," Nick acknowledged. "I just passed the place and the cops are all over. Will they find your fingerprints?"

I cringed and showed him my gloved hands, for once grateful for my thin Irish skin. I couldn't remember if EG had taken off her gloves after we'd entered the apartment. "EG was into everything. Scoggins will say he found the body when he was showing the rooms. No big deal." I hadn't even given him my business card. I debated changing my ID again in case he actually remembered the name I'd given him.

"Tudor says Graham is fuming. Do you intend to go back or do you want to hide out with me for a while?" Nick asked cheerfully, producing a size small, camel-colored cashmere three-quarter coat that matched the boots and hat perfectly. He's good like that.

In gratitude for his understanding, I even accepted the offering. The coat fit, it was warm, and even though the hat and boots called notice to me—which I hated—I didn't want to shop more.

"I'll go back, but I promised EG shopping. Help her find some other color besides purple, please." I re-directed our male fashionista to the youngling.

While they shopped, I reluctantly turned my phone back on and opened Sean's message first.

SCORE! It read. DEAD BODY=STORY

Glad I'd made someone happy, I opened Graham's e-mail.

Adam Herkness awake. He knows I was there.

Well, swell. The police would be on our doorstep, toot sweet, as they say in the cartoons.

Eight

FOCUSING ON "NORMAL" for EG's sake, I steered the conversation away from dead bodies and let her chatter over our purchases on the ride home. She mocked my Russian faux leopard hat. I wrapped my wool scarf around her mouth.

Mostly, I enjoyed my half siblings. It's keeping them out of trouble that turns me into a nagging harridan. But for this little while, I could pretend disaster didn't consistently loom on our horizon. We actually laughed as a normal family does as we walked up to the house.

I sent EG upstairs with our packages, ordering her to do her homework. I headed down to the basement. Mallard intercepted me in the hall between my office and his kitchen lair. A frown wrinkled his wide forehead clear to his balding scalp, giving him a look not too different from a bloodhound's.

"The police have indicated a desire to interrogate Mr. Graham," Mallard said in his professionally disapproving tone. "He is not available."

So much for normal.

Mallard-ese wasn't quite the same as butler-speak, one of the many reasons I'd concluded he was former CIA. Each word often contained layers of text I could choose to decipher—or not.

"All right, give me a second," I said. A few of Mallard's wrinkles relaxed while he waited.

I hadn't even had time to see if Graham's information on the Maximillian bank account was legit, but I trusted him under these circumstances. Graham knew I had enough information on him to fry his hide if the files were fake. So this was where Girl Friday earned her maybe-millions.

"How long before the cops arrive on the doorstep?" I asked, all brain cells fully engaged.

"A car has been dispatched. I expect them momentarily," he replied.

His tone was as formal as ever. If he was relieved that I was stepping up to the plate, I couldn't tell.

"All right, perform the grandiose butler act for them," I said, thinking aloud. "If they get insistent, allow them into that mortuary you call a front room. I doubt they have a warrant, so you know the routine. Tell them you'll see if the lady of the house is available. Stall and give me a few minutes."

His bushy brows drew down in disapproval. His lips curved up in the corners. I took that mixed reaction to mean I was on the right track. Seeking approval from a butler was deranged, but I'd never had a real father figure.

I dashed back-upstairs to the second-story study I'd turned into my bedroom. When we'd first moved in, I feared we'd be heaved out in a week. So I'd chosen the room that seemed closest to my grandfather—his study. I slept on a futon and used a filing cabinet for drawers. I wasn't ready to get permanent, yet.

EG had dropped my shopping bags on the carpet of my room. The doorbell rang downstairs as I rummaged through them. Mallard would stall visitors at the front door intercom for a while. The intercom annoyed the hell out of me, but mechanical interfaces had their uses.

I checked out the window overlooking the street. Sure enough, I saw an unmarked cop car out front and boys in bad suits admiring our Gothic façade, while looking grim.

I stripped off my usual dowdy duds, left various personal defense items secured to the chain around my neck, and dragged on the leggings and skimpy attire still laying out from last night's dinner. I'd watched my mother perform this routine since I was a toddler. I knew how it was done. I despised the necessity, but when my family was at stake, I performed my mother duck act to divert danger.

When had Graham become family?

When he agreed to house mine, I assumed. Maybe I should rethink living here, but not right now. I dashed into the bathroom and rummaged through a drawer full of make-up that Nick had insisted I buy.

I grabbed a tube of what I'd dubbed Magda-red lipstick and smeared it across my mouth. Since I spend most of my time in windowless offices, I'm so white as to be almost transparent. The red slash of color on my lips drew attention to my sharp cheekbones and long-lashed green eyes. I preferred anonymity. Attracting attention was Magda's routine, not mine.

But I could do it. As a pale, pathetic virtual assistant, I'd never be able to distract the cops. But I'd learned at my mother's knee how to be what I'm not.

I pinned my long braid into loops at the back of my neck and yanked on the Russian hat. It nearly reached my inky eyebrows and covered every bit of hair except the exotic braided chignon. I looked pretty close to Slavic—which is probably my grandfather's ancestry. Most excellent. Even I didn't recognize me.

The three-quarter length camel-colored wool coat came to the hem of my short skirt. I tugged on the fuzzy leopard boots with the modest three-inch heels. I found a perfume sampler and doused myself. Heavy musk and roses. Yuck. I'd have to take a shower later.

Purse. *Crap.* I carried canvas totes. This outfit required designer leather. As long as I was going to this much trouble, I might as well make the act work double time and use it for my next stop— after I'd steered the cops away.

I crossed to Nick's old room and rummaged through his closet. He'd left a ton of stuff, apparently claiming this room in case the new job and apartment didn't work out. I found a slim leather portfolio case I could tuck under my arm. The gold corners and fastener were a nice touch.

I added my keys, wallet, and larger defense items, and snapped it shut. It couldn't match the weaponry I carried in my army coat, but I was hoping I wouldn't need hand grenades today.

From the hall, I heard male voices carrying up. Mallard must have finally opened the door.

EG was peering out from her doorway. I smiled and waved. She frowned back. Smart kid. I held my finger to my lips in the universal sign for Keep Quiet, adjusted my skirt, and donned pure poisonous Magda. EG knew enough to back off when my inner vamp emerged.

I practiced placing one foot precisely in front of the other, giving my hips maximum swayage, as I sauntered down the enormous staircase.

Mallard had limited our visitors to the foyer, so they got full view of the performance. They kept their expressions professionally blank. Nice—Graham apparently rated cops experienced enough to be unimpressed by swaying hips.

Which meant I had to scowl, check my nonexistent watch, and pick up speed a bit. I became busy, important Magda, not sex-kitten temptress. My heels clicked authoritatively as I descended.

"Gentlemen," I nodded coolly. "How may we help you?"

"Mrs. Graham?" the older, larger cop asked. Iron-gray hair, gray eyes, fancy tie and the white shirt of an officer.

I frowned again. "Anastasia Devlin. And you are?"

"Captain Theodore Donovan. We would like to speak with Amadeus Graham."

"Wouldn't we all?" I asked in boredom. "You might wish to contact our lawyer, Mr. Oppenheimer, since Mr. Graham's name is of necessity on our lawsuit. Ask Mallard for the number. Is that all?"

The captain didn't intend to be dismissed so easily. I hadn't thought he would, poor man.

"This is Mr. Graham's residence, right?" he asked with a little more thunder.

I gestured vaguely. "As I understand it, that is the name on the deed, but this house has always belonged to my family. If you'll dig around in your files a little, you'll see that—among other things— we're *suing* the law firm that allowed their coke-head shyster to steal our grandfather's estate. You will note—the same shyster you allowed to die in your jail cells after we went to all the trouble of locating him for you. If anyone knows Mr. Graham, it would have been the late Reginald Brashton. So sorry that I can't help you. Now, if you'll let me by, I'm already late for an appointment."

"I've told the car to wait around the corner, Miss Devlin," Mallard said deferentially. "Shall I call the driver to bring it around?"

Oops, yeah, a rich bitch wouldn't walk to the Metro.

"By the pub?" I asked with just a hint of condescension. "I'll walk over. It will be faster."

I raised my eyebrows expectantly at the good men in bad suits. What were they going to do? Had I been my usual self, they would have blustered and demanded a search and otherwise been obnoxious. They might still do that.

But for right now, they saw a fabulously wealthy pain in the ass who liked to sue people and held a reasonable grudge against officialdom. For all they knew, I'd have Oppenheimer down here chewing their butts if they got in the way. And they had utterly no good reason to be here. Yet.

They strategically retreated, holding the door so I could sway away.

I'd better warn Oppenheimer that they'd be calling him next. We really were suing Graham. I hadn't lied at all, except by the omission of one crucial fact.

Tudor's take:

ON ONE OF GRAHAM'S WALL MONITORS, Tudor watched Ana strut down the front walk in a barmy hat with two cops glaring after her. Tudor grunted. "If she was six inches taller, I'd say that was my mother."

"Not to demean your mother," Graham muttered, switching screen views to show a hectic restaurant kitchen, "but that's Ana's collie dog act. She just herded the big bad wolves from her flock. Text and tell her the car really is around the corner, ready to take her to the hotel's restaurant."

Tudor did as told while thinking their host had lost his very expensive marbles. No one told Ana what to do. "Do collies bite the noses off bullies?" he asked, trying to warn his host, because, like a nutter, Ana had done just that to a bully when Tudor had been four. Watching the massive tosser's blood spurt after contact with tiny Ana's teeth had been a defining moment in his childhood.

"Yup," the madman said with satisfaction.

Oh well, he'd tried. "Isn't she better off digging into MacroWare with us? She's a devil behind the computer, and that stupid worm needs to be stomped before it mutates or goes any further."

"Why waste that outfit on a basement?" Graham's tone almost sounded appreciative and certainly not worried about Tudor's problem.

Tudor shot him a suspicious look, but the swot was flipping channels like a game pro. "I don't think she'll eat in a pricey restaurant by herself. She's pinching pennies."

"Did she answer your text?"

Tudor glanced down at the el cheapo phone Ana had given him so he didn't have to use his international call plan. "She wants to know the chef's name."

"Adolph. Adolph Nasser." Sounding chuffed, Graham settled back with his keyboard and began typing. "Go back to digging into those names I gave you."

Not understanding how a chef would save him from being arrested by half the governments in the world, Tudor slumped in his seat and did as told.

Ana takes a limo

I WASN'T ABOUT TO QUESTION how Graham had pulled off the limo when he'd commandeered helicopters in the past. Exiting the hired Lincoln in front of the downtown hotel where Stiles had been poisoned, I handed the hotel valet a ten and asked to be directed to the catering director. I preferred working from the bottom up, but if I was dressed like a ridiculously wealthy socialite—even I recognized the designer name inside my new clothes—I might as well behave as one and go straight to the top.

I'd talked to Sean on the way down here and knew he'd harassed the kitchen staff without result. He was now parked in a bar across the street, writing up the story I'd given him about Kito and waiting to see what I'd turn up. He'd earn his pay eventually.

I didn't have a business card saying *Patty Pasko, nouveau-riche,* so I merely introduced myself as Patricia Pasko and smiled coolly at the catering director. "I need to hold a reception for two-hundred-fifty people. Tray assures me that your kitchen staff was in no manner responsible for the unfortunate incident earlier this week, but I expect to interview them before I make a final decision."

Roger Tulane, according to his name tag, appeared to pale beneath his stylishly-gelled blond hair. "Tray?" he asked with careful curiosity.

Huh, so he knew MacroWare's private chef, interesting. "Yes, of course. The function will be a memorial in honor of Mr. Stiles for local MacroWare employees, coordinated with the west coast service. Low key, just chairs and a light buffet. We expect a substantial discount, naturally. Before we discuss details, may I see the kitchens? We don't mind helping you with public relations, but we have to consider the concerns of our employees first."

I think I stunned him into submission, then roller-coastered him into action when I got up and walked out the door. Never give the enemy time to think.

My childhood wandering embassies, hotels, castles, tents, and hovels across half the world had given me access to any number of kitchens. I'd never been inclined to examine them, except to avoid men with big knives. That didn't mean I couldn't pretend to know what I was doing, sort of.

Tulane hurried to open the staff elevator for me and punched the buttons to the lower levels. We walked out into a dim corridor in the bowels of the hotel where cacophony reined. Shouts, slamming pans, and the rumble of big machines gave a nice impression of hell.

My escort looked nervous as he murmured apologies and tried to keep me from marching onward. Given the level of discord I was hearing, I guessed that he wanted to calm his employees and talk to the chef first. So did I, except chaos was my friend. I had arrived at a convenient time—probably right after news of Kita's death had broken.

My smile was cold as I kept walking. Magda had been known to bring grown men to their knees with that look. I was too short to pull off intimidation but that didn't hold me back. "If Adolph is available, I would like a word with him while I'm here," I told him, upping his anxiety another notch. Name-dropping came in many grades.

"It's early yet. I'll be happy to give him your number..." His voice trailed off as we reached the overheated, noisy underworld that was the hotel kitchen.

A small woman of Asian descent shouted in what sounded like Korean—and hurled a pot of liquid at a tall, skinny young man with a really bad goatee.

White-coated staff scattered. Goatee Man dodged the pot, but the liquid apparently scalded. He screamed in pain and grabbed one of those huge knives I preferred to avoid.

I sighed, pulled my police whistle from beneath my clothes, and blasted the room with a shrill shriek.

Nine

THE CATERING DIRECTOR and most of the kitchen staff covered their ringing ears after my whistle blast. One of the larger male chefs had the sense to use the distraction and grab knife-wielding Goatee Man.

I separated the hysterical soup-flinger from the crowd. I admired her style. If I couldn't talk to Adolph, I wanted someone furious enough to spill everything she knew.

"You're a friend of Kita's?" I asked curtly, steering her toward what appeared to be a back exit.

Behind us, Tulane shouted at his kitchen staff. I left them to it.

My hostage stiffened and muttered in Korean. Over the years, I'd learned a few curses and basic pleasantries in numerous languages. "Please shut the shit up" in proper Korean was the first one that came to mind and was probably not an appropriate response. I stuck with "Please," opened the exit, and practically shoved her out of the kitchen into a dim basement corridor.

She was willing to go, so willing that she kept on moving, leaving me to hurry after her. Fortunately, her legs were as short as mine.

"Look, I'm on your side," I told her in English as she slammed open a locker.

Flinging her white hat on the floor and stomping on it, she uncovered her short, ragged black hair. Silently, she retrieved her purse and coat.

"You'll need a new job after that diva performance. I might be able to help. Let's get a cup of tea and talk."

She rattled in more furious dialect that I recognized as curses. Since they seemed directed at the hotel and men in general, I followed her to a different elevator that took us to a staff exit. Outside, she crossed a graveled alley, turned left on the street, and entered a Starbucks. So much for tea. At least my new boots and hat were keeping me warm.

"You know Kita?" she asked in angry, accented English after I'd bought her some obscenely expensive espresso concoction. "They insult a good, good man."

My over-priced tea landed me solidly on the side of deciding Graham owed me an expense account. I followed her to a table near the window.

Given the lady's level of hysteria, I assumed she knew Kita was dead. "You know the police found him?" I asked, treading carefully in case flinging hot liquid was her hobby. Boiling coffee in the face wouldn't be any less painful than soup.

She bit her lip and stared out the window. "He wanted too much, too fast." She wiped away a tear.

"That's the American curse." I blew on my boiling tea and went with my gut instinct in prodding her. "You have to choose your friends wisely."

She stiffened and glared, so I knew I'd hit pay dirt. "He was a *good* chef. He deserved this position. He should not have to pay anyone to get it. If he'd just waited for his papers to be fixed..."

Paying someone to land a job smacked of all sorts of illegalities. What kind of place was this posh hotel? I shrugged in response to her cry. "Waiting for papers might have taken years unless he knew people in the right places."

She wiped angrily at her eye. "Americans are bad as Communists. Everyone has hand out. Tray say he get him this job. Kita just need to do favors for these men." She glared at me suspiciously. "I don't want job for favors. I am excellent saucier. My papers are correct."

"You're not going to get a great reference after scalding Goatee Man. Who is he?" I let her change the course of the conversation until she was feeling more confident.

"Goatee Man." She snickered. "He is Nazi Adolph hired."

I bit back a snicker. Nazi Adolph was even better than Goatee Man, but she was referring to Goatee as the Nazi. Because he was German? I needed names.

Unaware of my distraction, she continued, "Adolph did not want to hire Kita because his papers were not correct. Now, Adolph fears he'll lose his position and reputation and everyone fears losing their jobs." She sighed. "I do not know what to think."

I thought we needed to talk to the police, but I was afraid she would shut up if I suggested it.

I held out my hand. "I apologize for my rudeness. My name is Patty Pasko. I have a rather large family with a lot of connections, some of whom are interested in finding the killers behind Kita's and Stiles' deaths. They can help you find a new job." I only half lied. I had every intention of following through.

She hesitated, then reluctantly offered a brief shake. "Euon Yung," she replied, half-Americanizing her name. "I was Kita's friend. We went to school together. Our families know each other back in Seoul."

I'd done my research. Yes, *fugu* was a Japanese dish. But Koreans fished the same waters. Their traditions were different and not as regulated as the Japanese, but they made blowfish dishes too.

"I know about large families," Euon said. "Why does yours want to catch Kita's killer?"

"We have a family member who may have learned too much about the murders," I improvised. It could be truth—who knew? "We won't feel safe until the killer is behind bars."

"I don't think American justice any better than Korean," she said regretfully. "Rich men brought Kita here. Rich men died. Now Kita dies. I do not see justice for a poor man like Kita. Rich men control too much."

I wouldn't argue that, but I was a cynical citizen of the world. I had a pretty good idea of how these shady immigration deals played out and how difficult it was to nail the villains. I still needed the names of the *rich men*.

I pulled out my Patty-the-accountant card with my public email address on it. "Send a resume to that address. When we're done here, I'll make a few phone calls about jobs. First, do you have any names you can give me? Who did Kita do favors for?"

"I don't know. Tray Fontaine was his boss in Seattle. He may know. Kita was waiting for his belongings. There might be papers there or in his room at the hotel. The police must have them." Sullenly, she sipped her caffeine.

I went for direct this time. "Would Kita have deliberately poisoned Stiles for cash?"

Euon didn't take offense but merely shook her head. "No, nothing like that. The request for the soup was made in advance, possibly through Tray from his superiors. This is not unusual. Kita practiced to be certain he remembered the details of cutting up the fish. It is very complicated knowing which organs to remove. Regulation requires that he test the soup on himself every time he made it. The police do not believe me, but it is so. If the soup was poisoned, it was done after it left his stove."

"Is that possible? Poisoned livers dropped in the bowls maybe?"

She shrugged. "Possible, I suppose. I do not cook fish. I am vegetarian. When he heard people got sick, Kita called me. He was scared. He said he must go to police. I did not understand then. I told him he did nothing wrong, let police come to him."

"But his reaction was not that of a completely innocent man. He knew something," I concluded, watching her expression.

She sighed and nodded almost imperceptibly. "I think so. I think he was frightened of those men. He made soup, like they ask, and people died when they shouldn't have."

"Do you know who served the soup?" That was the best way I could see that the poison could have been delivered.

She shrugged. "I was not there that night. Maggie O'Ryan, probably. She's our best server, and they usually call her in for VIPs."

The woman in the video? I made a mental note and continued while we were on a roll. "Have you seen these men? Or did Kita describe them at all?"

She pondered a moment. "He said once that businessmen were like sharks, and he was swimming in deep waters, but they got him his papers, and now he could work anywhere. These do not sound like people who poison."

"No, they sound like predators who hire poisoners and cover their tracks with the bones of the innocent. I'll need your resume so my people will know what kind of job will suit you, but let me start the process so you know I'll hold up my end of the bargain."

I knew I had to establish trust. It's a necessity in any business, not just with potential witnesses. While Euon watched, I texted Tudor to tell him to look into positions for *sauciers*—Graham could figure that out. Then I called Nick at the embassy, so she could hear me asking about chef positions for a hotel cook.

He laughed at my request. "Oh, right, in case we want to poison any foreign diplomats? I'll get right on it."

"Not funny, Nicholas," I said, using his full name so he knew I had an audience. "I'll forward her resume so you can see where she'll fit in. She already has a low opinion of American authority. Let's not reduce it. Come to dinner tonight and I'll explain."

He cackled again but agreed to ask around. I hung up and offered my hand again. "If you learn anything else, you can reach me at the number on my card. If you run into any trouble, don't hesitate to call. Women in the work force must stick together."

She almost smiled at that. She shook and carefully placed my card in her pocket. "You are one of the sharks, correct? Perhaps I will return to Seoul."

I tilted my head and tried to think of dowdy me as a shark. I couldn't. "No, I believe I'm more of a puffer fish. Treat me with respect, and I'm good."

She laughed then. "I am but a minnow. I will stay out of the way of sharks."

That was probably a safer attitude than mine. And more normal. But doing nothing just wasn't in my genetic make-up.

I picked up my portfolio and walked out, carrying my undrinkable tea. I wandered around the block until I found the tavern where Sean had said I could find him. I glared at the blaring sports TV and almost walked out again. A wolf whistle from a dark corner made me roll my eyes, but I turned to study the interior and found him.

"I almost didn't recognize you," Sean said as I approached. He scanned my outfit in appreciation. He stood like the gentleman he usually wasn't and pulled out a chair for me. His dark curls looked rumpled, as if he'd been ramming his hands through them. It was a good look, but he wasn't Graham.

"It takes a skirt to make me unrecognizable?" I asked sourly. I appropriated a spoon from his side of the table and lifted ice from his iced coffee to drop in my tea.

"It's the hat. You look like a Russian princess." He turned his laptop around and shared the screen.

I skimmed the story he'd written. "Tell me you've learned something new and interesting since you sent this." The story didn't mention Graham.

"The kitchen staff stops in here before and after hours to complain about Adolph," Sean said smugly, retrieving his toy. "I've compiled a dossier on him and sent it to you. Patra gathered a few nice tidbits from her celebrity contacts. The head chef's an asshole with numerous drunk driving convictions, but he's never poisoned anyone that we know of."

"He didn't want to hire Kita," I said, texting Tudor to ask about the limo's whereabouts. "It sounds like Tray Fontaine at MacroWare may have had something on Adolph that forced him to employ our dead fish chef. Adolph has hired a tall lanky fellow with a pathetic goatee. Has he been in here?"

"No, but the staff hates him and think he's Adolph's lover. Name is Wilhelm but the staff calls him Wee Willy. Don't have a full name yet." He two-finger typed on his tiny keyboard. "Patra can dig the dirt on Tray. West Coast is more her bailiwick."

"It's really MacroWare we need to get inside," I mused aloud.

Sean laughed. "Right-o. There's a job for Superman."

"Or Superwoman." I glanced down at my phone and Tudor's text, then up at the window. "My car's arrived. Keep me in the loop, and I'll do the same."–Up to a point, I amended mentally as I stood.

Sean didn't gape as I left him for the gleaming black sedan outside, but I liked to believe he was internally gawking—because *I* was. I knew Graham was filthy rich and accustomed to limos and maybe even Air Force One. He and Mallard had picked us all up in a Phaeton after one dangerous evening. I was pretty certain Graham had not taken the Metro to the hotel the night he met with Stiles. So apparently he had a car regularly in service, like all the other D.C. diplomats.

I had a sedan at my disposal. How cool was that? The luxurious leather black seat concealed by smoked glass was almost as relaxing as my private hidey-hole. Here, I could look out on the world and pretend I really was invisible.

But invisibility wasn't always useful, especially if Tudor's future was on the line. I wasn't sure I trusted Graham to protect my brother before himself. I didn't know how messed up his head was, and he didn't owe us anything.

While I pondered world—or at least, familial—domination, Graham actually deigned to call me. I stared at the phone in incredulity. We were hitting new firsts all over. His masculine baritone grumbling in my ear generated a visceral thrill.

"Interesting hiding place for your hard drive," he said in greeting. "I've provided a better solution so you don't have to make people suspicious with an empty computer."

"You've been in my office again," I said accusingly, knowing I'd locked my door.

"I kept the cat out," he offered without repentance. I'm allergic to cats and he had a bad habit of letting his into my room when he sneaked around. "Delete this number from your phone. I have Tudor's number set up to show as your mother in Poland. Use that to reach either of us."

"Aye, aye, *mon capitaine*," I mocked. "I want inside MacroWare. Can you arrange that?"

I was nuts asking for that. I didn't work well with others. I wouldn't know programming code from Mandarin. But I couldn't send Tudor into a nest of vipers, and I needed faces to put to names.

"Possibly," Graham agreed with reluctance. "The hole appears to be in random versions of the new beta software they're testing—or maybe not so random. I need to process their files to see who arranges the distribution. The leaks are only planted in DC sites currently, so I'm concentrating on the local sales office."

"No apparent connection between the sites affected?" Knowing I was thinking people and he was thinking computers, I added, "Same repairmen, salesmen, IT department, anything?"

"Huh, I'll get back to you on that."

I gave an unladylike snort as he clicked off. So, we were both so messed up that we understood each other. Scary, but workable.

My mother's lack of success in the relationship department prevented me from ever thinking about finding a permanent partner. Note, it did not keep me from thinking about sex, and currently, Graham was the only man stirring my hormones.

The car dropped me off in front of the house. The driver gave me his card in case I needed him again. If he was billing Graham, I'd certainly consider it. I liked the anonymity of the Metro, but sometimes, speed was a factor.

I hadn't eaten lunch and headed for the kitchen when my phone pinged again. I opened it to a text from Tudor.

WORM INSIDE NSA. DATA ANNIHILATED. I'M GONNA DIE.

Ten

CYNICALLY THINKING THAT TOTAL ANNIHILATION of NSA's spy files couldn't be all bad, I continued down to the kitchen. Tudor's frantic cry barely registered on my personal Richter scale. Teen boys were always going to die. It was an adolescent hazard. I didn't intend to handle world domination on an empty stomach.

We'd known the cookie monster had fallen into government servers and done some damage. It must have done more than Tudor had known for him to go ballistic.

I had paid just enough attention after 9/11 to understand that Congress had passed incomprehensibly complex laws allowing our own government to spy on every single citizen in the country and probably the world if they were feeling particularly paranoid that day. Since I could only take care of myself, not the stupid among us, I did what I had to do to prevent privacy invasion at the time. Until recently, I hadn't even owned a cell phone.

Graham had apparently gone even further. He'd erased his existence from cyberspace.

Leave it to Tudor to wipe out the entire populace—or just their mindless phone conversations. I was hoping that the worm had only consumed data from his Brit servers—which would be whatever he and his fellow boarding school nerds had been up to these last ten years. A nice size package, but not the Holy Grail. I had no way of knowing the actual extent of the destruction from his panicked text, but I assumed the media would soon be blasting doom and gloom if the NSA's entire database had been destroyed.

Mallard was nowhere in sight when I reached the kitchen. A lovely salad with a slice of grilled salmon on top was neatly covered and waiting in the refrigerator. If it was meant for Graham, tough luck.

Carrying the salad back to my office, I took a break from crime solving.

First, I investigated the external hard drive that had been added to my Whiz. All Graham's Sooper-Sekrid files had been transferred into the removable drive, leaving the Whiz showing only my virtual assistant accounts.

Graham and I had come to uneasy terms over sharing information. He left his satellites open for my use. I didn't try to use them for anything dangerous. I had my old Dell laptop for my more personal files, but we both knew we could access anything the other did if we wanted to bad enough. Mostly, we were too busy to poke into each other's business, and neither of us had a private life to hide.

I really didn't want the cops messing with some of my admittedly shady clients, but it would look strange to have a blank computer. The external would easily pop out and go into my hiding place or my tote. I moved my private email files into it as well. Graham might not care if I'd been hunting my missing siblings in Africa, but the police might get wrong ideas if they saw my sources.

For my lunch break, I checked on personal matters. I studied the Swiss bank account files that Graham had sent me. He'd apparently copied transfer slips from our grandfather's bank account before Rotten Reggie took it over. The number of digits to the left of the decimal point on each slip was gratifyingly enormous, well beyond my ability to spend immediately. If the money actually existed, we could educate our entire tribe, including the missing African twins, and still buy back this house from Graham.

We'd be the ridiculously rich I sneered at. I'd figure out how to handle the irony when it happened. Investing the million in funds we'd already retrieved was difficult enough. I needed it to be safe, but I also needed it to grow to achieve all our goals. I chewed nails over every stock market mood swing. This MacroWare glitch wasn't making my nervous stomach very happy.

I returned to admiring dollar signs. I had no clue how to hack Swiss banks, but at least these transfers narrowed down the accounts to two different firms. I sent questions about finding lost passwords or accessing old accounts to some of my Swiss contacts and e-mailed the banks with similar inquiries.

Salad consumed, I turned back to the files Sean had sent. The dossier on Adolph Nasser, the hotel chef, was pretty much as he'd said—a few drunken driving convictions, complaints from former employees, a checkered employment history. I didn't think this was highly unusual in the restaurant industry.

Adolph had worked briefly with MacroWare, before Tray Fontaine's time and only as a line chef. Apparently Stiles didn't like drunks on his staff. The date of one of the convictions on the west coast coincided with his departure from MacroWare and his hire in D.C. as the hotel's head chef. That had been a couple of years ago.

Since Adolph had come out ahead in that deal, I couldn't see why he'd carry a grudge worthy of killing anyone, but I opened my summary case document and added him to my suspect list.

MacroWare's private chef, Tray Fontaine, looked like a golden boy who could do no wrong. Graduated from a fancy west coast culinary school, interned under a chef even I'd heard of, he took his first big position at an L.A. restaurant known to be frequented by Hollywood stars. How he'd ended up operating MacroWare's private dining room was unknown. Sean had noted that Patra was looking into it.

I went back into the hotel's employee files and searched on "Wilhelm." I didn't find anything. Interesting. Biting my thumbnail and narrowing my eyes at the screen, I put together a few scenarios in which "Wilhelm" might not show on employee rosters—none of them legal, if that was his actual name.

Had the mysterious Wilhelm been working at the hotel Wednesday when Stiles was poisoned?

I sent an email to the hotel's HR department from my Patty Pasko, accountant, address asking if Wilhelm "Nasser" was employed in their restaurant, using the chef's last name to catch their attention. I hinted that "Wilhelm" might be in for a windfall. Hey, if phishing worked for Nigerian bankers, why not me?

Next, I dug around in the police files Graham had been sending me. Nothing new on the medical front. The PR guy who didn't like salsa had emerged from his coma and still wasn't talking much. It had been hotel staff who had mentioned the ambulance had been called to a meeting room hired by a Thomas Alexander.

Thomas Alexander, huh. Graham had said *he'd* booked the meeting room, but naturally, he wouldn't use his own name. I made a note to check out his alias, just to see where he'd picked it up.

So, why had the police shown up on our doorstep asking for Graham if they only knew about Thomas Alexander?

I dug deeper and discovered the PR/salsa guy, Herkness, had given the cops a list of people who were supposed to meet after the dinner. He hadn't given Graham's full name. He'd just listed him as Day—short for Amadeus—and said he was head of a security team Stiles had hired. He'd clammed up when the cops had asked him why the outside security team had been needed.

MacroWare wouldn't want news of a spyhole in a test program to go public. This whole case stunk of cover-up.

It had actually been the FBI that had connected the dots between Thomas Alexander, "Day," security, and Graham. The police files didn't provide *how* they'd made the connection. I only saw the transcript of the phone call between the feds and the police captain who'd come knocking on our door. So they really didn't know anything and were on their own phishing expedition.

No wonder the good captain had showed up personally and backed off so easily. It hadn't been my acting abilities that had driven him away so much as his doubts and distrust of another agency.

My ego could take the blow. And distrust didn't mean the cops wouldn't follow through. Without my cooperation, they just had a really tough job getting a warrant on this crummy bit of speculation. They'd have to dig deeper.

I sent Graham a message asking for Thomas Alexander's files, just to annoy him.

Most of the files on Kita provided details of what I already knew or guessed. His faulty immigration papers prevented him from working at MacroWare, but Kita had worked with Tray Fontaine in several of his restaurant ventures.

Tray's statement to the police said he'd hired Kita as an independent contractor upon occasion after Stiles developed a taste for Asian dishes. When Tray had heard Adolph needed a *poissonnier*, he'd promised to send MacroWare's business Adolph's way if he hired Kita.

That call sounded perfectly legit, the good-old-boy network alive and well. Of course, that network often involved blackmail, bribery, and the usual male score-keeping, so I couldn't totally disregard the connection, especially given Euan's hints of sharks and immigration papers in return for favors.

So far, the police had determined that Kita had been shot with a high-power Magnum handgun and a silencer. He'd been gunned down in the apartment and shoved into the closet—a professional job. In a town filled with wealth, spies, and military, a professional hitman was feasible but required *sharks* with lots of money.

I was enjoying that fishy image too much.

A few weeks ago I'd come across a professional hit job sponsored by a mysterious cabal called Top Hat. Sean and Patra had helped me catch the local Mafia connection, but we couldn't touch the wealthy bad guys who did the hiring.

And so far, I couldn't pin down a connection between a purportedly good corporate executive like Stiles with the rotten greedmeisters in Top Hat.

The police interviews with the rest of the hotel's kitchen staff were less than enlightening. Stiles' server, Maggie O'Ryan, claimed not to know the new fish chef's name. Even Euon's interview merely said Kita was a hard worker who tested his soups before serving. She didn't mention that they were old friends.

Poor Kita had no public mourners—which didn't mean there weren't private ones. The information trail I needed to follow wasn't on paper or in computers. If I'd learned nothing else since coming to D.C., it was that I had to hit the streets far more than I liked.

I had pretty much spent the last ten years in Atlanta researching from a musty basement, sometimes 24/7. Hibernation was fine when the research involved ancient history and nothing more vital than someone's PhD thesis.

But we were talking Tudor's life and career here, not to mention that of a hardworking chef and a couple of gazillionaires. And Graham. Sitting still, reading other people's research, just wasn't cutting it.

Since MacroWare had yet to publicly admit the flawed beta-ware, I worked on the assumption that Stiles had died over the discovery of the spyhole Tudor had reported. It didn't make logical sense just yet, but it was all I had.

Someone inside MacroWare knew where the bodies were buried, so to speak.

I was about to dig deeper to see what the police had found on Kita's phone and computer when my mobile rang.

The screen didn't display the caller, which wasn't unusual. No one I knew revealed their phone identity, although I had EG and Nick's numbers in my contacts so I could recognize their calls. But the international phone code was warning enough that it was my mother. I debated not answering, but Magda and I had developed a truce when she'd allowed EG to stay here. I owed her the respect of listening.

"Is Tudor there?" she demanded the instant I answered.

"Who's asking?" This was not me being snide. This was me knowing Magda wouldn't sound this upset if she'd learned on her own that Tudor wasn't where he should be. Someone had *told* her. Given the multiplicity of her government contacts, I could only guess which one.

She let out a sigh, signaling that she'd got my unstated message. Most families have their own shorthand communication. Ours was more like telegraphed code.

"My line is secure, so it doesn't matter who asked. I just want the answer," she said.

"Tudor has proved that no computer is secure," I warned. "Some dangerous people want his discovery covered up. He's safe, for now."

"The state department is looking for him," she admitted, revealing her source. "I can get him out of the country. Just let me make the arrangements, and I'll get back to you," she said briskly, with no obvious relief.

I rubbed my brow. The feds had already called Magda—so very not good. Wasn't that just a little far beyond paranoid?

But this was business as usual for our mother. She'd find a friend of a friend who would provide a military helicopter that would fly him to an undisclosed base and disappear him in a jungle somewhere, where he could probably bring down the internet in truth.

My goal was to break that pattern. "He's been accepted by MIT and Stanford. He's going to school, not living in jungles," I informed her.

"Don't be ridiculous. What does Tudor need with school? They need him more than he does them. He's far better off—"

"He's *sixteen*. He may have a skull full of complex gray matter, but he has no clue what he wants out of life. If he wants to run around playing spy when he gets older, that's fine. Right now, he gets a home and an education until he's had a chance to study his opportunities. Heaven only knows, half the countries in the world could use his skills just to update their antiquated websites. He could unite all the health organizations and get them communicating with each other. Wouldn't that be more useful?"

"Not if he's in prison," she said grimly. "Or blown up by people who think he's too dangerous."

"That's your experience. You made your choices for your reasons. Nick and I were forced to follow along when we were too young to do otherwise. But we have other choices now, and I intend to let the kids explore them."

I'd run away from my half-siblings when I'd been too young and helpless to save them, and they'd been breaking my heart. I was older now—and not quite so helpless. I might not have a real education, but I had a better grasp of what I could do. They could still end up breaking my heart, but at least I would know that I'd done all that I could to give them the best life possible.

Magda went silent for a few seconds, digesting my argument. It was similar to the one she'd lost over EG. Our mother wasn't dumb, just defensive. "You call me the minute the pigs get anywhere near my boy," she finally said in her best menacing tones.

"I will teach him to respect the *authorities,* until such time as they don't respect us," I corrected. "I prefer working within the system."

"You prefer manipulating the system," she retorted. "Just don't let Tudor get taken. How is EG?"

"Excellent. She's enjoying all her studies and teachers. And she's no longer wearing Goth black. She's starting to explore fashion as well as dinosaurs, medical anomalies, and geometry." I gave Magda those tidbits to chew on so she wouldn't start in on the sad state of American education. "Nick is doing brilliantly at the embassy, and Patra seems to be settling in at CNN."

"That's what I call working within the system," she said with almost a hint of admiration. "Just don't let any of them go near politics."

We both knew that politics was a ridiculous impossibility for our family. We clashed with authority too often to be useful in public office. But "going near" had many connotations—*undermining* being our expertise.

Magda didn't bother sending her warm wishes to her offspring. She shouted directions at a cab driver—or a cart or rickshaw driver—and hung up. I'd long ago decided that Magda—whose mother had died young—had never been hugged as a child. I barely knew my grandfather, but I suspected my mother was a chip off the non-sentimental old block. We knew she loved us, because she looked out for us. Sort of. When she could.

It was nearly dinner time, and after that call, I didn't have the will to dig back into musty files. Time to wield the family whip. I texted Tudor that he was expected at the table promptly at six.

He texted back that he wasn't hungry.

I might not know how to program software, but thanks to Tudor, I have an arsenal of juvenile hacking and worming devices, and I'm not afraid to use them.

I hit the intercom. "Boot him out, Graham, or your computers are hash." I happily pictured the noisy intercom blaring through Graham's concentration.

It was Saturday night, and we were having a family dinner, even if Graham refused to descend from his lair.

NICK ACTUALLY SHOWED UP TO JOIN US. He was dressed in a suit and tie, so he was either going out or on his way home. EG glanced up from her tablet to study his sartorial elegance. "Get tired of noodles?"

He tugged her hair and took his usual seat at the head of the table. "I miss Mallard," he told her in a manner that indicated he hadn't missed EG.

She grinned, knowing he didn't mean it.

I was already sitting at the other end of the table when Tudor arrived with his frizzy red hair slicked back and wearing a school blazer over his black t-shirt. "Thank you for taking time out from your busy schedule," I said without sarcasm.

"Where's the bolt hole if the cops come?" he replied sullenly.

"Basement stairs, just the other side of the swinging door. Or the dumbwaiter on the far side of the buffet," Nick answered cheerfully.

We'd been trained at an early age to always locate the exits. "Didn't Graham show you his?" I asked innocently, fishing for information. I knew one of his bolt holes. I was betting there were others, but I had no excuse to explore the third floor.

"Yeah, one, but I don't think anything will help me. Now that the feds are involved, it's all over but the handcuffs."

So, Graham was keeping him informed. I hoped that was a positive. I got itchy when I wasn't in control, but I accepted my limitations. The NSA had probably been very unhappy to find a worm bearing Tudor's signature eating through their data. But after the State Department debacle, we'd known they'd find out sooner rather than later.

Tudor eyed the vegetable soup warily but tried a spoonful.

Mallard's cooking was one good reason to never leave this house. I made certain the kid was digging in before I replied. "That's your inexperience talking. Once we have the evidence that government computers have been systematically corrupted by sophisticated data thieves, and you adapt your software to look like a new kind of virus protection, you'll be a hero."

"We're not James Bond," he said gloomily.

"*Au contraire, mes enfants,*" Nick took up the family banner. "We are better. Only peasants use blow-'em up cars and laser guns. We simply need information. The FBI is looking for you, yes. You stupidly used your US passport to enter the country, and I can't erase that. But if you choose to leave using your Brit passport, I can arrange your disappearance. So quit worrying."

Fortified by the rich soup, Tudor looked a little more hopeful. "The FBI went to the embassy looking for me?"

"Naturally. They have quite an entertaining dossier on you." Nick stopped talking to admire the roast beef and Yorkshire pudding Mallard presented, presumably in honor of Tudor's appearance.

I'm not a vegetarian. My upbringing included a lot of rice and noodles, beans and insects, not much beef. I have adventurous tastes as a result, but I'm more appreciative of greens and fruit. I'd seen real carnage and didn't need blood on my dinner table. So I didn't simper over the beef as the men were doing.

I concentrated on the deliciously spicy roasted broccoli and cauliflower and let Nick play role model.

"They probably have a dossier on all of us." Tudor said with a shrug. "My father is both English and Australian, and I was born in London. My mother is American. So I have three passports and a dossier. Can I leave here on the Brit one and arrive elsewhere on the Aussie one?"

"Stop it," I scolded. "You're not going anywhere except to MIT.

Just give us time."

"My worm ate the NSA!" he cried in frustration. "Don't you take that seriously?"

"Nope," Nick and I said in chorus. Anarchy had been our upbringing.

EG flashed her school tablet that shouldn't have Wi-Fi but now displayed a news headline: GOVERNMENT DATABASES DESTROYED. GOP CANDIDATES DEMAND EXPLANATIONS

Oops.

Eleven

SUNDAY MORNING, I DID LAUNDRY. EG had gone to her father's house for an outing. For whatever reason, EG idolized her adulterous, pompous dad, Senator Tex Hammond. Letting her get to know him had been one of the reasons for my settling in D.C.

Tex had lost his conservative halo after EG turned up as product of his adultery, but his wife and other daughter were gradually accepting her existence. I tried hard not to judge EG's paternal family, but it involved a lot of tongue biting and assuring myself that she needed a well-rounded social education.

The feds might be after Tudor and the cops after Graham, but we still needed clean clothes, and I wouldn't stick Mallard with our undies. So I did laundry. Pondering whether we could hire a maid if we were rich, I wiggled out of my work bra, added it to the wash, and tugged my sweater back down.

Only then did it occur to me that Graham probably had a security camera even in the basement laundry. I raised my middle finger in salute in case he was watching and sauntered off to my office.

Bored with reading other peoples' research, I started an analytical search of my own. Under Graham's instruction, Tudor had adapted his cookie monster program to deliberately locate all systems containing the spy hole in the betaware. He'd sent me a list of the contaminated websites that he'd found to date.

I took his list a step further. I sorted out the government systems by server, and using one of Graham's illegal programs, infiltrated their computers through the holes in their operating system firewalls. I didn't wipe out anything. I just ran a systematic search through the documents of two dozen government agencies, looking for similarities. I was operating under the theory that whoever had arranged to spy on these computers had a motive other than general nosiness. Data mining this extensive would be worse than NSA's phone files. No human could reasonably process it—unless they had strict search parameters.

Almost all the government computers connected to the server I'd chosen were used by boring financial committee personnel. There was no point in hunting for common word similarities because "money" or "funds" would come out on top—not useful. The key to a good search is to be specific.

I started just by comparing all proper nouns. Senator Paul Rose—the leading presidential candidate—cropped up in a statistically abnormal number of instances. But a megabank, a stock brokerage, and their related executives also appeared high on the list, so Rose's name wasn't unusual in conjunction with the others. They were all filthy rich and powerful and had interests in banking.

I'd first run across Rose and his cohorts in tracking my grandfather's stolen funds—and developed a pretty extensive database on the senator and his pals. Know thy enemy and all that.

A quick search revealed Rose's trust fund owned substantial numbers of shares in both the bank and brokerage ranking highest on my list. He also owned a large piece of Goldrich Mortgage, which was being examined for various fraudulent sales of bad loans to the government. The banking committee appeared intent on blocking sale of Goldrich to the megabank—yawn. Nothing new there.

Further down my search list was a number of other large financial institutions. With a little work, I could probably tie all of them to Rose's supporters, but this wasn't leading me to murder.

I sent my findings to Graham with the ungrammatical question: "Ya think maybe Rose likes to monitor banking legislation?"

I could almost hear his snort in reply. If anyone could pay to add corrupt operating systems to government computers, it would be Rose and his old-boy Top Hat network. The shadowy connections between politicians, bankers, and powerful corporate executives had first landed on my radar in my grandfather's dying message mysteriously mentioning *Top Hat*. Later, I'd caught glimpses of the alliance when they'd tried to influence EG's dad over an infamous textbook deal. People who thwarted them tended to die, but the Top Hat cadre was always clean.

If this powerful group had planted the spyholes, they might have reason to kill Stiles to prevent discovery of their spying, but motive was nothing without evidence.

I'd let Graham and Tudor figure out if Rose had corrupted MacroWare to keep an eye on banking regulations—and why.

Legislation made me snooze. In my world, laws were made so the crooks knew which way to dodge. I just wanted to get back to my life.

My goal was to find the bottom-feeders who had actually killed Stiles and company. I'd leave it to people better trained than I am— like Graham—to follow the money.

I was nose deep in MacroWare crap when the intercom sputtered. With Tudor upstairs, I was afraid to shut it off as I often did. I waited expectantly.

"The feds have added two and three and developed a logarithm leading to you," Graham said solemnly.

"A joke, he makes jokes," I answered, still waiting for the ax to fall.

"They no doubt have your family tree tacked on the wall," he retorted. "You might give Nicholas and Patra a head's up. In the meantime, it might be advisable to take Tudor to the movies."

"How much time do we have?" I was already messaging my siblings and shutting down systems. I knew cut and run. Would EG be okay at the senator's house?

"The feds have no grounds for a search warrant," Graham continued ominously. "They only wish to speak with you about your missing half-brother. I'd give them an hour to post spies in the bushes."

"Sweet. Get Tudor bundled up. What about you?"

He chuckled. He actually chuckled. The madman was enjoying this. I wanted to be a fly on the wall up there. Naturally, he didn't answer.

I don't know why I worried about Battyman. I'd stick to keeping Tudor out of jail until he could figure out how to fix the software or kill his multiplying worm.

Removing my external drive, I dropped it in one of the many canvas totes kicking around my desk, and ran upstairs to collect my coat.

I cursed Nick for talking me into buying the totally inappropriate leopard boots. They were much too glamorous for my overalls and heavy black sweater. I pulled on combat boots and my army coat instead, new plans formulating as I did. I tied on the hood to hide my braid.

Tudor met me in the upper hall looking pale but determined. I yanked his knit hat further down over his distinctive hair.

"Graham said there's a better way out through the coal cellar," he said, twitching away from my mothering gesture.

"I was going that way anyway. Lead on." Ha! I'd known the spider in our attic had more secret exits. I gloated that I was finally about to learn another.

We clattered down two flights of stairs to the basement. Tudor headed to the windowless cellar that had once housed coal, and I raised my eyebrows. The coal cellar, really?

I flicked on my LED flashlight—my army coat was well equipped—and we noted the rusted coal chute. The room was entirely underground. I didn't know how we could get out through here. I double-checked to make certain I couldn't be locked in, but the old wooden door into the chamber was rotten. Even a baby could smash through it.

Tudor took the light and ran it across the back wall. "There. Brill." He ran his ungloved fingers along the edge of a crack around the chute.

To my utter amazement, the concrete block wall opened.

"Why the friggin' heck didn't he tell me this was here?" I muttered as I followed my baby brother through a six-foot-high cement tunnel.

"I think he likes watching you on the security monitor when you sneak out through the back yard," Tudor said with a male shrug. "You trigger an alarm every time you go out the kitchen door."

"Remind me to wear a sheet over my head and give him the finger from now on." That was attitude speaking. I actually got off on knowing that Superman was watching me—as long as I had control of the situation. Yeah, hormones aren't rational.

"He's a boffin, but if he's got our backs, that's what matters," Tudor said sensibly, examining the recessed lighting in the tunnel walls—presumably looking for their source of power.

I wouldn't call Graham a nerd, precisely, but the latter part had been my conclusion—he had our backs. I still didn't fully trust an unknown cipher in the equation of my life.

The tunnel didn't seem to run further than the length of the back yard, maybe a little more. At the end, we climbed a short flight of stairs to a metal door. I had a pretty good sense of where we were and really wanted to smack our uncommunicative landlord. I slammed the door open instead.

Gaping at the vast open space we entered, I swore. Well, at least I now knew what the warehouse/churchlike building was on the block behind us. I'd stupidly thought it abandoned.

Men who kept secrets like an enormous carriage house suitable for hiding limos—and possibly helicopters, tanks, and an arsenal— ought to have their heads chopped off. You had to know men like that were up to no good.

I examined the gleaming antique Packard Phaeton I'd once seen Mallard drive. Then I studied the empty concrete floor that could have held a private plane had there been a runway and uttered a few more choice words that I tried not to use around the kids.

"You didn't know this was here?" Tudor concluded, whistling as he examined the gleaming classic. "Is this ours?"

"Like, I know?" I glanced overhead, wondering if the Mansard roof would hold a helipad. That would explain Graham's magical disappearances and appearances. Cops, doctors, Google Earth, newspapers—all had helicopters around here, so I wouldn't have noticed one extra drone from my basement hideaway.

"A Phaeton isn't exactly invisible, is it?" Tudor said wistfully. "Maybe I could buy a motorbike and keep it in here."

He was talking about our pattern of travel, learned at our mother's knees. When we wanted, we could be very, very inconspicuous.

"Should we live long enough for you to get a license, a bike works for me. But that Phaeton screams 'Look at me,' so very not Graham. It may be our grandfather's." I scouted around for the exits and decided on a small door at the side.

"There's a good film in Georgetown," Tudor said, following me and punching the door lock with a code that I memorized. "How difficult is it to get there?"

Leave it to a kid to have a show already picked out. "I don't suppose you mean *The Three Musketeers*," I said in disgruntlement.

"*Monsters*, in 3D," he suggested with relish.

I politely refrained from rolling my eyes. "How about we do some sleuthing instead?"

"Sleuthing?" he asked in incredulity. "Who says *sleuthing*?"

"I do. While Graham is covering your ass, we can help cover his. How about a ride to our part of town?" Tightening my hood, I headed for the street.

"I thought *this* was our part of town," he grumbled.

"Did you earn the money to live here? Do you have money for your own place?" I asked as we aimed for the Metro. I liked the kids to stay humble.

"No. Dad gives me just enough allowance to buy games." He glared at my gloved hand when I held it out for money for the Metro. He didn't offer any.

"Exactly." I slid my card through the ticket machine. "On our own, we don't even have enough money to travel by subway. So we'd be living in the working man's part of town."

"That's where you've been living until you got here?" he asked with curiosity.

Worse, but he didn't need to know that. It had been my preference at the time. "In another city but similar housing, yup. And it's where we'll end up if our lawyer doesn't beat Graham and our grandfather's lawyers into submission. The law is on Graham's side on the house. All we can do is hope he'll do the right thing once we have the funds to pay him back. He laid down over a million in cash."

Tudor didn't like that answer. A silent Tudor was a dangerous Tudor, but I let him stew for the train ride down to the apartments I'd visited a few weeks ago for different reasons. I knew the neighborhood and the police district. I'd feel right at home if we ended up renting there.

"Who are we looking for?" he finally had the sense to ask as we got out at a station well past the usual tourist areas.

In the November gloom, the apartments looked dirty and tired. At night, they were worse, I knew.

"Maggie O'Ryan." I checked my phone directions and aimed down a main thoroughfare.

Whereas Kita, the hotel's fish chef, had found expensive lodging in fashionable Adams-Morgan, the hotel's best server lived two steps above a slum. I'd done some cursory research into Maggie, knew she had grown kids, an ex-husband, a bad credit record, and her last house had been foreclosed on. Kids are hard to raise on tips.

"You going to just walk up to her and ask if she poisoned Stiles?" Tudor asked.

"Lesson one: if you want people to talk, you have to be on their side. Innocent until proven guilty should always be your motto."

"You want to give me a clue of how we're approaching her, if she's there?" Tudor took in our surroundings with interest, as if he was learning a new video game.

"By knowing our witness," I said, turning down a narrower street lined with old junkers, mostly pickups. "She has a teen with an unusual form of multiple sclerosis. He needs a new wheelchair. I think we can find better use for our rainy day fund than paying taxis."

Of course, since I was working Graham's case, I'd probably charge what I was about to do to his account.

"Taxi drivers have to live too," Tudor muttered, but even he couldn't argue too much when it came to a kid with a harder life than his own. Despite his last few years in a posh boarding school, Tudor had lived in slums and seen the catastrophic results of war. He wasn't completely rotten yet.

"My name is Patty Pasko, so yours is probably Paul Pasko," I told him. Tudor had been well trained in aliases under our mother's aegis and knew what I was telling him without further instruction.

Locating the building number, we studied the situation. A row of cheap tin mailboxes lined the outside wall. Junk mail stuck out of half of them. A walkway led along each side of the four-story brick structure, and I sincerely hoped Maggie and her son had a bottom floor, because I didn't see evidence of elevators designed for wheelchairs.

Door numbers had been left to the whim of tenants, apparently. We located 1G at the front left but the other doors had only empty spaces. I followed the walkway around, looking for 4G.

I turned the corner to the back of the building. A paved lot was apparently meant to be a patio. A rusted grill, a tattered sunbrella, and a few filthy, dilapidated lawn chairs littered the cracked concrete, along with half a dozen rusting bicycles.

Tudor studied the junk with disgust. "They don't have rubbish pick-up here?"

"They're renters. Stuff gets left behind. If you don't have money to buy better, then you use what you find," I said pragmatically, finding a neat black metal 4G on the first door at the back. "Quit judging."

I could hear yelling before I even knocked on the door. Out of caution, I stepped aside after I knocked, motioning Tudor to do the same.

The door opened, and an old hand-driven wheelchair crashed out, bumping over the threshold, onto the broken patio, and around the corner as fast as the kid could wheel it. I caught a glimpse of a mop of dark brown hair, a tall, skinny boy with bad acne—and no coat.

"Michael!" someone inside shouted.

A moment later, Maggie O'Ryan appeared. Graying brown hair straggling from a loose ponytail, she looked weary as she saw us on her doorstep. "If you're the police, arrest me, please. Jail has to be easier than this."

Twelve

TUDOR GRIMACED when Ana ordered him to go after pimple-face, whose name was apparently Michael. Not having any good excuse not to, he jogged out to the street and found the tosser making for the Metro. It was boringly easy to catch up.

He didn't have Ana's handle on people, so he just said the first thing popping to mind. "I think my sister hoped to have some barmy production where she hands you a check for a new chair," he said, strolling alongside the frantic escapee.

The twit was running out of steam already. He glared at Tudor. "The proceeds of crime already?" he asked in disgust.

Tudor's interest picked up a notch. "You think the non-profit is run by a *crime* syndicate? That would make a cool vid. I could work with that."

Michael slowed down to stare. "You write video games?"

"Sometimes. School gets in the way," Tudor said, voicing his dream as if it meant nothing.

"How about a game where your mother kills people for money?" the kid asked furiously.

Bugger it! That whacked him back to reality. Was the kid saying his mother had actually *killed* Stiles? What the hell did he do now?

Tudor shrugged and played up his Brit accent, although his nerves were now jangling. "For all I know, Mum has fragged dozens of pillocks, but she'd make sure the buggers deserved to die first. So it's just the usual Robin Hood rubbish and would make a boring game."

The kid looked glum and stopped wheeling at the corner. "Yeah, if I'm translating correctly, that makes sense. Still, she'd go to jail if she got caught."

"Not if it was self-defense. My sister once drop-kicked a—" He started to say *nanny* but realized that wouldn't go over well in this part of town. "...a prat out of a second floor window after he set fire to our apartment. She didn't go to jail."

"Mom couldn't drop-kick a dog," Michael said in disgust. "So, was that your sister at the door?"

"Yup. She's tougher than she looks. Want to go back and see if they're plotting murder?"

The kid looked resigned. "I didn't bring my Metro pass anyway. You're really here to give us a check? That doesn't make sense."

Tudor shrugged as the kid turned around. "You've got a sister who makes sense?"

"Nah, she just took the cash Mom gave her and paid off credit cards. I wanted to buy a car and get out of here."

Crikey, that did sound daft. Tudor wondered how he'd convey that info to Ana without getting them both killed—if his mother really was a murderer.

Could Ana be in danger? Tudor picked up speed, forcing the kid to wheel faster.

Ana gives away Graham's money:

"LET ME GET THIS STRAIGHT," Maggie O'Ryan said as she poured tea from flowered china. "You work for some fancy non-profit who wants to give *me* a check for a new chair for Michael—out of the clear blue sky and the kindness of your heart. But you come here without a check and dressed like an undercover cop. Am I getting this so far?"

I slid my Patty Pasko business card across the plastic coffee table. "You want me to walk around here in Armani? Why are you expecting cops at the door?"

"Because that's how my life is. Until I see cash in my bank account, I'm not believing you. And if you ask for my bank account number, I'll have to shoot you." She tightened thin lips and stuck out a pugnacious jaw. Weariness had carved as many lines in her face as age.

I liked her a lot already. "If you want to shoot scammers, I can direct you to a nest of them in Canada. But getting guns across the border isn't easy these days."

Maggie almost laughed. She'd returned her graying black hair to its ponytail while the water boiled. She still wasn't relaxed, but she took a seat on the scuffed vinyl sofa and poured tea for herself. "You learn to look gift horses in the mouth these days. I apologize if I've offended."

"You'll only offend if you insult my intelligence or my siblings. And I'm not entirely certain about the latter." I sipped the tea—strong Irish breakfast, of course. "I didn't bring a check for multiple reasons, one of which is that sometimes we can get a group discount on whatever appliance is needed. We might be able to upgrade your choice or give you a little cash back instead of leaving it all up to you to figure out. I was afraid if I arrived bearing catalogs, though, you wouldn't open the door."

"You've been doing this a while, haven't you?" she said tiredly. "How did my name get drawn?"

"I'm not on that committee, but it's often teachers or local cops who make recommendations. They're in a better position to notice who needs what. If you thought I was hauling you off to jail, I assume you've been in touch with the local precinct recently?"

She rubbed a rough-looking hand over her forehead. "Not the locals. The ones near my work. They're more uptown and probably think I'm a murderer. I doubt they know about Michael or care, but he's got a few good teachers. Who was that you sent after him?"

"My little brother. I promised him a horror flick if he came with me today."

I prayed Tudor remembered not to give out his name. It could be in the newspapers any day now, and it wasn't as if everyone in America was named after English kings. Our mother had a thing about historical royalty, which is why I'm Anastasia, named after a Russian princess—one who got murdered, I might add. The life of royalty tends to be short.

"They look as if they might be the same age," Maggie said. "Ever since he ended up in a chair, Michael has been having difficulty with bullies at school. We're thinking of moving to a district with better policies for children with disabilities." She shifted uneasily in her seat.

I recognized nervousness when I saw it. But the boys burst through the doorway, not leaving me time to gauge the cause.

"I don't want a new chair," the wheelchair-bound kid declared. "We just need the money."

I nodded slowly, as if pondering the possibility.

Maggie hastily jumped in. "Don't be foolish, Michael. You need a chair. If we move, your new school will require multiple classrooms, and it will be easier for you with an electric chair."

The boy looked mutinous. I glanced at Tudor, who crossed his fingers in our family warning signal to be wary. Right. I'd get on that—as soon as I figured out how.

"You have to understand..." I said slowly, groping for what was at stake here. "Some families... might not use cash in a manner conducive to our purposes."

"She means people gave money to their fund for wheelchairs, not drugs or groceries," Maggie bluntly told her son. "We'll look at the catalog and see what they can get us at the best price."

"That would be your best choice," I agreed apologetically. "I know moving is expensive. What if we find someone to help with that? How soon are you moving?"

"Not fast enough," the kid said gloomily, wheeling off and disappearing into the back of the house.

"I apologize for my son," Maggie said, wearing a taut expression. "We've been through some tough times lately. I'm hoping he'll come out of it. I have a deposit on a nice place for the first of the year. The chair would make a great Christmas present."

Tudor sat silently while we discussed dates to meet again. I liked Maggie. I was pretty certain she was in a nervous frenzy because her conscience was eating at her, but I couldn't come right out and ask. She had to trust me first, and she didn't—rightfully so. How much time and patience did I have to spare before the feds caught Tudor or the cops came after Graham?

And if time and patience were all I had to offer, I was in need of a better modus operandi than befriending witnesses. I'd forwarded several offers of job interviews to Euan, but she had yet to come forward with additional information. Fine detective I made.

We offered our farewells and departed, Tudor practically leaving me in the dust as he rushed to escape on his long legs.

"Your movie runs all night," I said dryly, catching up with him.

"He thinks his mother got paid to murder someone," Tudor spat out. "You were sitting there, drinking tea, with someone who may have poisoned Stiles."

I affectionately punched his shoulder. He winced. Oops. We needed to introduce him to Graham's third floor gym.

"I appreciate your concern, but I watched her make the tea and drink it before I touched it—an unnecessary precaution in this case, but it's always good to stay in practice. What makes Michael think his mother murdered someone?"

"She apparently came into some money, but that's all I know." He hunched his shoulders and glared sideways. "What happens if we don't deliver the goods?"

"We'll deliver. That part is easy. The hard part is establishing trust. That's the point you and Graham don't get. You want information to be inside machines, but machines have limits. It's face-to-face talk, watching body language, developing a connection, that makes the difference."

"Right, like you get out so much," he grumbled.

"I used to. I fell out of practice for a while, but I'm trying to get back in the swing again." *Now that I wasn't hiding from Magda* was my unspoken rationale. "Computers are easier than dealing with people, granted, but they don't have all the answers."

But we'd learned Maggie had come into unexpected money—at least enough to make a deposit on a better home. That could potentially be traced. So we hadn't totally wasted our time.

"Let's make a stop before we hit the Metro," I suggested. I hadn't planned this, but I knew how to do impromptu. I steered him toward the precinct station and the cops I'd helped to bring down a local mob king. In my books, that meant they owed me.

I didn't recognize the sergeant at the desk, but I asked for Detective Azzini or Sergeant Jones. Tudor hung back. I doubted that he'd ever been inside a police station, but he was looking a little green. Guilt does that—another reason I was here. He needed a hard dose of reality.

Warning the sergeant that I had no useful news, just charity in mind, we talked schools while we waited. I had his name and number and ordered wrapping paper from his kids' school fundraiser by the time Azzini arrived.

The good detective looked harassed in a hunky TV detective sort of way, with his clipped tight black curls and beard shadowing his dark skin. He led me back to his cubicle. "No hot leads today?"

Azzini knew my real name, but he had no reason to connect me to Graham or anyone else. I introduced Tudor as Paul Pasko, who looked teenage awkward as he shook the cop's hand.

"I'm working on a big one, but there isn't anything you can do yet. I thought I'd ask you and your guys about a holiday feel-good case instead." I told him about Maggie and her kid and an anonymous donor wanting to help out. I knew the good detective would look her up the minute I left, but that would have happened anyway. This way, she was a person to him, not a perp.

"And you want us to find someone to deliver the chair and maybe help her move out of this slum? We've got a community group that can probably do that." He studied me through narrowed eyes. It was a sexy look on him, but I wasn't buying it. "You gonna tell me why?" he demanded.

"Call it a hunch. She doesn't trust cops. She's all alone. And I think she's an innocent caught up in some deep shit. We don't want her disappearing into the night." *In more ways than one*—I hadn't forgotten Kita.

Kita had come into a job and expensive immigration papers recently. *Follow the money* kept ticking in the back of my head.

The detective rubbed his tired eyes but nodded. "You know this won't stop us from arresting her if we need to, right?"

"As long as you're aware that I believe she's innocent until proven guilty and will act accordingly, we're good," I said cheerfully.

"I don't make promises. You're not really a lawyer, are you?" he grumbled, standing up to lead us out.

"Half the professors would have quit if she'd gone to school," Tudor said grumpily. "You won't believe what she can do to a law book."

I smiled proudly that he thought this of me.

"Knows how to keep you in line, does she?" the good detective asked sympathetically. "Maybe she ought to teach classes to delinquents."

I laughed. Tudor didn't.

I wanted my brother working on *this* side of the law, if possible. Magda had her agenda; I had mine.

We made our way back to the Metro. I texted Graham to ask if it was safe to return. He ignored me. I assumed that was a no, so we went to Georgetown. I even endured the really bad 3D monster flick with Tudor, in appreciation for his accompaniment.

I was a little less enthusiastic about dinner at a burger joint, but I was still waiting for an all clear from Graham. Stupid me. He'd probably changed the locks while we were out.

After the burger joint, I scowled at my watch and made an executive decision to return home. Tudor was leery but none of his cell phone tactics landed him any more info than I had. We couldn't wander out in the cold all night.

It was after eight and dark as we took the back street by the carriage house. Worried about Graham's claim that the feds would place spies in the bushes, I sent Tudor in first, while I watched. I didn't want to tackle a fed, but I knew how.

Half the street lamps were out on this back street, but I noticed no movement, no camera lights or glints of binoculars following Tudor as he slipped into the carriage house.

Tudor texted me when he was safely inside the cellar. I ambled across the street and slipped into the darkness beside the carriage house like any homeless bum looking for a safe nest for the night.

No men stepped out of the shadows to interrogate me. I used the key code to enter the side door.

Graham was there. I couldn't see him in the complete darkness, but his presence was strong. Maybe it was his elusive musk or my nerves making me antsy. Either way, I wasn't going anywhere until I'd had a word or two with my overlord.

I produced my flashlight and signaled my location. "I know you're here," I said aloud.

He came up from behind, grabbed my waist, hauled me back against his hard chest, and kissed my ear. I should have had a heart attack, but I didn't even scream. I elbowed him. He just chuckled.

He smelled of subtle cedar and rosewood, and I was trying hard not to swoon. He had to lift me off the ground to kiss my ear.

Since I'd given up one-night stands, I'd been without sex way too long. So maybe that influenced my thinking—what little of that was happening right now. But Graham was everything I wanted in a man—physically. He'd been haunting my dreams since we'd first met. My heart pounded harder in foolish anticipation now that he had his hands inches from my breasts.

"Mallard has temporarily convinced the feds that you and Tudor are touring MIT. You're now officially confined to quarters." He nibbled my ear then brushed hot kisses along my cheek. "Want to do something about it?"

I was in serious danger of melting and grateful for my heavy army coat keeping his hands off vital parts. I'd done promiscuity in the past. I was getting too old for that stupidity, but I didn't know how to do relationships. I was pretty sure this wasn't a good start, no matter how much I wanted it.

"No way," I warned, to both his suggestion and innuendo. "Hiding is a form of retreat, and I'm no longer there. Hiding is what *you* do. I did it all day for you and Tudor. I won't anymore."

There had been a time when I had hid, and he knew it. But I was learning how unhealthy that was.

Graham growled and dropped me like a hot potato. "You don't know the danger you're in."

I missed the strength of his arms and mentally called myself a dozen names. I could have laid down my ultimatum *after* we'd done a horizontal tango. Why did I have to develop scruples now?

"Living is dangerous," I said scornfully, hurting from his abrupt rejection. I didn't like being left cold after he'd got me hot. But I didn't kick him like he deserved. I was unfortunately starting to understand the depths of his paranoia. "We all have to decide what risks to take for the rewards we want to achieve. You make your call, I make mine."

I stalked away, leaving him to pout or whatever men did when women wouldn't listen to them.

Thirteen

How Ana spends Sunday night

"WHAT KEPT YOU?" Tudor asked in irritation once I slipped into the coal cellar.

My little brother had been worried about me. That was kind of sweet. Little did he know.... Sighing, I slapped his back and pushed him onward. "I was reconnoitering. I don't see any spies, but you'd better lay real low for a while. Go upstairs, let EG in when she arrives, and send her to bed. It's a school night. Then get some sleep and let that gray matter process a brilliant solution to all our problems."

He gave a teenage snarl at the babysitting duty and ran up the stairs. That was okay. He was old enough to shoulder a few family responsibilities.

I entered my office and opened my computer to check on new files. Graham had been haunting the carriage house for more reasons than me. I expected to find answers in his latest documents.

He'd thoughtfully gone in and tagged my incoming mail in levels of importance. Really, I needed to strangle the control freak, but I admired his efficiency—and his intelligence—too much.

Graham had highlighted three attachments in red for *important*. The first was a police file on the contents of Kita's laptop and phone. In the stolen document—assuming he was hacking police files and a mole wasn't handing them to him—Graham had bolded Kita's correspondence and calls to Tray Fontaine at MacroWare's HQ. They looked legit to me. The guy would have been thrilled with his mentor for finding him this new job.

A welcome-to-your-new-job email from hotel management asked Kita to stop by the office and had been highlighted in a bright magenta. Funny, ha ha, Graham. Rainbow colors denoted what? But I noted the name of the manager—one Brian Livingston—and figured on running a little research on the boss. Someone had invested in immigration papers to obtain Kita's position as fish chef.

Livingston's phone number showed up on Kita's contact list

after the date of the meeting. How often did luxury hotel managers call their chefs? Or vice versa?

Kita's laptop records also turned up the place where he'd purchased the puffer fish and the research he'd done to remind himself of the intricate steps necessary to remove the poisonous organs.

I needed to investigate how to put the poison back in. If Haitian voodoo priests could create zombies with dry puffer fish guts, I assumed some other knucklehead would have figured out a drying process or worse.

My imagination conjured an image of billionaire CEOs in Italian suits rising up like zombies from the podium and shoving botulism-laced salsa down each other's throats... But puffer fish actually *paralyzed* the nerves, and I had no proof that the salsa was bad.

The next highlighted file was a police dossier on Thomas Alexander, the alias Graham had used to book a hotel room. Apparently MacroWare had been paying a computer security firm owned by one Thomas Alexander.

According to the dossier, the *real* Thomas Alexander, the original owner of the security firm, had died in the Pentagon fire in 9/11.

So had Graham's wife, but that wasn't in this report. If the police had the ability to put two and two together, however, they might see the connection, flimsy as it was.

If Graham had actually bought the company and hadn't changed the name, that was hardly a big deal. People bought established businesses and continued under the original name all the time. Of course, they didn't usually assume that owner's identity as Graham apparently had.

Right now, the police report was pretty thin and didn't include Graham's name or who had bought the firm after Alexander died. Sloppy, sloppy, sloppy. They just noted that the credit card used to book Alexander's hotel room was in the name of a dead man's company.

The third highlighted document was the real eye-opener. An email from "Thomas Alexander" had been sent to the police *today* with the possible motivation for murder: *He'd told the cops about the operating system defect.*

I stared at that email in awe. Graham had guts, I'd give him that. He did what had to be done, provided the cops with motive for murder—even if it got his ass fired by MacroWare for exposing their cover-up. Because by golly gee, MacroWare certainly hadn't announced any flaw in the system yet. My guess was that they were discreetly updating the beta programs—destroying all evidence of the breach.

Except neither Tudor nor Graham had found any evidence of the operating system being patched, despite the warnings Stiles had received and passed on to his now incapacitated staff.

Graham was taking a huge risk by passing the information to the police. If the media learned about a spyhole in MacroWare's operating system—the scandal could affect national security *and* cause a global economic melt-down.

Graham had just e-mailed the information equivalent of an atomic bomb.

Seeing the need for speed, I dug back into Graham's files. Using Thomas Alexander's email, he had sent the cops the name of three computer firms that could be trusted to verify the operating system defect and recommended that Kita's laptop be checked for the flaw.

Wow, just wow. Graham had actually exposed himself to the world—albeit under an alibi. He'd had some pretty bad crap dumped on his head nearly a decade ago when he'd tried to disclose political irregularities and got publicly kicked out of his influential office. The potential to blame him again instead of the real culprits was huge. No wonder he was feeling a little wound up.

How long would it take the cops to track down the "Thomas Alexander" who was handing them this loaded bomb? Those computer firms Graham had recommended could probably trace his email—eventually.

I had a thousand questions, like: if Kita's computer was affected, had Kita possibly sent an email or document that might have scared the real bad guys into fearing he was a danger to them? There were so many "ifs" attached to that my head threatened to explode, so I didn't try to come up with more.

Despite the explosive potential, I didn't see anything in these files that I could work on now. Sundays were useless for getting anything done. I sent my queries to Graham and shut down.

I toddled upstairs, and after checking that both Tudor and EG were in their beds, I went to mine. Not to sleep, mind you—Graham had done a real number on my libido. Sleep was out of the question.

MONDAY MORNING, I was interrogating EG over breakfast about her Sunday visit when Tudor tore into the dining room looking paler than his usual ghost-white. Even the freckles across his nose looked pale pink instead of brown.

"He's gone!" he cried. "Vanished! He's left us all to hang!"

Well, yeah, that's what spies did. "Graham?" I inquired, just to verify before I gave in to frantic heart palpitations.

Tudor nodded and looked as if he'd knock the cup from my hand if I didn't get up and run. "*Everything* is gone."

Oh, filthy bad word. That couldn't be good. I practiced a meditative technique I'd learned in India. It didn't work. I would go ballistic if I didn't act on my explosive energies. That was the reason I so admired Graham's gym. When I needed to kick something, I could. This wasn't the time, I accepted, as I dragged out of my chair.

The spider in the attic—gone? Did I change the locks and take possession of my grandfather's house? Or worry that he'd left us to take the blame for whatever he'd done now? Most likely both, plus all the other scenarios I could conjure.

"Can I see?" EG asked eagerly. She'd never been inside the lair.

"Let me first," I said with relative calm. I'd learned at an early age to hide panic and my fear of dead bodies lurking in dark corners. "Tudor, sit, eat, keep EG company."

Mallard was normally in the kitchen at this hour. I didn't want to run down there first without seeing the evidence with my own eyes.

I took the stairs two at a time—not easy given my short legs but fear gave me wings. Graham had given the cops leads that could potentially lead to proving his existence—and his proximity to the murder victims. Had he decided to move on and start over?

I refused to think—*leaving us in the lurch*—but it was there, buried in my psyche. I should have realized it the instant I'd read those files. Or figured something suspicious was happening when Graham had grabbed me in the garage. None of this was normal Graham behavior.

Upstairs, all the doors were open. The third floor had been a mysterious place of closed doors that we'd been ordered to stay out of. I, being the nosy and impertinent one, had poked around, but once reassured nothing lethal had been concealed up here, I'd obliged and mostly left Graham alone.

Putting off the scary emptiness of computer central that Tudor had reported, I glanced in the bedrooms, looking for evidence of hasty retreat. I opened doors on old narrow beds, stripped to the ancient mattresses, probably once used by children or servants. I knew about the gym and passed it by with only a cursory glance inside. Near the far corner room overlooking the back yard and carriage house I started sneezing, evidence that Graham's cat had been here recently. Would he have taken it with him? This room had a king-sized bed with no linen. The closet was empty as if no one had ever lived here.

My heart had reached my throat by the time I entered the largest room on this floor. The one at the center, at the top of the stairs, had been Graham's computer lair. Had last night been Graham's warped way of saying farewell? Had he been waiting for a ride when I'd strolled through?

With leaden feet, I entered the windowless cave where Graham normally resided. The lights were on for the first time since I'd moved in. As Tudor had said, the room was essentially empty, with none of the blaring screens, beeping alarms, and staticky voice connections to make it the heartbeat of the house.

My heart did a nose dive, and I couldn't stop sneezing. So far, I hadn't found the cat.

Where once there had been an entire bank of monitors there was now a beige wall with vividly colored, impressionistic sports paintings. Even I recognized the artist from the sixties—my grandfather's time. They were probably worth a fortune or two.

A row of circular glass lamps vaguely resembling flying saucers hung over a long, curved console. The console had a higher counter on the painting side and a lower one on this side, like some kind of Star Trek prop except made of polished teak. It was empty of keyboards or anything that indicated it had been used any time this century—although not a speck of dust marred it. That was a good indicator that Mallard had been in on the move.

I yanked open a drawer and found the antihistamine box. Oddly reassured, I popped one and continued studying the bizarre situation. Just yesterday this room had been the beating heart and brains of the mansion. It was as if all the life had been sucked out overnight.

The cheap computer desk Tudor had been using sat in one corner, out of place in this expensively masculine—den?

Den. All it needed was a round poker table. I narrowed my eyes and tried to picture the dark lair that I remembered. Graham had had monitors pretty much along the width of the space now covered by art. The low counter was about the right height for his keyboards and accessories. He usually sat on this side of the desk, facing the wall of artwork. His desk chair was now abandoned in the corner with Tudor's computer, but I suspected it would fit neatly under the low counter.

I tried to recall the windows from outside of the house—they'd all been shuttered—probably to hide the fact that they'd been walled over.

I crossed the room and examined the art work, then the console.

It took me a while. The latch was part of the wood, not visible, and hidden in a reasonably inaccessible underpart of the console. I pushed, and the entire panel opened up to reveal his network of wiring, keyboards, and computers.

He hadn't intended to have his secrets easily discovered. A cursory police search would reveal nothing. The FBI—well, that would depend on how badly they wanted him. By the time I closed the console, EG and Tudor were in the doorway, watching.

Figuring it was probably better not to give Tudor unfettered access to the satellite feeds probably wired behind the wall, concealed by art, I didn't hunt for the switch that would lift the art work. I gauged there was just enough room around each painting for a sliding panel. Revealing how the console opened to expose Graham's equipment was dangerous enough.

"Don't touch his stuff," I warned. "He may have gone on walk about, but he'll have access and will know if you've tampered with anything."

They both eyed the artwork with interest. But *we* knew what had been in here. Others wouldn't. Anyone unfamiliar with the layout would just see my grandfather's archaic man cave. Now that I looked at it, I could see the high side of the console would pass for a bar. It just needed liquor. The shelves were empty—because everything was hidden behind them.

I frowned at Tudor's desk. "I don't like you working up here alone."

He sat down and opened his browsers. "My stuff is all here. The connections he lets me use are still operating. I'm still inside MacroWare. I'm getting closer to the engineer who could have designed that hole, and I've almost got a patch worked out."

"OK, granted, that's big," I admitted. "If the cops or feds arrive with a search warrant, how quickly can you disappear?"

"The hidden stairs are right over there." He nodded at an empty wall of glass-cased bookshelves beside his desk. "I can hear anyone at the door through the intercom. All the important information is on the external drive, so I can just shut down, unplug the external, and hide inside the wall. The main drive is just games." He opened his screen to reveal the contents of his C drive—everything a kid could love.

"Pink Pony?" I asked dubiously, scanning the list.

"He stole that from me," EG said, her eyes wide with awe as she contemplated the bookshelf. She hadn't known about the hidden stairs. I'd have to buy a lock to keep her out.

"Right. Let's get some of your toys and books up here, make this look like a play room—just in case," I advised.

Fireworks were going off in my head, but now wasn't the time to reveal the level of my confusion. The kids needed me to be confident and assured.

How many times had Magda been in a state of total panic but still ushered us calmly out of a country on the brink of explosion? I didn't want to count the number. Mostly, I didn't want to sympathize with my mother.

"You think he's coming back?" Tudor asked uncertainly.

His own father hadn't. Damn, but my siblings made my hard heart bleed.

"Graham will be back, and we'll live to regret it," I assured him. "He's protecting us right now."

I liked that idea. I'd practice believing it, right up to the time I killed him for leaving me to cover his ass.

Fourteen

SINCE TUDOR AND I were supposed to be visiting MIT, I needed to lie low. If we had feds in the bushes, I didn't want to leave EG open for questioning. That meant I needed to find backup for her trips to and from school. I hunted down Mallard in his kitchen.

Speakers under the cabinets were blaring opera, and our hefty butler smiled with the serenity of a monk as he obliterated a chicken breast with a mallet. I did not underestimate Mallard's killer instincts.

"I don't suppose our lord and master has left any instructions with you, has he?" I asked.

"Only that I recommend that you and your family take a long vacation until he has matters in hand," he replied respectfully.

"And you know that we have no intention of obeying orders, right?" I knew Mallard's loyalties were with Graham, but he'd worked for my grandfather first and worshipped my mother. We tested his allegiances regularly.

"I would not consider questioning your choices," he said with dignity, producing another raw piece of meat and smashing it.

"Right." I eyed the flattened bird with respect. "Would it be too much to ask if you'd walk EG to the Metro? Or I could hire a taxi."

"Miss Elizabeth Georgiana ought to have a car and driver. The Metro is too dangerous in the current situation. I have made arrangements."

I opened my mouth, but for a change, no words spilled out. I'd seen the ancient Phaeton. I prayed that wasn't what he intended. I still managed a grateful "thank you" and beat a strategic retreat.

I could be vociferous, bold, and outright deranged in the face of danger, but kindness knocked me for a loop—shows what my experience has been.

I shivered at realizing that even Mallard thought we had a problem. I had a notion that Graham wasn't feeding me all I needed to know.

I watched at the door with EG until the sedate black sedan that had carried me downtown arrived. I recognized the driver. EG was suspicious, but I promised she was safe.

This was Monday. We had less than a week now to get Tudor back to his London school. The timing on when the cops came after Graham was unpredictable. I just knew I had better get cracking.

After I'd shipped EG off and sent Tudor back to work upstairs, I directly called Patra, figuring I'd be dragging her out of bed at this hour.

"What's this about EG having her own limo?" she cried as soon as she answered.

From Patra's irate question, I deduced she'd already been up and reading her messages and EG had told her about the limo ride. The brat had probably been texting the world. I'd hear from Magda next.

"Graham's call," I said insouciantly. "We've got to get to the bottom of this Stiles thing, and he didn't want me taking time out."

"BS," Patra said succinctly. "She'll be rotten. I need to snag that DC job and move back in there. The flat here is hideous."

Since I'd lived in Atlanta and was aware of the cost—Patra's entry level journalism job paid squat—I understood her complaint. "Tell me you've found out about Tray Fontaine. Prove your worth, grasshopper. This is a huge case and could be a career booster."

She grumbled while she apparently opened her files. "Not that you're feeding me anything useful, but—Tray Fontaine just came through a messy divorce and declared bankruptcy. He lost his house and his Ferrari and partial ownership of some fancy LA restaurant. He's clinging to majority ownership of a small restaurant in Seattle and just bought a more modest condo nearby, modest as in Seattle millions."

I whistled. "He lost everything and now he's buying million-dollar houses?" Money inevitably raised my suspicions. "Any record of how he got the funds?"

"Credit reports show two mortgages against the property that nearly equal the purchase price. He must have wealthy friends the bankruptcy court would like to know about."

"Possible," I agreed. "Million-dollar loans are fishy under those circumstances."

"Fishy, har-har. Since I was already in Seattle databases, I ran some searches on the poisoned guys," she continued. "Adam

Herkness, the PR guru who doesn't like salsa, is part owner of Tray Fontaine's remaining restaurant. He's recently divorced as well and is hurting for funds."

"So it isn't likely that he loaned Tray any."

"Exactly, but—" She hesitated, apparently hunting for another file. "Bob Stark, the financial officer who is still comatose, is rolling in riches. Wealthy parents, never married, heavily invested in the market—although he sold all his MacroWare options last week."

Uh-oh. Remembering my thought on MacroWare's stock plunging even more once the police revealed the spyhole, I opened my suspect file and started typing. "Do you have a date when he sold them?"

"Tuesday, the day before the poison dinner," she reported. "Why?"

"Because that's when the internal problems started to unravel." I hadn't told her yet about the spyhole, so I fudged. "Aren't there laws about insider trading?"

"Yeah, except Stark wouldn't poison himself," she pointed out.

That had been the reason I'd left this research to Patra. I figured the five poisoned men weren't suspects. In theory, they had been a danger to the real killer. So far, Tray Fontaine was the only connection to MacroWare who had walked away—except he hadn't been in DC. His stooge Kita had.

Tray went to the top of my suspect list—but he had utterly no motive. He was a chef, for pity's sake. What did he know about operating systems?

"Any reason to believe a wealthy accountant like Stark would loan money to a bankrupt chef like Fontaine?" I asked.

"Tray was blackmailing Stark?" she suggested. "I'm grasping at straws, but Tray's ex-wife moves in the same circles as Stark's family. Stiles liked his employees to be straight up good guys. Stark's family are heavy duty loan sharks who have skirted the law for decades. Maybe Bob was involved in financial shenanigans and Tray found out."

"Insider trading is not straight-up behavior, so you may be on to something there, except I can't see a chef and a finance guy communicating on the same level. Stiles was an ass if he hired a financial officer with that background, no matter how much he liked the guy," I concluded.

"They went to the same school, different years," Patra added.

I pondered old school connections and tried to douse my bias, but I read the papers and understood the old boy network of "you scratch my back, I'll scratch yours." Had Stark "scratched" Stiles' back at some point? With funds, probably. Nothing new there.

"At the very least, we could conceivably be dealing with stock fraud," I decided. "Check with the SEC. Still, Stark wouldn't murder himself to save his family."

"You said there might be some connection to government financial committees," she pointed out.

She might be my sister but she was a journalist first and foremost. So I was limiting what I fed her. Now that Graham had given our information to the cops, could I tell Patra? The news of a spyhole in government computers would create an international sensation and make her career.

It would probably also cause a stock market crash and panic, for all I knew—

Sorry, Patra.

"Possible connections," I agreed cautiously. "But the Stark family wealth doesn't lead directly to government fraud."

"Understood, but MacroWare's current operating system software is viewed as problematic by most businesses. Sales are way down, which means there aren't any lucrative government contracts pending either. Consumers are waiting for the new roll-out. If MacroWare could tell corporations that the government was upgrading to the new version they're supposed to be testing—"

"Or vice versa," I added, thinking hard. "I'm not making the dots connect," I admitted, "but I think you're on to something. Except why would Stark sell now if the new roll-out will put them back on top? Think Sean can dig into the financials?"

"On it. I'll send him what we have here. He's pretty good about sharing the glory." This last sounded tentative.

There was roughly ten years difference in Sean's and Patra's ages, but I wasn't entirely certain there was a vast lot of difference in experience. Patra had lived what Sean had only heard about.

I tried to give her what she wanted. "Sean still believes in truth and justice and apple pie. He plays fair."

I could almost hear her grin. "That's what I thought. Keep me updated. I want that DC bureau position."

As I hung up, I wondered if the feds could tap our lines. I had to hope Graham's security prevented it—for now. If he'd really disappeared, we were up the proverbial creek. Technology might be my friend, but I didn't have Graham's expertise or maniacal preoccupation with keeping people out.

I was trying not to panic, but this scenario was playing too close to my life before I ran away. Life and death with the kids in between and no protection other than poor pitiful me... Not a road I wanted to travel again.

How had I let Graham give me the confidence to think I had someone at my back? That was crazy thinking.

Rattled, I stuck to researching from my underground office, where I felt safest. I let my lizard brain ponder action while I read up on everything that came in overnight. Somehow, Graham was still forwarding his various feeds, so I knew he was alive—at least until I found and killed him.

The hospital report showed Enrique Gomez, MacroWare's security guy, had come out of his coma but wasn't talking yet. Could I hope they'd start ratting on each other and solve all our problems? Of course not—because the bottom line was that even though Stiles' close compadres had the most to lose, they wouldn't poison themselves.

So if I accepted the motivation for murder was that someone didn't want the spyhole revealed, the number of suspects was too huge and too anonymous to investigate from that angle.

Which brought us right back to—who had the *opportunity* to poison? Kita and Maggie—one dead and one not talking. Who else might have had access to both the soup *and* the vegetables? Botulism was far more likely to be found in vegetables—like canned tomatoes or minced garlic. Anyone who made salsa from canned tomatoes and bottled garlic probably deserved to be sent up for murder.

I was scrolling through the files on Tray Fontaine that Patra had sent and thinking I really needed to get into the hotel kitchen—when I struck pay dirt.

From the list of stockholders in Tray's restaurant that Patra had sent, it appeared our Seattle chef had borrowed or coerced all his restaurant pals into buying a share. Kita had a tiny share, so did Adolph, Kita's boss here in D.C. And also—one Wilhelm Vokovich.

We had a winner! I didn't need the hotel's HR to respond to my inane attempt to phish the new cook's name from their records.

I gleefully dug into Wilhelm—and came up with almost zilch. I needed Graham to hack through immigration files, because as far I as I could tell, Wilhelm hadn't been born here. He had no credit record and no tax files. I opened the hotel's HR database again but couldn't find Vokovich on the roster. No social security number would be my guess. Adolph was paying him under the table. Why?

I really needed into that kitchen, which reminded me of Euon Yung's resume. I texted Nick to ask if she'd found a job yet, and on a whim, I asked Mallard if he knew of anyone who needed a cook. I really wished she hadn't quit her job. I needed inside information on that hotel restaurant.

Mallard studied her resume and nodded solemnly. He occasionally met at the pub with a bunch of other upper crust household personnel. If anyone needed a cook, he'd know about it. Even if Euan turned out to be useless, I could feel as if I'd held up my part of the bargain.

And then from the depths of cyberspace, Graham sent me the Holy Grail—a pass into a memorial service for Stephen Stiles and Henry Bates, in the hotel in which they'd been poisoned. Holy Irony, Batman.

How did I work this.... Let me count the ways.

I studied the invitation. It appeared to have been on formal paper originally, but there was a barcode on it for electronic use. The geeks quite possibly could have assigned a different code to each invitation to identify the guests as they entered rather than ask everyone for their ID. Or possibly not.

However—the disadvantage of barcodes is that if they're bent or damaged in any way, a scanner can't read them. Or... if I ran the image through my photo program and smudged the code, it would force security to ask for ID. This wouldn't work for expensive theater tickets, but this was a memorial. If I had the bad luck to meet a truly anal guard who knew how to track down a guest list, I'd lie—or hope Graham had my ass covered.

He'd sent this invitation expecting me to use it—and as Thomas Alexander, he probably controlled security.

The service was scheduled for two, today. Even though the memorial was likely to be nerd city, I couldn't go in as my normal

nerdy self, not with the feds believing I was out of town. My
distinctive black braid was probably on every wanted photo in their
system.

My slanted eyes and high cheekbones were also giveaways, but
they could be played down with make-up and glasses. I'd already
used the Russian hat. I didn't want hotel management recognizing
me.

I was seriously conflicted. I wanted in the hotel kitchen, but I
also wanted to hobnob with the people who had known Stiles. For
all I knew, the murderer would attend. How did I dress for both?

I ran upstairs to contemplate my limited wardrobe.

I had the dorky black designer silk suit that Nick had made me
buy to impress EG's last fancy-schmancy school. With that, I could
wear my hair up in a roll and slap a veil on it. Not that I owned an
actual veil, but Nick had also shown me the value of accessories. I
had a lacy black scarf that I hadn't figured out how to use until now.
Bunched up with pins and stuck on top of my hair—it would conceal
my widow's peak and eyes.

With my face hidden, I could circulate in the memorial
reasonably well, but not in the kitchen. Maybe I could bring the
kitchen to me. It had been a long time since I'd exerted myself to
mischief. I was supposed to be a grown-up now. But old habits are
ingrained and a natural fallback position.

Humming to myself, I returned to my computer and began
multiplying the pass to the memorial service. Stiles had invented cut
and paste for good reason, I'm sure. He would be proud of me. By
the time I was done, Graham's invite had been copied onto good
card stock. I was wagering the fancy stock went on the invitations to
special guests, and security wouldn't even ask for ID when the
smudged barcode failed.

If they didn't get past security, I'd come up with another
solution. Half of my job relied on luck anyway.

A list from Tudor on additional corrupted websites reminded
me of how hard he was working. He deserved a reward. I IM'd to ask
if he'd brought anything suitable for a funeral. He returned the
graphic of an upraised middle finger.

I laughed and saved the graphic. Then I ran back-upstairs to
rummage in his backpack and Nick's leftover wardrobe. I left khakis,
a black t-shirt, and Nick's blazer on the geek's bed.

Tudor's hair was as much a problem as mine, though.

I ran up to where he sat alone in that ugly room, staring at his monitor. I dropped the cardboard invite on his desk. "If you want to go, you have to get your hair cut."

His eyebrows rose to the aforesaid curly mop. "Really? An official MacroWare invite? All the local office will be there!" he said in drooling awe.

"Exactly," I said in satisfaction. "And possibly the families of some of the poison victims, since they've flown in from Seattle for bedside duty. Opportunity knocks."

"You could at least pretend you're offering a little respect," he chided, running his hand regretfully through his thick curls.

"I can't think of a better way of showing respect than to find out who killed them. Now, can you get your hair cut before lunch? We can probably run some dye over it so you won't look like you. A knit cap is probably uncool at an indoor funeral."

"A cap is never uncool. It's a badge of honor," he muttered. "How much do haircuts cost?"

Triumphantly, I handed him some cash and reminded him to leave through the garage, preferably looking like a bum. That wasn't hard for him to do given his current state of grunge.

Heading back down to tell Mallard we'd be gone all afternoon, I realized I was actually *anticipating* mischief and mayhem. My, my, how times change.

Fifteen

GIVEN THAT THERE WAS A BIG EMPTY HOUSE being renovated across the street that was a haven for anyone watching our front door, I called Graham's car service again. Tudor and I walked out via the backyard tunnel and the back street to meet the limo on busy Massachusetts where we could blend into the crowd and traffic.

I'd persuaded Tudor to rub some men's hair dye on his newly-scalped hair, but he still kept a black knit cap in the pocket of Nick's overlarge blazer. We all had our own comfort zones.

I missed Tudor's red curls, but the dark military cut and blazer emphasized his long nose and sharp cheekbones. His big glasses added years, and he almost looked distinguished sauntering into the hotel lobby—well, compared to all the other slouchy, badly dressed nerds. I was starting to understand Nick's obsession with making me dress properly. It was pretty easy to stereotype the bigwig families and the worker bees just from their differing attire.

Earlier, Tudor had dug out the hotel schematics and memorized the floor plans. He more than happily ditched me in the crowd to work his way down to the basement kitchen with pockets full of mischief.

I produced my phone and invitation from my attaché, then balanced the case under my arm as I strode across the lobby. My stupid veil brushed my nose and got in the way of studying my phone as I joined the stream of mourners heading for the ballroom. Half the people here had their phones in hand. Some of the women even wore black feathery fascinators and several wore hats, so my veil wasn't a total give-away.

And Tudor was right. Some of the dorks honestly wore knit caps which they left on even inside the ballroom. Incipient baldness would be my assumption in the case of a few older men. Bad hair day for the women. I really wanted to join my tribe, but it was the CEOs I needed to talk to.

There were ushers at the door wearing black suits and mics that screamed security. I had to hope they were Graham's minions. They were scanning the invitations as expected but some of the guests received special treatment. I watched security escort a stylishly garbed matron to the front of the room. They knew their audience, so I was betting at least some of the guards were "Thomas Alexander" hires. From all I'd discovered, Graham's firm had pretty high-profile clients.

I watched Brian Livingston, the hotel manager, and Roger Tulane, the catering director, enter together and take seats toward the back. I texted Tudor to look for a seat near them.

I stood to one side and read my messages until the usher returned. Then, with an air of impatient importance, I stepped crisply in front of someone fumbling for their invite and handed over my stock one.

He didn't even raise his eyebrows as he offered his elbow for me to take. I'd guessed right—one of Graham's plants. The invitation had probably been coded. It was interesting working *with* the madman for a change, instead of thumping him upside the head to get his attention.

And it was a major relief knowing the spider was still alive, just in someone else's attic for a while.

The usher placed me in the same row with the elegant woman he'd brought in earlier. *Nice.* Her ruby-studded rose brooch seemed out of place on her severe black suit, but I was no fashionista and just admired her attitude.

Several men in tailored suits nodded in my direction. The women mostly ignored me. There were no young children, although I recognized several as adult children of the victims. Setting my portfolio attaché on the floor, I took a chair next to a plump Latino woman in her forties who watched me with unabashed speculation.

"Linda Alexander," I murmured and held out my hand. "And you are?"

Heads perked up all around me. My murmur had been deliberately carrying.

"Victoria Gomez," the plump woman said aloud, almost defiantly. "Are you one of Mr. Stiles' associates?"

"In a manner of speaking." Well, I was working for Graham who had been an associate, close enough. "How is your husband? I heard he's awake." That wasn't a guess. I'd done my research on the families and knew she was Enrique Gomez's wife.

"They say he will recover," she said in relief. "It will be months. The poisons caused so much damage—" She drew a deep breath. "We are luckier than others," she added sorrowfully, nodding at the stylish matron with the ruby brooch.

A tall man in a charcoal gray suit sat between me and the woman I'd followed in. He'd been conversing with her, patting her hand in sympathy. Now he reached over to shake my hand. "Pleasure to meet you, Mrs. Alexander. I'm Wyatt Bates. Will Thomas be joining you?"

Bates. "No, I believe he's in Belize, looking into a situation there," I said warily. "He sent me in his place. Are you a relation of Henry's?" Henry Bates was the man who had died with Stiles—one of the few men capable of overseeing the programming of a spyhole, or repairing it. I tried not to eye this personage with suspicion.

"I'm Henry's brother. I live here in D.C. He only came to the conference so our families could visit." He looked a bit gloomy and harried. "In a way, it's my fault he's dead. His family has gone back to the west coast to arrange the funeral, so I'm sitting in for them."

"I am so sorry for your loss," I said, thinking fast. I didn't think *Thomas Alexander* was exactly a well-known figure, but this man had brought up the name with familiarity. "How do you know my husband?"

"I'm with the D.C. office of MacroWare. We've heard his reputation. I was hoping he was coming close to finding the madman who did this." He said this loudly enough for everyone within hearing range to tune in.

Interesting that MacroWare execs thought the killer had to be insane instead of purposeful.

"I'm not able to discuss my husband's business, Mr. Bates," I said. "But I can't imagine your security would allow Thomas to continue working on a case in which he was potentially implicated, like this one. I can't think Thomas would approve either."

I didn't want killers thinking Graham had any answers. It was bad enough having the feds and cops on our doorstep.

The stylish woman on the far side of Bates unexpectedly spoke up. "You are quite correct, Mrs. Alexander. Until we know if my husband's death was an inside job or the act of a madman, we must be scrupulous about whom we trust. Thank Thomas for understanding that."

Oh, wow, this was Stephen Stiles' wife. What was she doing here in D.C? Even I didn't have the nerve to ask.

"Let me convey my husband's deepest sympathies, Mrs. Stiles," I said. "He held your husband in the greatest respect." Well, Tudor did, anyway. Who knew what Graham thought?

She nodded graciously and returned her attention to the stage. I couldn't tell from her stone-faced expression if the widow was grieving, furious, or on medication—the true mark of class in my mother's world. Scary. Bates returned to murmuring sweet nothings in her ear. She didn't appear to notice.

An older woman leaned over my shoulder, offering her hand. "Good to meet you, Mrs. Alexander. I am Hilda Stark, Bob's mother. If you would be so good as to give your husband my card..." She produced a gilt-edged one. "I would most like to speak with him."

Bob was the wealthy VP of finance, the one with a loan shark family. I wish I could swivel around to see his mother better.

"Now, Hilda," Louisa Stiles said disapprovingly, sending a warning look over her shoulder. "The police have told us not to speak to outsiders, and Mr. Alexander must be considered an outsider."

"My Bob may never be the same," the older woman protested in her deep voice.

I had an ear for accents, but hers had been buried beneath decades of flat west coast dialect. She could have been German, Russian, or Scandinavian for all I could discern.

"I have a right to find out who did this to a good man," she continued.

"*Five* good men," I said peaceably. "Thomas assures me that the best people possible are on the case. But I will happily give him your card so he may reassure you, if you like."

Personally, I was hoping her card had fingerprints. One could never have too much information. I tucked the neat square into my attaché case.

That Hilda Stark had actually elicited a reaction from Louisa Stiles spoke of previous unpleasant encounters. MacroWare might not be one big happy family after all—a point to ponder.

The memorial began before I could learn anything else. I kept an eye on the service doors to the left side of the ballroom, an aisle away from where I was sitting. Those were the doors wait staff had entered during the fatal dinner, so I assumed our kitchen guests would arrive through there. My seat was angled so I could see this entrance.

I couldn't tell if Tudor had entered behind me yet. He hadn't responded to my text about sitting near hotel management, but I hoped he was watching my back. I waited to see if my extra invitations had reached their uninvited targets.

A few minutes into the service, Maggie O'Ryan in a white serving uniform slipped in through the same service door she'd used at the banquet. She stood unobtrusively behind a pillar and bowed her head when the minister opened with a prayer. My bet was that her prayer was genuine.

A black suit accosted her, and she handed him one of my printed invites. I smiled proudly as the suit accepted it. Tudor had done well. Staff would never have been invited to this event, but I needed them up here where I could see them—the ones who interested me, at least.

Adolph arrived a few minutes later through a door closer to the chairs. He flashed his faux invitation boldly and stalked to an empty seat somewhere behind me. I hadn't met the hotel's chef, but I'd studied his photos—tall, stout, commanding dark eyes, thinning brownish hair with too much pomade. He was wearing his chef's whites and didn't look grief-stricken or guilty, just officious.

I was wired and impatient, ready for the next act. But I waited respectfully and was rewarded half an hour into the service when still another kitchen worker slipped through the doors on my left. This one, I recognized, Goatee Man—Wilhelm—although he wasn't wearing a white coat.

He couldn't carry off Adolph's arrogance, not with those skinny, slumped shoulders. He glanced nervously in the direction of his presumed lover but waited for security to accept his faux invite. He took a seat along the wall. Adolph hadn't taken a row with an empty chair where Wilhelm might join him.

I waited just a little longer, until the crowd started to rustle and murmur during a particularly long-winded speech by a well-known conservative politician. Presumably, the widow had invited him. Interesting. Stiles had been a well-known liberal, so this really wasn't the right audience.

The guests were making that obvious. They shifted and looked at their phones as the windbag prosed on.

I set my attaché in my lap and removed my phone, glancing down just long enough to unlock it and find the app Tudor had programmed for the occasion. Not for the first time, I wished Graham had been available to help me organize this better. My level of mischief sophistication is nowhere near his.

Within seconds of my phone signal, Tudor set off the first of my pranks. Graham would seriously regret not staying in contact.

A round of loud pops reverberated like gunshots in the high-ceilinged ballroom.

Alarmed, the politician ducked and ran for the stage door. The rest of the speakers hurriedly filed off the stage under the direction of security, raising the room's level of fear. Frightened murmurs rippled through the crowd. Trapped in their chairs, the intelligent guests anxiously looked for the source of the disruption rather than panic. A few of the more hysterical types stood up and tried to push their way out even though there was nothing to be seen and they were trapped by a mass of bodies.

Another round popped. People hit the floor or threw chairs out of their way in their effort to escape. Security drew guns and motioned everyone down as they edged toward the sounds.

My group in front had plenty of room to escape—and me to shepherd them. I waved off a security guard coming our way and grabbed Mrs. Gomez by her elbow. "Gunfire," I said curtly and authoritatively. I stashed the awkward attaché under my arm. "There's a safe room to our left. Hurry."

Tudor had located the small reception room on the maps before our arrival. Presumably it was too small and not any safer than the ballroom or security would be rushing us toward it. Considering Tudor was in charge of the noisemakers, it was safe for our purposes.

I shoved Gomez in the right direction, released her arm, and whispered the same to Bates, Mrs. Stiles, and the other immediate families. Once I had them moving in the right direction, I hurried in front of my little lambs to open the concealed door.

Another round of "shots" fired, and my captives scrambled for safety.

Rounding up my kitchen help wasn't as easy. I couldn't tell if Maggie recognized me, but she followed when I signaled Adolph and shoved her in his direction. Adolph had no reason to respond to my signal, except he'd seen the VIPs go that direction. Human nature being what it is, he followed them.

Tudor, blessedly, hurried into the fray. He caught Wilhelm and urged him to follow his fellow workers.

Our departure raised the level of urgency, even though there was still no visible gunman. The black-suited ushers were attempting to wrangle the panicked crowd toward the main doors. A few intrepid independents broke free and followed us. I couldn't blame them. I just slammed the door closed after Tudor and a few of his geek buddies entered.

I had hoped Tudor would steer hotel management in this direction, but they knew the floor plan and had apparently found better exits. Dang, I really wanted their reactions.

The lights were already on in the salon we entered. Tudor's map of the hotel had worked excellently. Apparently designed for the privacy of important guests, the salon sported shiny chandeliers and gilt-edged plaster molding, and no windows.

Most of our guests actually relaxed in the illusion of safety. Wilhelm attempted to depart through a far door, but Tudor, tall and officious in Nick's pricey black blazer, blocked the exit with enough authority to deter him.

"We're safe here," I announced to the crowd. Even in my heels, I was shorter than everyone. But I stood against the white door and looked enough of a grim authority figure in my black suit to command attention. Heads swiveled my way. I set down my case and crossed my arms.

"Thomas was afraid of this and arranged for your comfort until security can clear the main room," I said solemnly, hiding my glee at stealing Graham's nom de plume.

"Thomas was afraid someone would *shoot* at us?" Bates asked incredulously. He was one of the taller people in the room. Maybe that gave him confidence. Or maybe Louisa Stiles clinging to his arm did. "Why didn't he warn us?"

"Madmen are not reasonable or predictable," I said in my best placating tones. Of course, if the killer was in here, he knew I was lying through my pretty white teeth. Guns were not his modus operandi. "If someone, for whatever reason, has a grudge against MacroWare, what better place to carry it out than a public occasion like this one? We can hope the police are closing in on him now."

"That is no madman," Hilda Starks said indignantly. "My son, he told me—"

Ah hah—so our execs *knew* what they were dealing with.

"Hilda," Louisa Stiles said sharply, dropping Bates' arm. "We do not know all the people in this room."

The attention of the expensively dressed crowd instantly zeroed in on Maggie and Adolph, the conspicuous white-coated kitchen staff. There were "others" in here that they didn't know, but the kitchen staff, for the most part, stood out. I wanted an Academy Award for improvisation.

"*They* are the people who poisoned the soup!" Hilda cried in booming accusation. "What are they doing here? Who invited them?"

Wilhelm ducked his head. I couldn't tell if he was hiding or embarrassed. He wasn't wearing white, so no one noticed him but me.

Angry murmurs rippled through my sophisticated crowd. Poor Maggie looked as if she wanted to run.

The intrepid outsiders who had sneaked in with us began to look longingly at the doors Tudor and I blocked. But screaming alarms and pandemonium could be heard on the other side of the wall, so they tried to make themselves invisible while verbal gunfire burst over their heads.

"The gentleman who cooked the soup is dead, you'll remember," I said with what I hoped was just the right note of regret.

In the back of the room, Maggie was now straightening her shoulders and looking at me strangely. Well, I knew I'd be taking a chance there.

"*He* hired the killer," good ol' Hilda insisted, pointing at Adolph. "Why is he in here and not out there with the shooter like everyone else? Did he know this would happen?"

She might be a loan shark, but I adored the annoying old lady for making my job easier. I left Adolph to defend himself.

"I hired Kita at Mr. Stiles' request," Adolph said stiffly. "Kita is dead and is not out there shooting now. We are all still in danger as long as the real murderer is free."

Yay, Adolph. I had thought he'd be an ingratiating toady to these people. Never underestimate the arrogance of an artiste, I reminded myself.

"It was Wilhelm who made the vegetables," Maggie offered with a clear gleam of malice in her eye. "Is that not where the botulism was?"

Presumably, only the kitchen staff and I knew who Wilhelm was. Adolph had managed to keep his name away from the cops as well as HR, so his name was new to the bigwigs. I hid my triumph at finally having his part explained and waited for Hilda to go after him with a big stick. But for a change, the tough old lady held her tongue and actually seemed to squirm.

Wilhelm edged for the door I was guarding, probably thinking I was a pushover. I hid my smile and waited for his move with anticipation.

"Don't be ridiculous," Hilda finally said with a sniff, constitutionally unable to hold her tongue or keep a secret. "Wilhelm is a good boy. A little misguided, perhaps, but he would not use anything except the freshest ingredients."

Oh, ho, a connection! I didn't know to what, exactly, but Louisa Stiles asked for me.

"Who is Wilhelm?" Louisa questioned accusingly, eyeing Hilda. "You know Stephen only allowed pre-screened personnel to prepare his food."

I hadn't known that. I tried to maintain impassivity and keep an eye on the tall, skinny cook with the pathetic goatee.

"*Your* Stephen hired the Jap who nearly killed my Bob!" Hilda shrieked, revealing her underlying ignorance, since there's a substantial difference between Korea and Japan. "Do not tell me of this pre-screening. My nephew had as much right to cook as the soup killer."

Wilhelm was her nephew? Cogs began to click.

Standing guardedly beside Tudor—she had us *sooo* tagged—Maggie spoke. "Wilhelm plated both the vegetables and the soup, but he's an *illegal*, just like Kita. Being illegal does not make them killers."

Except Kita purportedly had obtained his papers. Wilhelm had not.

Maggie shoved Tudor aside to walk out. Tudor let her go.

At the same time, Wilhelm dived for me. I'd been waiting for this moment. I didn't like being thought weak just because I'm small, so I took down aggressors with great glee.

I kicked the much taller cook in the nuts with my pointed pumps. Once he bent over with a groan, I karate-slammed the back of his neck.

And that was when the fire bomb fell through the ceiling.

Sixteen

CRIKEY! THE WHOLE BLOODY CEILING CAVED in a spark blast. Chandeliers fragged into flying glass knives. Plaster dust spewed. Electric wires arced like a game gone 3D. And of course, the blooming lights went out.

Coughing on smoke and dust, Tudor had no clue what was happening, but he opened the hall door and began steering out the coughing, screaming prats who'd just been bickering like first-termers. If he caught their hands or coats, he yanked them toward the exit.

With a sickening twist in his gut, he heard what sounded like real gunfire—and not his barmy fire crackers.

Ana!

Hadn't she just taken down the bad guy with one of her wicked kung-fu moves?

A big man almost knocked Tudor over, shouldering him aside in his haste to escape. To avoid being trampled, Tudor had to retreat to the hall with his back against the wall. The crowd spilled past him in panic, nearly bowling over police and hotel security rushing this way. Heart pounding in terror, he waited to see if Ana emerged. She had been on the far side of the room, next to the ballroom. Maybe she'd escaped that way.

Mrs. Stiles finally stumbled out, coughing, her jacket coated in dust and smoking with little holes from the sparks. Swallowing his fear for Ana, Tudor peeled off the wall and offered a respectful arm in the smoky darkness. If he couldn't reach his sister, he could aid his hero's widow. "There's a ladies room just ahead. I'll tell the police you're there after they've cleared the area."

She nodded shakily and actually clung to his arm to let him escort her. Tudor felt six-feet tall and... terrified.

What the bloody hell had they done?

***

Ana's perspective:

BEFORE THE CEILING COLLAPSED, I had seen Tudor at the far door. Once the lights blacked out, I couldn't shove through pandemonium to reach him. He was smart enough to get out on his own. I kicked around where I'd last seen Wilhelm, but he'd apparently crawled out of reach of my feet. I grabbed my attaché instead.

Without light, we were all stumbling around in the dust. I heard what sounded like Mrs. Stiles properly castigating some poor peon. Others of her wealthy cast and crew were cursing at each other and making a push for both exits. I heard Hilda's accent grow angrier and the toad who'd been sitting beside me raised his voice. I ignored them in favor of escape before the ceiling collapsed.

Whatever had scorched through the plaster had burned out quickly. Maybe it had only been an electrical fire, but it had damned well kept me from learning anything useful. I was furious enough to want to punch someone, but I couldn't tell who I'd be punching.

The lights in the ballroom had been doused as well, I discovered when I finally located the door grip. Pure blackness greeted me, but no smoke.

I froze at the gunshot in the salon behind me.

A woman screamed, and a dozen people attempted to trample me in their rush to escape into the ballroom. I had no means of holding back a panicked mob, even if one might be a murderer—or at the very least, Wee Willy.

Double foul word.

Without my handy army jacket, I was essentially weaponless. I clung to my attaché case, but I hadn't thought to add a flashlight to its contents. I needed to know what was happening, dammit. I flattened myself against the door jamb and aimed my cell phone light into the dust cloud, hoping to see Tudor or maybe a silhouette with gun in hand.

Following the light I provided, my captives shoved past me to stumble into the darkened ballroom. The main doors on the far side of the ballroom crashed open to reveal squares of light from the central atrium as hotel security dashed to the rescue.

I couldn't see any guns in the dim beam from my phone.

A hand grabbed my arm and yanked me in the opposite direction from the incoming police. I could have broken his wrist, but I sensed Graham in that masculine grip. Since I wasn't in any humor to be interrogated by cops, I followed him.

Graham wasn't a talker at the best of times, and this certainly wasn't one of our better moments. We ran to the back of the ballroom and out the stage door through which our distinguished guests had entered—and departed—an eon or so ago. Time was irrelevant. My heart was pounding too hard for my brain to hear myself thinking.

"The gunman is escaping," I finally pried past my tongue as he tugged me into one of those dreadful concrete block stairwells.

"He'll have washed his hands of residue by now. You practically offered him his victim on a silver platter." He nearly jerked my arm off when I tried to pull away.

I didn't even know who the victim was.

Graham's insult got my blood flowing again. I ran up the stairs after him, while trying to dig my fingers into the pressure point above his elbow to make him release me. The maneuver would have brought any normal man to his knees. Graham deflected me without a flinch, damn the man.

"The whole friggin' memorial was a set up," I argued, although I'd only just realized that. "Were those *your* men leading us all to the front?"

"I had security by the podium—not in the damned salon." On the landing on the floor above the ballroom, he pushed open a fire door. The lights weren't on up here either.

"Yeah, well, your security sucks," I retaliated, still frightened but growing more irritated.

I could see flashlights on the far end of the corridor and hear men shouting. Graham yanked me through a doorway into a laundry room. He opened a rear door into an unlit service hall. It was a damned rabbit warren back here. He flicked on a handheld LED to keep us from falling over laundry bins and cleaning carts.

"Where's hotel management?" I asked. "I saw them in the ballroom. They should be in charge of fixing this mess."

I was almost back to normal now. I hoped he was leading me to the area over the not-so-safe room so I could see how we'd been invaded. "That side room *should* have been secured. That's what it was designed for. Your communication leaves a lot to be desired."

He didn't argue with my conclusion. *Ha*! Of course, he really

We halted behind the service wall when we heard the voice of authority shouting commands on the other side. I sighed with impatience as I realized the cops and firemen and hotel management were all shouting conflicting instructions.

"Do they even know someone may have been shot down there? Don't you have a friend to buzz?" I asked in disgust, finally hearing Brian Livingston, the hotel manager, yelling at his maintenance workers. By the time his maintenance crew got finished trampling around, there wouldn't be a shred of evidence left.

"I don't have friends," Graham said coldly, dropping my arm.

But I noticed he got out his phone and texted someone.

I pulled out my phone and texted Tudor.

Tudor responded instantly. "Cops everywhere. I'm guarding Mrs. Stiles."

I showed the text to Graham, who cursed and started punching out another message. I was getting bad vibrations from his urgency.

"Tell Tudor to get the hell out of there," he ordered as he typed, keeping his voice low.

My thinking, too. OUT NOW I text-shouted in all caps. With no ID on him and the feds probably plastering his face all over the internet, we really didn't need Tudor anywhere near the police.

Tudor didn't immediately reply. I didn't want to contemplate what he was doing. That was his hero's widow in there. He might have some stupid notion she would listen to him about the spyhole. He didn't need to be revealing that to someone else who could get murdered for the knowledge.

Although after this past hour, I had the edgy notion that the refined Mrs. Stiles already knew more than I did. The lady was one tough cookie.

I breathed easier when I received a message curtly saying GONE.

TAKE THE LIMO AND GO HOME I typed back. I'M GOOD

I got a crusty K in return. You gotta love cryptic texts.

"We won't accomplish anything with all those people out there," I told Graham, once I was reassured Tudor was out of the way. "Shouldn't we make ourselves scarce?"

Admittedly, I had a fondness for enclosed spaces for spying, but this dark corridor didn't seem a particularly healthy harbor.

"I need to check something." He ran his pocket flashlight across the wall. Wires and plumbing ran everywhere.

His light hovered over what appeared to be a jury-rigged electrical connection—now burnt to a crisp.

"Old trick," he said in disgruntlement, switching off his light. "Let's go."

"Stuck a penny in and shorted it?" I asked dubiously. "All that commotion for a simple short?"

"Bad wiring, heavy chandelier, weak ceiling. Someone knows this part of the hotel hasn't been recently updated." He grabbed my arm again. "Quick thinking on their part."

Hotel management came to mind. I checked the clock on my phone. I could bail now and go after Livingston—or indulge my sick curiosity about Graham and his habits and let him drag me away.

He hauled me to a freight elevator. Guess that answered that. I was practically humming with anticipation to see how Graham worked, although that might have been hormones. Even in the dark my pheromones were loving his.

We took the elevator up two floors and walked off into a well-lit, carpeted office area. My good black silk suit was covered in plaster dust, and the stupid veil had slipped over my ear. I hurried after Graham's long strides while trying to remove the pins with one hand and hold my case in the other.

Graham glanced back to see what was keeping me. His Superman jaw was set in a grim lock—not unusual. His black t-shirt and jeans exhibited none of the dust that covered anyone close to the mayhem, so I knew he'd come running at the explosion.

Mostly, I was too busy engaging in pornographic daydreams gazing at his broad, muscled chest and shoulders to yank the veil off. I had a thing for big shoulders.

He grabbed my lace and ripped it off, flinging it into an open trash bag in a maid's cart. "A blind man could see through that disguise."

"Only if he knows me," I countered. "And nobody does. By the way, I'm now Linda Alexander, Thomas's wife, should any of your pals ask."

He suffered a fit of coughing as he hurried on, but I suspected he was covering a laugh. He's rusty at it. He opened the door to another stairwell and we continued upward.

"Is this your way of telling me you've not hiding anymore?" I asked, half in curiosity and half in aggravation as we climbed still more steps.

"There are very good reasons that the Secret Service is secret and the CIA doesn't announce their presence," he grumbled, using a card key to enter an unmarked door on the landing. "My existence doesn't need to be known either."

"I didn't think fire exits could be locked." I chose not to acknowledge his reference to agencies I knew my mother aided occasionally.

"These aren't fire stairs. They're private ones for the security around the presidential suite. This is the reason foreign dignitaries stay here."

He had keys to presidential security. I wouldn't want this man as an enemy.

We walked down a plush maroon-and-gold carpet in a hallway so insulated we couldn't hear ourselves breathe, much less a toilet flush. Genuine artwork adorned the discreetly papered walls, not the cheap knock-offs most hotels displayed.

I knew there were spyholes or cameras behind half the wrought iron sconces between the paintings. This was the world I'd grown up in.

"Are they filming every move we make?" I asked warily.

"There's no one staying up here now. I set the film to loop," he said casually, as if making a mockery of hotel security was a matter of snapping fingers.

Using his card key, Graham opened one of the unmarked mahogany doors and dragged me inside. If he meant to murder or ravish me, I'd go out in style.

Or not. I stared in disbelief at the wall of computer monitors where there really should be plush sofas and a baby grand. "You're kidding, right?"

Heavy draperies along the long far wall covered what was probably a spectacular view of the Capitol. Graham flipped a switch over the wet bar for light and rummaged for bottled water. He flung one at me before opening another for himself.

From the bar counter, he flicked on the monitors. One showed the ballroom, now illuminated by big police lamps. The memorial guests were gone. The chairs were knocked over and scrambled.

Anxious hotel execs conferred with maintenance men. Cops did whatever cops do. The firemen had gone away.

Several other monitors focused on closed hotel doors.

"You've tapped into hotel security?" That wasn't really a guess given what he'd just told me about looping the cameras.

"The families of the MacroWare execs are staying here. Henry Bates has stopped by to suck up to them. Beyond that, they're not talking to each other. The atmosphere is as poisonous as that dinner."

Ah, so my suspicion that MacroWare was not one big happy family was right. Interesting.

Graham lit up another monitor. That one came up black. He cursed more out of habit than surprise—probably the salon. He hit another key. This time we saw a plain room full of desks, computers, black suits, hotel security, and a really official looking Captain Theodore Donovan. Oops.

"Does security know you've bugged them?" I rummaged through the fridge and appropriated some high-end cheese and crackers. I tried to look nonchalant as Graham listened in on the man who had come to our door looking for him.

Graham didn't answer. I took that for a *no*. Graham apparently thought his security was more valuable than the hotel's. For all I knew, he was right.

Knowing Tudor was safe, I had time to reconnoiter. The elegantly upholstered blue and cream sofas had been shoved to the wall opposite the monitors. Graham had dragged a crude collection of tables and consoles from around the suite to create the line of monitors along the window wall—similar to his office at home. So, this was what he did in his spare time.

On one of the tables, I found an array of flashlights and dropped a few into my attaché. I needed to find a fancy leather tote if I was doing this again. The leather portfolio was too small.

I wasn't much used to actually being part of the action. After appropriating what I could, I collapsed on a sofa cushion and swigged my water to watch the monitors. I checked the time and texted EG that I was running late. I got the ubiquitous K in reply.

Graham turned up the sound, but I wasn't much of a listener. On all those little screens, people hemmed and hawed and talked in circles. I liked my info condensed, summarized, and neatly edited into factual lists with bullet points.

I sat up when Graham opened a screen showing a stretcher carrying a covered body being unobtrusively rolled down a service corridor. "Who?" I demanded, thinking of the gunshot and all the people crowded into that little room.

"Hilda Stark," he said as nonchalantly as if he'd just said "Big Bird."

For his callousness, I flung a water bottle at him. It smacked him on his brawny shoulder and bounced to the thick gray carpet. He didn't even turn around. "Why?" I cried. "She was just a loud old lady."

"Exactly." He switched on another monitor showing Louisa Stiles delicately dabbing at her eyes while a police woman handed her a glass of water. Anxious security and hotel staff hovered nearby. The room looked like a private salon with gilt-edged French chairs and a writing desk.

I got the message. Lady-like Louisa, who kept her mouth shut, got star treatment. Loud-mouth, argumentative Hilda, who'd been on the verge of revealing company secrets, got shot. I ground my teeth in frustration.

"Why weren't there metal detectors or searches to prevent weapons?" I asked, belatedly. I should have questioned everything about this memorial instead of spending my time designing appropriate costumes.

"That was the point of invitations—so we didn't have to strip search executives. Everyone on the list had high security clearance. How would you have reacted if we'd had to search your attaché case? We couldn't put detectors on fire and service doors. I expected you to use a little judicial wisdom in handing out the invitations."

"I don't think it was my invitees with the gun. If anything, they would have used knives and gutted their victim. If you were listening in, then you know this looks like a spur-of-the moment murder. The killer is getting nervous." Finishing off my crackers, I finally formulated a plan and stood up. "I have to catch Maggie before she goes into hiding."

"You are not going into that slum at this hour," he said with conviction, not looking up from his keyboard.

"Don't be ridiculous. It's a perfectly respectable residential area. She'll run if I don't get to her. She *knows* something. Did you hear her talk about Wilhelm? Our murderer didn't care if she pointed her finger at staff." I shrugged out of my dusty jacket and looked around for a mirror to inspect the damage. This was a bad outfit for the Metro.

"Hilda and Kita knew *something* too, and you see where that got them. Maggie is better off hiding."

I winced, wondering if he was right. Maybe we should all hide and sneak around behind the cover of Graham's computers. My gut said *no*.

If Graham had any expectation of us working together, he'd have to listen to someone besides himself.

I turned my back on him while I yanked my loose tank top from my skirt band. "Maggie will be better off when the murderer is caught," I insisted. "Hiding is not her style."

"This is why I can't get a damned thing done with you around," Graham muttered from right behind me.

He walked on cat feet. I hadn't heard him approach. Before I could react, his big arms circled my waist and turned me around as if I were no more than a computer monitor.

His kiss stunned any other reaction except lust.

Seventeen

OH, BLAST, THAT MAN COULD KISS! Graham hauled me off my feet and devoured my mouth. I retaliated by wrapping my legs around his hips and rubbing. Spontaneous combustion happened.

He didn't falter but shouldered open the bedroom door.

I yanked my mouth away. "I'm still going after Maggie," I warned him.

He dropped down on the bed, crushing me between his heavy weight and the dreamy mattress. "That's the problem here. I can't protect all of you, all of the time, and get my job done!" he said in frustration before he returned to smothering my mouth.

I wiggled beneath him and caught his attention by yanking his hair until he let me speak. "Your job isn't to protect us. That's *my* job. And we can't always be successful."

I knew that from harsh experience. We'd lost a sibling to a terrorist bomb. He would have been twelve about now. That had been one of the many reasons I'd abandoned my family after EG had been born. Old story, but I understood his complaint—Graham hadn't been able to protect his wife or hundreds of other people in 9/11. For control freaks like us, who care too much, that's the end of the world.

Like *us*. Graham and I were too much alike in too many bad ways.

I didn't want to think anymore. I just wanted to feel.

He chose to drop the argument once I ran my hands under his t-shirt. Thinking went straight away once he fastened his hands on vital parts.

This was nuts, but I was doing this, no question about it. I didn't know about Graham, but I hadn't had sex in so long that I figured I needed to clear my hormone-fogged brain.

Not that I was thinking anything that logical when he opened a foil packet.

***

LESS THAN HALF AN HOUR LATER—I think Graham had been as sex-starved as I was—I was a puddle of wax lying half under one heavy naked dude. I'd seen his scars when we'd worked out in the gym, so they weren't new to me. The rest of all that gloriously muscular maleness—I'd have to examine another time.

I wriggled until he lifted his hip. I slid out from under him even as he grabbed to hold me down. "Save Maggie, first," I told him, heading for the bathroom.

"Send Sean," he shouted after me. "The two of them can out-Irish each other."

He had a point there. I didn't know if it was enough of a point to persuade me to crawl back into his bed. I was pretty limp but still hungry for more of what he had to offer. Like sugar, sex is addictive. I didn't need either, but boy... I *wanted* them.

I showered and grabbed a hotel robe. When Graham staggered into the bathroom looking gloriously rumpled, unshaven, and way too tempting for my own good, I sashayed back to the bedroom. While the water ran, I hunted through his drawers and stole one of the black t-shirts he must buy by the dozen. It fell nearly to the hem of my skirt, but that was okay. I was aiming for grungy.

I braided my hair into two plaits and wrapped them around my head, pinning them close to my scalp. My stockings had a run, but I needed them to go with the sensible but despised pumps. Grumbling about women who let fashion dictate misery, I shook the dust from my suit jacket. At this hour of the afternoon, it would be too cold to go without it.

Graham stalked out wrapped in a heavy white hotel robe. I nearly melted all over again. Just imagine every square-jawed, steely-eyed, rugged movie star you'd ever admired rolled into one whiskery grouchy hunk... And I happened to know he cleaned up well too.

"Meaningless sex," I informed him before he could say something even nastier. "I needed that. So did you. Discussion over."

"Adrenalin rush," he agreed, eyeing my outfit with displeasure.

While he was grudgingly communicating... "Adam Herkness referred to you as *Day*. Does he know your full name? Will he give it to the feds?" I opened my attaché and produced a black knit hat and gloves. So, Tudor wasn't the only nerd around.

"Stiles and I went back a few decades. He knew my name. Herkness heard him call me Day. He's a salesman. He remembers names. I don't know if Stiles told him more, which is why I'm here. Did you call Sean?"

"Sean wants a news story. So does Patra. How much are you prepared to give them?" I dug out my phone and scrolled to Sean's name.

"Not my name," Graham said dryly.

"He already knows that. And he won't buy the empty attic if I show it to him, although the cops might. But I'm talking about the flawed operating system. You told the cops to keep it undercover, but it can't be a secret much longer now that the sheep are bleating about the destroyed NSA files."

He ran a hand over his scruffy jaw. "It's a national security issue. Sean will need to confirm it with other sources. Go ahead, but tell him to keep the sensation down low until the facts are substantiated—which they aren't at this point."

I hate voice mail so I texted Sean to see if he was available. "All right, but I'll need a safe house for Maggie and her son until their new apartment is ready in January. I can ask Nick to move back in with us and let her have his place, I guess." I was thinking out loud more than anything.

"Tell Nick everything we know and have him pass it on to the British consulate," Graham actually agreed without my twisting his arm. "His moving back in will be safer until the news is out there—*if* the killers were out to keep the OS flaw quiet. We still don't know that for certain. Kita was gunned down by a hired assassin—not as well planned as Stiles' death. I need to see if Hilda was killed by the same weapon, but that wasn't a professional hit. Someone panicked." He rummaged in a drawer and pulled out fresh boxers— black Calvin Klein knit, if I wasn't mistaken. Yummy.

I kissed his cheek and ran before he could drop his underwear and grab me. Too much of a good thing makes Ana a dull girl.

Still feeling abraded and satiated from the unexpected sex, I hurried down the hushed corridor, pretending I had a clue of where I was going.

Thank goodness, the elevator worked normally and didn't take me into a Secret Service closet somewhere. I took it downstairs and hid my attaché under my suit jacket. My knit cap helped me blend in as I sauntered through the crowded lobby like any of the nervous, milling nerds, pretending to talk into my phone while not making eye contact.

I carried Graham's warmth and the memory of great sex into the cold November gray, still without a hint of what I meant to do. With the limo shepherding EG home from school, I headed for the nearest Metro.

When he didn't answer my text, I left a suggestive message on Sean's voice mail, then called Patra. When I got her voice mail, too, I told her I was about to give Sean the scoop if she didn't call right back. Then I pinged Nick to give him the bad news that he had to move home if we found Maggie.

Nick always answers his phone, when he's not in the depths of a bad love affair anyway. He chirped cheerily on the other end, so his love life was currently good.

"Is your phone secure or do you need to call me back?" I asked, just to get his edge up.

"This one's safe," he said, a little more warily. "Did you just blow up the Stiles' memorial?"

"Close. But apparently keeping secrets just got a woman killed, so I'm passing on ours. Graham still insists it's a national security issue. If nothing else, if this news gets out, it will blow the hell out of MacroWare's stock price and probably Wall Street, but you can pass on this much to your boss. Someone has programmed an opening into some, but not all, of MW's new OS's to make them easily hacked from the outside—that's how the NSA's files got deleted."

"Whoa, back-up, I'm not Tudor. How does that translate into simple English?"

"Can't make it any simpler. Some of MacroWare's new trial operating systems have a built-in spyhole for anyone who knows how to find it. We don't know who knows about it, besides us. Tudor's cookie monster program found the flaw, he told Stiles, Stiles died, but we have no proof there's a connection. Essentially, whoever knows about the security defect can go in and rummage around in any computer using the faulty software."

"And destroy the computer's contents?" Nick asked in incredulity.

"Presumably. Tudor did it accidentally," I said with a casual shrug he couldn't see. "We need to keep Tudor undercover in case they realize that. Besides Tudor, any hacker"—like me—"can potentially read the contents of the vulnerable hard drive, download anything they want, introduce Trojan horses, whatever."

Nick may not be technologically competent, but he knows how people behave. He added two and two pretty quickly. Actually, he was something of a card shark and could add the entire deck if necessary. He came back with a swift summary. "You think Stiles was killed to keep this flaw secret? So they can keep using it?"

"They killed Stiles, and the guy who could repair it, and the chef who cooked the poison soup, and mother of the guy who sold all his MacroWare stock this week. But we can't find the logic yet. The O/S hole will be discovered by others eventually, so the deaths may be a delaying tactic, however improbable that sounds."

He whistled. "The ambassador should give me a bonus for this."

I rolled my eyes at this selfish assessment. "You'll have to earn my cooperation. I have a potential witness who needs a safe house. I'm nominating your apartment. You need to move back in with us until we get this nailed. Graham has left the building."

"A family confab is needed," he said ominously. "We'll talk later."

He hung up on me. I get that reaction a lot. I hopped the Metro heading home to EG. I really needed to make lists and do more research, if only Sean would call and tell me he could find Maggie.

Sean rang back as I got caught in the rush hour crowd at Dupont. The elevators on the Metro were out of order, so I elbowed my way up the stairs as we spoke. I filled him in on everything we knew and gave him the national security spiel. He's not dumb and could figure out the rest on his own. Then I gave him Maggie's address.

I was nearly breathless by the time I reached the top. I needed to find more time for exercise.

"Maggie won't believe me at this point," I told him. "I don't know if you can talk her to safety, but we've got Nick's place lined up as a safe haven. It's a first floor walk-up with a handicap ramp, so her kid can get in and out. I don't know about schools. I'll look into it if you can get her out of there. Detective Azzini knows guys who will help, if she needs persuasion."

Sean had met the good detective when we'd helped him bring down the mob boss, so he knew who I was talking about. Sean asked a few pertinent questions so I could tell he was on top of the game. I spotted a black suit with a bulge under his coat out on the street, near our corner. Pulse escalating, I idled past in the crowd, holding the phone to my ear and tilting my face away.

Hanging up on Sean so he could get to work, I debated the best angle to reach home. Without Graham there to monitor the situation, I had no way of knowing if there were feds on every corner and cops in every car.

I needed to be in my basement, hooking my Whiz up to his security network so I could assess the extent of the problem. *This* was why Graham never left his lair. Paranoia required constant monitoring.

I stopped and thought about that.

Unlike Graham, I'd learned my lesson—I hoped. Paranoia was like hatred—more harmful to the person suffering from it than to the object. Besides, as I'd tried to tell Graham, we couldn't protect everybody, all the time, and it wasn't healthy if we tried.

I'd be danged if I'd let a bunch of cops shove me back into my childhood defensive modes.

Instead of defense, I opted for offense.

I called Tudor. "You're in charge of EG. She should be home shortly. Nick is on his way. I'm about to hunt an illegal immigrant. There are feds on the corner and probably more under every bush. Don't go out. Hold the fort."

He growled something obscene. I didn't listen. I was already circling the block, heading back to the Metro.

Graham would have a cow.

Eighteen

LATE AFTERNOON CLOUDS dimmed the streets, and I shivered in the November cold. I needed my army jacket, not a damned suit coat. If I meant to kick myself out of my warm basement office, I ought to at least stash a closet elsewhere.

I found a café with free wireless, ordered a large hot tea, and defrosted my hands enough to type. My attaché contained my trusty laptop. It wasn't a sleek new model, but it had a huge processor and programs that blocked the idiots who sat around coffee shops, trying to hack my wireless.

Really, sometimes the world is out to get you. Paranoia isn't all wrong.

I wanted to ask Graham to hunt Wilhelm's address, but he'd roar like a wounded lion if he knew I hadn't gone home. Understanding just how incompatible we were served to remind me that great sex was just that, nothing more. We each had our own separate neuroses and never the twain should meet.

Now that I had Wilhelm's last name—Vokovich—I had a little more to work on.

He didn't show up on any of the search engines I could access from this limited network. I needed Graham's satellite connections. So I looked up Adolph's address and proceeded under the assumption that Adolph and Wilhelm were getting it on in the same house.

I took the Metro to Adolph's upscale community. As I hit the street and checked my phone map, I noticed a Goldrich mortgage center on the corner. Recalling that company as high on the banking committee files I'd searched, I pondered connections as I hurried down rush-hour-jammed sidewalks.

I knew that Tray Fontaine and Adam Herkness had mortgages on fancy houses that didn't seem affordable given their high level of debt. Judging by this neighborhood, it looked as if Adolph was also living on a scale higher than his chef's salary could command. I'd skimmed his HR file and could do the math. Kito had also been planning on moving into a high-end community, although it would just be his rent and not his mortgage that pushed his budget. How did these pieces fit together?

Adolph's posh condo had no yard, just a planter on the steps containing a skinny evergreen. Land is too expensive to buy more than one needs, and what city dweller had time for a lawn? But condos made life difficult for sneaky rats like me.

I circled the block, looking for a rear entrance to the complex. I was shivering and about to consign this notion to the trash pile of stupid ideas when I encountered an automatic gate sliding open to allow in an Audi. In the fading daylight, the driver didn't notice as I slipped through the closing gate behind her.

Other than trapping myself in the parking lot behind the condos, I wasn't certain what I'd just accomplished. I wore no disguise. Adolph and Wilhelm could easily recognize me, especially after I'd karate-chopped Wilhelm into submission. Great stupid idea, Ana.

I was playing on the impression that Wilhelm had just lost his aunt, possibly his guardian angel in the world of illegal immigration. The police would want to question him. Had he slipped away before the cops found him? He had to be feeling trapped like me—and paranoid.

In the interest of getting the heck out of the cold before I became an Ana-sicle, I dialed Adolph's phone number. I stationed myself against the wall of his unit, beside his garage door, where no one could see me from above.

On caller ID, my cell phone number would only show as unknown with a local area code, like almost everyone not in their address book. No harm trying.

"Ya?" a male voice answered cautiously.

I hadn't heard Adolph speak a lot, but I knew he had been born and raised in this country and was unlikely to mock an accent.

"Wilhelm Vokovich?" I asked in a voice of nasal authority. "This is Linda Lane in Human Resources. It has come to our attention that we do not have your green card on file. Immigration authorities are asking for your documents. I believe they are on their way to your home. If you could fax or scan—"

"You have wrong number," he shouted, then slammed the phone in my ear. Landline, nice. I missed the days of slamming phones.

I occupied myself wondering where one bought a dial phone for slamming while I rearranged a few of those big rolling trash bins in front of Adolph's garage door. While I was at it, I scouted the area for potential weapons. Workmen who left unlocked toolboxes behind—thinking this was a secure area—were my friends.

This was by no means one of my better ideas, but I was freezing, and the exercise warmed me up.

Ten minutes later, the garage door rolled up. By then, I'd created a reasonably impressive barrier blocking access to the drive behind the condo units.

A Mercedes sports car backed out at high speed— and screeched to a halt upon hitting the first big plastic bin. Garbage bags flew out of the cans, over his trunk, and spewed chicken guts onto the blacktop. Little cars aren't meant for crashing into tall objects, so the trunk looked a little worse for wear.

I waited until Wilhelm leaped out, cursing, before I made my presence known.

He visibly startled as I emerged from behind a neighbor's patio trellis. Adolph's new chef was a scarecrow figure of wild blond hair and towering skinniness. I'm a sturdy, tidy shrimp. But I'd brought him down once, and judging by his widening eyes, he hadn't forgotten me.

"You!" he said intelligently.

"We need to talk," I told him. "We can do it here or at the police station."

"You cannot make me!" He started to climb back into the car.

From behind my back, I produced the hammer some poor workman had stupidly left at the end of the day. I sauntered to the front of the pretty Mercedes and swung the hammer dangerously near the headlights. "Does Adolph know you're driving his baby? Do you even have a license? If the police catch you driving it, they can impound it."

I didn't even know if it was Adolph's car. I was lying as fast as my frozen tongue could flap. I'd never owned a car or a license, but I understood fear. I'd lived with it long enough.

"What do you want?" he asked, obviously debating whether to run over me or the cans, and the risk to his relationship if he messed up his lover's pricey toy.

"My only agenda is to find who ordered Stiles killed," I said reassuringly. "I assume the same person is responsible for the death of your aunt."

I thought he might weep. His shoulders slumped, he leaned against the car, and covered his face. I remained wary. Trapped animals usually fought back.

Not Wilhelm. "You will find who killed my Aunt Hilda?" he demanded, uncovering his face and finally revealing anger. "She was goot woman." He growled something in German that I couldn't decipher.

"I liked her," I agreed. "But whoever killed Stiles apparently thought she knew too much and was in that room with us. What did she know? Give me anything that will help me find this murderer."

He shook his head wearily. "I know nothing. It is all money and..." He shrugged, not knowing the word. "I do favor for Adolph. He does favor for Tray. Aunt Hilda does favor for me. It is all one thing and nothing."

The man wasn't as stupid as he looked. "What favor did you do for Adolph?"

"I come in and work that night, even if I have no papers, that is all. I make my vegetable risotto, but there is not enough fresh tomatoes."

"Because the risotto wasn't originally on the menu?" I asked.

He nodded and pushed his crinkly blond hair off his brow. "Kita's onion soup was on the menu, but those rich pigs asked for *fugu chiri*. If you ask me, they got what they deserved. But Adolph could lose his position because of that stupid Jap."

I didn't waste time sorting out nationalities while he was talking. I puzzled over why he thought the puffer fish was a last minute addition when Kita had been practicing for days. "It may have been your risotto that killed them. Who provided the ingredients?"

"It was *not* my risotto," he cried. "I used some cans, yes, but they were good. Any... moron... would know a bad can of tomatoes. What does this do with my aunt?"

His accent was worsening. I needed to keep him talking. "One killer leads to another," I said. "What about the salsa? Who made that?"

"I did. Adolph says the fresh basil and garlic would hide the canned taste. We disagreed, but he is top chef and I am not. After we argue, he chopped the basil and onions for me, in apology, to show it is not all about the money, I think."

He didn't look at me as he said this. Either he was lying, or he was embarrassed—or both. I wasn't making progress on motivation, but the salsa was looking even better as the weapon of executive destruction.

"Was the salsa and risotto only for the head table, then?" I asked, hunting for a means of injecting botulism into this joint project. "I can't think you'd have enough for everyone at the last minute."

"Of course," he said bitterly. "Everything for MacroWare so precious Tray will hear how good we are. But no more! I could not work for pigs like that," he said, facing me again and making a rude gesture of disgust.

"So who was doing whom a favor by pleasing the execs and Tray?"

He looked rightfully puzzled by that mangled question, but my teeth were chattering. It was dark enough that the street lamps had come on, and the wind was picking up, wafting the stench of garbage my way.

"Adolph wanted to open a kitchen in the MacroWare office in D.C." Wilhelm sounded sullen as he figured out my question. "Tray said he would talk to Stiles if their hotel dinner was good."

"You said this was all about money. I'm not seeing it yet," I said patiently, under the circumstances. "I'm just seeing good ol' boy scratch my back syndrome."

He wrinkled his nose to puzzle his way through that. His grasp of idiom was pretty sound, as reflected by his reply. "My Aunt Hilda knew Tray from Seattle dinners. As personal favor, she arranged big loan for him so he would hire me and help me get green card. Tray could not hire me because of MacroWare security, so he asked Adolph to help. Adolph wants to open kitchen in MacroWare office here. If he does that, I can be head chef. Because they know Adolph drinks too much, MacroWare would not hire him as chef, but they would not care if he *owned* kitchen. Aunt Hilda would help us."

This was making absolutely no sense on the murder front. Well, it wasn't as if Wilhelm would say, "Adolph used bad tomatoes for the salsa to kill the MacroWare bastards who fired him for drunken driving convictions"—especially if Adolph was hoping to gain a restaurant from *live* execs. I wasn't even seeing a way to arrange botulism poisoning from this scenario, provided Wilhelm was truthful. I had my doubts about that.

"You handled both the soup and the vegetables, correct?"

He narrowed his eyes. "Kita was slow. He wanted to clean before filling bowls. Adolph said to serve now. So I did. I know nothing of puffer fish."

"Serve—as in dishing the food out, not taking it from the kitchen?" I was running out of questions. I'd never worked in a kitchen and couldn't really puzzle out at what point tainted tomatoes or puffer fish could be added.

"Exactly," he said impatiently. "I filled bowls like peon because Adolph ask me. I add risotto to plate with chicken and top with salsa. Servers add dishes to tray and serve tables. No poison, nowhere."

"And you know of no one in the kitchen who might want to poison Stiles?" Now I was fishing without bait.

His hand gesture indicated his opinion of my question. "You think I would not tell police if so?"

"I think you told the police nothing because they didn't know you were there. Adolph threatened his staff to keep your presence quiet. Do you have any idea how suspicious that looks?"

"It is so," he said gloomily. "I should go home now and forget new life here. It is not much different from old life."

"I can't help you there. It will look like you're running away, though. Maybe you should just try to figure out how to be legal without your aunt bribing people." I looked at my watch. Time to be moving on. "Open the gate for me, will you? And if you think of anything else that will help, call me." I handed him one of my fake realtor cards.

I left him to clean up the garbage bins.

Patra called as I trudged back to the Metro debating my next stupid move.

"We can't find anyone to verify the operating system leak," was her opening volley. "But MacroWare stock is falling on rumors."

"Not news," I retorted. "Can anyone get their hands on the beta program and test it?"

"I had a nerd at our bank score a copy from their D.C. office. I just sent it to Tudor to see if it's one of the flawed ones. I've made enough brownie points with this case to earn a travel budget to follow the story. If I fly up there, will Maggie O'Ryan let me interview her?"

"You want to get her killed?" I asked in horror. "Send her a bodyguard. I know it's not Hollywood exciting, but see if you can find out who held the mortgages on all the major players. I'll get back to you when I know more, okay?" I wanted Patra working on our side, but I was too tired and disgusted to come up with a more challenging job for her other than doing the tracking I didn't have time to do.

"That's too easy. Come up with something better soon."

Yeah, like visiting Maggie again.

Or better yet, returning to Graham in his suite and having hot monkey sex.

I went home by way of Metro and hid in a pizza delivery truck that conveyed me to the carriage house garage, avoiding the goons with guns watching the house.

Nineteen

TUDOR GLARED at prissy Nicky and turned his tablet face down on the dinner table as ordered. He could argue that Nick wasn't his father and couldn't tell him what to do, but he didn't know his half-brother as well as Ana and couldn't judge his reaction. "People could die while we're stuffing our faces. Why isn't Ana here?"

"Probably for the same reason Graham isn't," his barmy brother said too cheerfully.

As if Tudor knew what that meant. The way he saw it, both adults had scarpered just when he needed them most—not anything new in his life.

"Graham never eats with us," EG pointed out. "Are we having a Thanksgiving dinner? Can I invite Mom? And Tex and his family?"

"That would certainly provide traditional family entertainment," Nick said wryly, without really agreeing.

Tudor didn't know EG's father and didn't want to. Since he didn't intend to be here that long, he didn't care who they invited. "I'm done. Can I go back to my program now?" He scooted his chair back. "It's kind of important."

"And we're not? You have much to learn, cherub, but run along and save the world while EG and I send photos of your empty chair to Ana." Nick produced his cell phone and waved it in Tudor's direction.

Tudor scowled but ignored the threat. "Saving the world is more important," he insisted. "Ana would agree." He thought. Being abandoned didn't give him warm fuzzies.

He left EG and Nick snapping photos of empty chairs and debating clever tag lines. Some other time it might have been fun to pretend he was part of the family, but not now, with the fate of the internet on his shoulders.

The attic echoed hollow without Graham's scary vibes. Tudor hadn't realized how much the silent dude had occupied the space until he was gone. He'd been kind of chuffed working with someone who appreciated how his head worked.

Graham wasn't completely gone though. His files had continued pouring into Tudor's mailbox through dinner. Tudor focused on the messages with Graham's analysis of the beta software Patra had nicked.

He remembered Patra as a silly teenager more interested in boys than news, but he was impressed that she'd scored the sacred program half the PC world drooled over in anticipation.

He backed up the program's files into an external drive before he systematically deconstructed the code.

Tudor was deep into C++ when Ana arrived bearing a foamy green drink he supposed was meant to be good for him. He snatched one of the brownies that accompanied it.

"Any way of detecting who wrote what part of the code?" she asked.

"Not without comparisons. So many people work on these things that it wouldn't be easy even then." Tudor tested the drink. There was enough ginger ale to make it potable.

"Wouldn't it have to pass a lot of tests before release? Someone in the company had to have seen the spyhole if they're any kind of techies at all, and we're talking the Taj Mahal of Geekdom." She nibbled one of the peanut butter brownies.

Ana had a way of drilling down to the core.

"The hole could have been planned," he reluctantly admitted. "This is test software. They might have been using it to test usage by particular types of consumers."

Ana grimaced. "Introduce a test hole, then kill everyone who knows about it? This does not compute. Any way we can use it to reverse spy on MacroWare?"

Tudor scarfed another brownie and thought about it. "Graham has access to MacroWare's servers. We can search their files without using the new software. What are you looking for?"

"Bad people." She sighed and rubbed her eyes. "I need to *meet* people to know who to spy on. Any luck yet on learning who was in charge of distributing the test software?"

Interesting. He'd always thought of Ana as a nerd like him. She actually *liked* going out and nattering with the gormless? Wicked strange.

"Got that one." He scrolled through his files and hit print.

Underneath Graham's massive console, a printer quietly whirred.

Ana retrieved the paper and turned on a recessed light to study it. She whistled. "Wyatt Bates is one of the honchos of the local operation? Why did I not remember that?"

"Why should you?" Tudor countered. "He's just a cog, but he's the cog who cranks the beta programs to end users."

"He's *Henry Bates'* brother. *The* Henry Bates, the genius who could have fixed—or written—the hole and would certainly have been in charge of the program's development. Henry was not a cog. Wyatt Bates was at the memorial, right next to Mrs. Stiles, cozying up to her. He was in the safe room when Hilda got killed."

"So were we and Mrs. Stiles and a lot of other wankers," Tudor pointed out, "including the twit chefs."

She shrugged. "See if you can find any more fun connections like this one. Then go to bed. Sleep is necessary."

Ana left, presumably to stay up all night going through the mail in her box.

Later, Tudor took another break to munch the last brownie. He'd discovered Michael O'Ryan's Facebook account when he'd researched Maggie. From the messages shooting back and forth between Ana, Nick, and the reporter Tudor hadn't met, he gathered that O'Herlihy had somehow persuaded Maggie to pack suitcases and hide in Nick's house. It might be good to check the page and see how the kid was doing.

Glancing at the posts, Tudor wanted to reach through the computer and shake the prat complaining that their Mafia safe house was *yellow*. Someone needed to take Mikey's's keyboard away and slam it on his braincase until he had some sense knocked into him.

Tudor direct-messaged Michael's account—PRACTICE TAKING CARE OF YOUR MOTHER THE WAY SHE'S TAKING CARE OF YOU, TWIT. START BY SENDING ME IMAGES OF ANYONE NEAR YOUR HOUSE NOW THAT YOU'VE TOLD THE WORLD WHERE YOU ARE. He added a secure email address.

The response was almost instantaneous. "Like this?" The email contained an image of a black sedan with tinted windows parked in the shadow of a row of multi-colored Victorian town houses.

Oh, bollocks. That was Nick's neighborhood all right. Black sedans were never good in Tudor's world. Was parking even allowed on a street that narrow? He didn't see any other cars.

Tudor IM'd Ana and Graham, because he could tell by the file exchanges that they were still working, then added Nick, just because. For good measure, he called the cops and reported suspicious drug activity.

Someone had to protect the prat.

Ana takes a ride

I WAS JUST HEADING FOR BED when Tudor's message popped into my box. I didn't quite catch the significance of a plain black sedan until I recognized Nick's neighborhood in the shadows. Black sedans regularly cruised our area, but they did not park in that Adams-Morgan alley where Nick lived. No one did. It was too narrow and littered with No Parking signs. Someone thought they were above the law and common sense—not a good sign.

I uttered a few foul words and ran for the stairs. I was closer to Maggie's location than Graham and more responsive than the cops. I pounded Nick's door and kept on running to mine. I wasn't going out again without warm clothes.

Nick emerged yawning sleepily and holding his phone. He held up the latest image from Tudor—a man standing by a tall bush. I couldn't recognize anything more. Nick pointed at a wrought iron mailbox hidden in the greenery. "Neighbor." He wrapped a cashmere scarf over his camel overcoat.

I texted Tudor as we crept down the stairs, trying not to wake EG. YOU'RE IN CHARGE OF EG. WE'RE ON OUR WAY.

He texted back symbols representing obscenities.

"Charm is his genius, right?" I murmured as I held up the phone for Nick to see.

He just snorted. "Which bolt hole do we take?"

"New one. You'll like this one. I'll show you." I led him down to the coal cellar, through the tunnel, and into the warehouse/garage on the next street.

He whistled as my flashlight swept over the Phaeton. "Let's take this."

I was about to ask if he'd like to steal a train, too, when my mischief gene kicked in. I really was getting too old for these jokes, but I can't think straight when exhausted, and riding sounded so much easier than hunting a Metro at this hour. "Keys?"

I couldn't see him grin in the darkness, but I could hear it in his reply. "What? You never took a keyless antique for a spin?"

He opened the unlocked door and almost whistled in disappointment. "There are keys in the ignition. Who puts a keyed ignition in a magneto classic like this?"

Having no interest in what he was talking about, I checked the garage doors. They looked like old-fashioned carriage doors, but what appeared to be an automatic opener produced a low glow to one side. I hit the button and the doors silently slid open on well-oiled springs.

"If we dent the Phaeton, do we get to keep it?" I asked through a yawn as I slumped into the ginormous front seat. No seat belts to hold me upright.

"I'm thinking the car is part of Max's estate and ought to be ours anyway." Nick checked the manual transmission, then smoothly backed the monstrous machine into the narrow side street.

"The underground tunnel is a good indicator," I agreed.

I still hadn't had time to do more than exchange a few emails about the Swiss bank account, so I didn't waste time speculating on our chances of being filthy rich and buying back the property. I wanted the house. The ancient car—not so much.

Nick studied the weird stainless steel dashboard while twelve cylinders growled at a stoplight. "If our grandfather was freaky paranoid enough to build a tunnel to his garage, he probably built a bomb shelter under the kitchen."

"Or the entire cellar covers a cemetery of dead bodies. All that concrete would be convenient for burying our enemies." I could almost fall asleep on the soft leather seat.

"The bodies would go under the *carriage house*." Nick actually chortled. "No wonder Magda is a piece of work."

As were we, but we were driving into the Adams-Morgan neighborhood now, and I was more intent on studying the streets than speculating on our many family idiosyncrasies.

TELL MICHAEL WE'RE IN A LIMO, I texted Tudor.

"Just pull right into the drive," I told Nick. "I'm tired of sneaking around. That's your house. Let's own it. It's not as if anyone in the sedan can trace this antique or connect it to Maggie."

"The drive is an alley in back. If you want storm trooper tactics, let's do full frontal exposure. It will be good for my cachet." He parked under the NO PARKING sign in front of his yellow apartment house. Honest, it was one of the most sedate houses in the neighborhood. Yellow is a good color, I thought, warm and inviting.

The black sedan was just down the street on the other side, where a streetlamp had burned out and sidewalk construction obstructed the corner. Probably as illegal as our blocking the street with the Phaeton, but that's the criminal mind for you.

"Do I look butch enough to enter with you?" I asked sarcastically when Nick flung open the car door and sashayed out as if this were Kensington Palace.

"In that knit cap, you look like a Russian spy. I'll tell everyone you're my driver but you were too drunk to drive."

The house looked quiet and dark, but we couldn't see the back windows from here. Nick let himself in with a key. He reached for the alarm system but it apparently wasn't activated. He muttered and swung his gaze disapprovingly to the stacks of boxes and suitcases on his pretty parlor floor.

Michael rolled down the wide hall from the back of the house. One good thing about these old Victorians, they had lots of wide open space for maneuvering a chair in. Behind him, Maggie wiped sleepily at her face. She was wearing a ratty chenille bathrobe, but the kid was still dressed.

"That's probably the FBI out there, trying to catch drug dealers," Michael said with disgust. "Aren't you supposed to carry automatics and drive them off?"

I rolled my eyes and glanced over his head to Maggie. "Take the TV away from him."

"He has a point," she said warily. "We have no idea what you are."

I pointed at Nick in his spiffy coat and scarf, looking all cosmopolitan. "Nicholas Maximillian, attaché to the British ambassador and renter of this little house of horrors. I'm just an assistant, and probably an enabler, to the man attempting to find a killer."

I pinned a glare on Michael. "The whole *purpose* of moving you here was to remove your mother from sight. Telling the entire world where you moved has rendered the arrangement pointless."

"I have to go to work anyway," Maggie said wearily. "It's not as if I'm invisible. I can't imagine I know anything anyone needs, so why am I a target?"

I pointed at the front window. "Someone thinks you're a person of interest. That sedan isn't from the local neighborhood watch."

Michael wheeled over to peer out from behind Nick's heavily draped front window. He whistled—badly. "Isn't that an antique Rolls? Is that yours?"

"Phaeton," Nick growled. He jerked the expensive draperies out of the kid's grubby hands and checked on our vehicle. I focused on Maggie.

"I've talked to Wilhelm," I told her. "He says there was a lot of horse trading happening on the upper level," I said, being deliberately obscure about MacroWare. "What did they offer you to do what?"

Michael was instantly back in the hall to listen. "What upper level?"

Maggie just shook her head. "None of this has anything to do with what happened that night. This is a nice place and all, but I know it's only temporary. I need the new place and don't want to lose it."

"Even if you have information that could expose a killer? Hilda Stark *died* today. Kita died to cover up what he knew. Isn't it better to have the information out there so there is no point in killers stalking you?"

"We don't know those are killers in that sedan," she said angrily, gesturing at the window. "It could just be some drunk who fell asleep at the wheel."

Still keeping an eye on the Rolls, Nick looked up. "Cops just busted the guy by the mailbox. The sedan is skedaddling."

Michael rolled back to the window to savor the action—or verify it. "Cool. The cops are undercover! They've got dashboard lights. They're chasing after the sedan! Did you do that?"

"Our little brother did that," I said scornfully. "Kid stuff and temporary. They now know the street is protected and will back off to regroup. We've got to fry the big fish before they return."

Maggie and I both knew that driving off one black sedan was meaningless, but maybe the cops convinced her that we were the good guys. She caved, anyway.

"The only thing I've done that involved that night was to keep my promise to Adolph not to mention Wilhelm to anyone—until you blew up the hotel ballroom. I accidentally learned that Wilhelm is an illegal a week before the conference. I understood them wanting to keep it secret. We do that all the time. It seemed simple enough at first. Adolph had me tell anyone who asked that Wilhelm was a new hire from our sister hotel in Germany. He gave me a bonus for my help that I really needed to pay the credit cards."

She hesitated, then continued. "But then those VIPs died... and I knew Wilhelm had prepared their vegetable risotto. At first, we all figured it was the soup that made them sick, so I wasn't too concerned. But the health department started asking more questions, and then the cops. I told Adolph I didn't know if I could lie anymore. He said Wilhelm was related to one of the men who died, and he would have done nothing to hurt them. I wanted to believe him. I mean, Adolph is a pretty big deal. He actually knows execs at MacroWare. That's one of the reasons the hotel got the conference."

I bit my tongue and let her babble. Sometimes, that worked better than leading the conversation.

Maggie continued reluctantly, "Adolph said he'd talk to Wilhelm's family about my concerns. The next I knew, he said the family understood and were grateful for my cooperation. They'd heard Mikey had been having problems at school, and they wanted me to have a new apartment. They made the deposit on one in a great neighborhood. What was I supposed to do, tell them they were full of shit?"

"But then you told an entire room full of people that Wilhelm had been there that night and Adolph hasn't fired you. So what are you afraid of now?" I waited expectantly. So did Michael.

Maggie sighed. "If Wilhelm isn't the problem and they really meant to help me, then..." She hesitated and stroked Michael's hair. "I don't want to say anything that might endanger Michael. Adolph has done nothing but help me. But Kita *died*. That must be related to the fish soup, not Wilhelm. What I saw... was nothing. I'm just afraid that if the cops start questioning me..." She glanced worriedly in the direction of the windows and sighed. "The cops won't care if the killers think I know more than I do."

Finally, we were getting somewhere. I held up my hands in

innocence. "Yes, I'm on the side of the cops. No, I'm not one and don't *have* to tell them anything. But even though you didn't tell them about Wilhelm, we still knew about him. You have choices— tell the cops whatever you're hiding is one choice. Or you can tell me and hope I'll find the killer first, before the cops learn you're withholding information. Or third, you can sit here like a duck in hunting season."

She tugged her robe tighter and caved. "Maybe the police already know and this is nothing, but it's the only other thing I can think of that's of importance. I saw one of the men at the table produce a salt shaker from his pocket. When I served the soup, I overheard him say that it enhanced some chemical in the puffer fish. I got the impression it would make them high or..." She glanced at Michael, then shrugged. "Increase their potency."

Puffer fish toxins were claimed to produce an artificial high *and* enhance sexual potency.

They'd poisoned themselves?

Twenty

NICK AND I EXCHANGED GLANCES. Given what I'd read about voodoo rituals and blowfish, I was pretty certain the fish toxin could be powdered and added to a salt shaker. That would explain the presence of tetrodotoxin, and exonerate Kita's soup.

The real poison had been botulism. Could that be powdered?

Nick shrugged. He didn't know either.

I pressed Maggie harder. "Which man? And did anyone else know this?"

"One man in a suit is just like another," she said angrily. "I thought they were being juvenile. Here they were, filthy rich men with the world at their feet, and they needed drugs to get through a gourmet meal. The cost of their dinners alone would have bought a chair for Michael."

"Preaching to the choir," I retorted. "But Stiles was known for feeding the poor in Africa and looking for cures for cancer. For all I know, the others contributed to those funds, too. None of them deserved to be poisoned. If one of those rich men killed the others, we need to stop him from killing again. Think! What did he look like?"

Maggie rubbed her forehead. "He was the one wearing nerdy glasses, I think. When the health department arrived after the food poisoning report, I warned Adolph about the shaker. He said he'd handle it, and I shouldn't tell anyone else or the cops might start questioning our illegals. That was before anyone knew about Kita and Wilhelm. He thanked me for my help. Since the salt shaker should prove they'd poisoned themselves, I figured it would get his kitchen off the hook. I assumed he would pass on the information. I was hoping that would mean another bonus next year, or at least a raise." She glared at her son. "I do not deal drugs. I just don't tell secrets out of school—until now, and I expect you to keep them too. I want to keep my job."

The kid looked embarrassed enough to retaliate by saying something he shouldn't. I stepped in before he could. "As far as I'm aware, that information has *not* been given to the police. Do you have any idea what happened to the salt shaker?"

Maggie grimaced. "It was still on the table when I carried off their soup bowls and entrée dishes. I didn't do the final clean-up."

Which meant someone had confiscated the shaker before the men went to the hospital, or it would have still been in their pockets or in their rooms for the cops to find. Adolph might be playing nicey-nice, but he was hip deep in shit. Just knowing about that shaker—even if all it had done was get them high or numb their taste buds—put Maggie's job and her life in jeopardy. She was smart enough to figure that out on her own.

Now I really had to worry about the men we'd seen lurking outside. They could be reporting to whom Maggie talked. Still, so far, all Adolph and company had done was pay Maggie for her cooperation. And maybe watch to see that she didn't talk to cops.

If Kita had called the cops—that had probably been the trigger that got him killed. It was beginning to look like that in MacroWare World, one got rewarded for loyalty, and eliminated for being a snitch.

"We appreciate your help," I said, as if I wasn't jittery over Adolph's role. "Detective Azzini says you've chosen a chair, and I've ordered it. It should be here by next week. I think you ought to tell the detective about the salt shaker, but that's your decision. I won't tell him."

I gestured at the house alarm. "Nick, show them how to set the system, so we can all get some sleep tonight."

Nick showed both of them how to use his guest codes. I assured Maggie that Adolph couldn't take back her bonus or take away the apartment if she told the cops what she'd told me. Then we left mother and son to have a good long discussion about ethics and morals—a discussion Nick and I honestly couldn't participate in.

At least we hadn't done anything illegal in front of an impressionable kid, other than steal a Phaeton that probably belonged to us.

Nick steered the ancient limo down empty streets, but quiet was not his natural state, no matter how much I longed for it.

"Why would Henry Bates poison himself?" he asked.

So, he'd figured out who the nerd with glasses was. "He wouldn't," I concluded. "Bates was an unmarried, aging, techie geek who probably liked getting high or had hopes for the end of the evening. Someone he trusted gave him that shaker."

There were half a dozen strong contenders for who had given him the poison, if poison it was. I only had motive and opportunity to work with. Unfortunately, real evidence was elusive. Without the shaker, I couldn't even prove that was the way either of the poisons was administered, much less which one.

"I was thinking it was the salsa that was poisoned," Nick continued. "Didn't the one guy scrape it off and come out alive?"

"Yeah, but he may have just not liked salsa. I'm still thinking the canned tomatoes in the risotto or salsa were where the botulism was, but Wilhelm says Adolph prepared the salsa and swears he knows bad tomatoes when he sees them. Unless Adolph provided the salt shaker, too, that would have to mean two killers and no motive for Adolph that I can see. That's just not adding up."

If I could draw a circle of evidence around Adolph, I could go in with all guns blazing and maybe pry the answers I needed out of him. But he was a man with a lot of powerful contacts on his side. He couldn't be intimidated like illegal Wilhelm. I needed proof and officialdom on my side so he couldn't swat me like a fly.

Crimes worked out so much easier in one of Tudor's computer video games.

"Are you checking on who the cops arrested in my bushes?" Nick asked, moving on. "Maybe that will tell you who is interested in Maggie."

"Half the world is interested," I said in disgruntlement, texting Graham to look into it. As expected, his reply was nasty. GET YOUR ASS BACK TO BED didn't sound romantic anyway. "For all I know, that was Patra in the bushes. Or Sean. I'm pretty sure Adolph doesn't command goons in sedans."

I rummaged in the Phaeton's stainless steel dash for the garage door opener as we cruised down the street behind the house. We circled the block, just to be certain all our own thugs had gone home. That they were gone proved they were underpaid, overworked cops and not the bad guys.

"They're after me, Graham, and Tudor," I reminded Nick. "They think you're harmless, and they can't connect a limo with any of us."

"*They* being half the world again, right?" He slid the car through the carriage doors and into the darkness of our private Bat-garage.

"FBI, cops, and the mafia for all I know. Nothing like having both sides gunning for us." I pointed at the stout figure stepping out of the shadows at the back of the garage. "And Mallard. I'll hide in here. You go talk him down."

I curled up on the lovely leather bench seat and conked out.

Ana's Tuesday Musings

THE PHONE RINGING jarred me awake. I bounced my head off the steering wheel, groaned at a crick in my neck, and fumbled about for whatever in heck I'd been hauling around last night that might contain my phone. I found it in the pocket of my army jacket and tried to read the caller information, but my eyes were too blurry, and the car was too dark.

But it was warm. Miraculously, the car was still warm. The garage had heat.

I finally swiped on the phone and grumpily answered, "Yeah."

"Cops at the door with a search warrant," Tudor whispered. "They have Graham's name and know he saw Stiles last. I'm in the stairwell. What now?"

"Join me in the garage, I guess. It's cozy. Don't suppose you have any breakfast bars you can bring me?" I rubbed my eyes but I was accustomed to coming alert at a moment's notice. Cops at the front door meant lots of bad news. I wanted to be fortified before I heard it.

"I should have time to snag something from the kitchen on the way to the cellar," he whispered. "Mallard is stalling. He had to find his reading glasses to read the warrant, and he left them on the porch."

I could hear his breath as he hurried down the narrow circular stairs. The kid needed more gym time. "Where's Nick?" I asked.

"Performing his best barmy drag queen and embarrassing Mallard."

Nick dresses well, not flashy. He's not a drag queen by any stretch of the imagination. But like me, he knows how to put on a good act.

"What about EG?" I asked.

"I think she's already at school."

I uncrossed my eyes and glanced at my lighted phone screen. It was after eight. EG was good.

"I hope Nick borrowed the robe Patra left behind. That should have their eyes glowing in the dark." The robe was pink and sheer and floated on feathers. I don't know where she got it or why but I was relieved she'd left it behind.

Tudor snickered. I could hear him open a cabinet door, presumably in the kitchen. I was trying to stay calm but I was about to crush my phone into toy parts. I needed Graham's monitors to know if the garage was surrounded.

I bet he had some means of checking. I dragged my weary body out of the Phaeton, found my LED light in another pocket, and began exploring while Tudor whispered his progress. That's our training—keep everyone aware of where you are at all times if there's trouble. At least then we know where to find the bodies in the ashes.

By the time Tudor stepped through the tunnel exit into the garage, I'd located the security panel in the back wall. It looked a bit like a basic electric panel with small screens above the switches. I studied the controls and decided they wouldn't blow up anything before I started flipping them on.

As expected, Graham had hidden cameras focused on every angle of the broken pavement surrounding the garage and a few more on the street. No wonder my grandfather had loved him. They were a paranoid match made in heaven.

"They're making cops smarter these days," I muttered, zooming up a monitor to reveal a nondescript sedan on the corner and men crouching in the weeds.

Tudor slumped in despair. "I was getting so close to finding a patch for that spyhole! How can I finish without a computer?" He indicated a leather bag over his shoulder. "I've got my hard drive if I can find someplace else to work. What about you?"

Good question. I really hated giving up our protective fortress. This introvert preferred doing her work from an isolated basement, and my grandfather's mansion was the safe nest I'd never had.

I was getting soft.

With a sigh, I checked the attaché I'd grabbed last night on my way out of the office. Good habits paid off, I noted, discovering the external drive in my cache. "I'm good, but I'd rather not hook these up in public. And we can't hook them up *anywhere* until we get past those clowns out there."

I took the apple and breakfast bar he handed me and munched while I read through the news on my phone. "Any notion what brought them back?"

"They're running out of suspects, and the FBI really wants to know more about us?" Tudor suggested. "Or they figured out we're not at MIT."

"If I could drive, we could take the Phaeton to MIT," I muttered, wishing the phone worked as fast as my computer. "Or we could send Patra with Michael O'Ryan in our place. Wouldn't MIT love that?"

I glowered at the phone screen.

"Ugh, no!" he protested, before he realized the real direction of my sarcasm. "What did Patra do?" he asked in resignation, noting the direction of my glare. He's smart like that. "Let the cat out of the bag, did she?"

"She or Sean got several competent nerds to verify there was a spyhole in the software. Both their names are on the article. Never tell a journalist actual facts," I said with a sigh. "I didn't think they'd find anyone to corroborate the story. So much for national security. The glory hallelujah politicians are screaming their heads off already. No wonder the cops are at the door. They have to blame someone soon or Congress will have to actually work over the holidays. IT departments around the world are now officially on overtime. I kinda want to be in the White House while they panic and check their computers."

Tudor snorted and watched the non-action on the street monitors. "If they'd just leave me alone, I could fix it, daft twits."

"Wouldn't solve the murder and get Graham off the hook, though. I'm betting we've got one day before the Russians and Chinese happily burrow their way into whatever's left of NSA files and the world market crashes. Your cookie monster problem will be irrelevant. Can you tell if anyone at MacroWare is working on a patch?"

"Mostly, I'm seeing a lot of hash from the top about PR nightmares. Not a lot of action on the program front. I haven't looked this morning now that the news is out."

This was Tuesday. We were running out of time and options.

Swallowing hard at the thought of our hard-earned mutual

funds reduced to rubble as the internet and the world economy collapsed, I thumbed through my email and found an urgent message from Patra.

GOLDRICH FINANCES HOUSES FOR ALL MW EXECS, PLUS TRAY, ADOLPH, AND RELATIONS. STARK'S LOAN COMPANY OWNS CONTROLLING SHARES

Ding, ding ding—bells and whistles rang, light bulbs flashed, and connections started popping together in my devious brain. I wasn't exactly sure what I had, but now that I had some evidence of financial shenanigans, I had direction. Maybe I wouldn't kill my sister after all. She and Sean were proving amazingly resourceful. Since I was spending so much time away from my desk, it was handy to have research back-up.

I called Graham's cell phone and got voice mail, damn him. "The cops are searching the house," I told him. "We need a place so Tudor can fix what no one seems to be in a hurry to fix. I need to head down to Goldrich headquarters. If you can't think of a safe place to stash Tudor so he can work, I'll send him to you."

I snapped the phone off and finished munching my breakfast. Threats were the only way to get through Graham's paranoid fixations.

LET SEAN HAVE HIM, he messaged back.

OK, so he was furious with Sean and didn't want to hear my musical voice at this hour. Got it. I could rearrange Graham's head if I had time, but I didn't. Family first. I called Sean and left a message saying I was sending Tudor his way and to have a computer ready. Then I faced the puzzle that was our friendly policemen in the bushes.

"Call in a murder on the corner?" Tudor suggested. "Wouldn't they be first on the scene?"

"And when they find no murder and trace the call and arrest you for filing a false report, how will you get back to school?"

I called Nick in the house. "Tell the cops with the warrant where the bodies are buried so we can get out of here."

He chuckled. I heard him shut a door. "I'm about to sashay to work and leave the blue boys with Mallard. They're singularly unimpressed with the lack of evidence that Graham exists, and they really don't like that they can't get into your computer."

"And they'd better have a good reason for searching or

impounding it," I said firmly. "Or we're calling our lawyers. Not that the drive there has anything except my client files, but it's the principle of the thing. The guys crouching in the bushes probably need coffee about now. What can we arrange?"

"Dogs or donuts," he suggested.

"Or both. I got it. Tudor and I will go exploring shortly. You may as well go on to work."

"Don't do anything I would do," he said cheerfully.

Nick didn't give me all that protective crap that Graham shouted. Nick and I had spent our childhoods creating diversions. He knew I could handle myself. Pity Graham didn't respect my brain.

Well, maybe he feared what my warped brain was capable of. He's not dumb.

I called a local dog walker and offered big bribes via my anonymous Paypal account. That was going on my expense report. Then I ordered a donut delivery to our front door. Mallard could provide the coffee.

The dog walker came through with flying colors.

Dogs big enough to yank leashes out of their walkers hands are a noisy and sometimes dangerous nuisance. Not long after my PayPal transfer, *oops*, the pack followed a cat and escaped their handler. They ran howling and yapping into the bushes surrounding the garage—where our men in blue were hiding.

I admired the chaos—pit bulls and poodles, nice.

On another monitor, we watched Mallard stoically open the back gate to allow the dogs in so the cops could herd them where their tearful handler could catch them.

While Mallard was passing out coffee and donut rewards, Tudor and I slipped out the side door and moseyed on down to the Metro. At least this time, I had my army jacket, although I'd slept in the clothes I was wearing.

On Massachusetts, I watched with wary interest as all around us, men in expensive suits frowned at their newspapers or fancy tech. Some had already taken to shouting into their phones.

I had a nasty notion that the stock market had started its plunge. The FBI would camp on our doorstep until they found Tudor and/or Graham. I needed to turn their heads in the right direction—pronto.

I took Tudor down to Sean's newly-remodeled newspaper office. Thanks to Patra's last little escapade with Top Hat's benevolent mobsters, half the offices had been burned or waterlogged a few weeks back.

The new tile and fresh paint had improved the décor considerably, I decided, as we took the elevator up. Sean had left a message giving us entrance under our Patty and Paul Pasko aliases. I wasn't about to give Tudor's name to a bunch of nosy reporters.

A secretary installed him in an office with a new computer. I admired the layout of shiny new machines in the cubicle farm and asked if anyone was beta testing MacroWare.

The secretary gestured toward a guy taking apart one of the desktops. "Just that one. He reports on new software."

No cookie-eating monsters or spy holes in here, then. I approved their tech guy's excess of caution.

Deciding I'd left Tudor in safe hands, I set out to develop a clothing stash for the next few days. For years I'd lived without phones and credit cards. I didn't have a driver's license and my phone isn't under my name. Family had ended my hiding months ago, but I still didn't like the world knowing where to find me. I was desperately trying not to be my rootless mother, but old habits die hard.

I took a membership at the Y. That gained me a locker and a shower. I found a thrift store—nowhere as upscale as the nifty consignment shops in our part of town but sufficient for a boring business suit. I stocked up on used walking shoes and a few basic no-iron clothing items that I carried out of the thrift store in a vinyl gym bag which would fit neatly in my new locker. I wasn't wasting money on hotel rooms as Graham was doing.

I glanced longingly at the boxing bags in the gym at the Y. I'd love to have a little attitude adjustment time, but the week was almost half over, and I had to get Tudor back to school. I resisted. I showered, put on my business suit, transferred some of my weapons from my army jacket to my attaché, locked up the rest of my clothes, and headed for Goldrich headquarters.

High finance, as I've mentioned, was not exactly my forte. I'd never had money, a mortgage, or a loan of any kind. Mutual funds pushed my limit and worrying about them gave me ulcers.

I recognized that experience divided the haves from the have-nots, and I vowed some day to educate myself about the money I'd never had.

I had learned that in my research that Goldrich was an enormous mortgage company right on the top of the list of companies the banking committees were investigating. Goldrich, along with several mega-banks and investment firms, also had a huge political lobby. Our congress-critters were stepping delicately as they discussed new regulations on fraud in a wealthy, powerful industry. Whether or not Goldrich was taking advantage of the spyhole in the government operating systems, I had no way of knowing, but two and two normally make four, so my calculated guess was that they'd take any and all information offered.

The fact that every single Macro exec and their families used Goldrich for their mortgages yelled collusion to me. I'd already seen how MacroWare execs traded favors. Bob Stark and Hilda owned controlling shares of Goldrich. That said they had a lot of influence on the banking front as well as the software level.

Adolph and Trey in their expensive houses were already high on my suspect list. Bribery by mortgage was innovative but not unthinkable. Murder for cover-up was logical, no matter how I disliked the thought.

Twenty-one

Ana doesn't get a mortgage

A FEW WEEKS AGO, Patra had nearly got herself killed by infiltrating a media conglomerate's office. Unlike me, she actually had credentials to land the job. Given my GED and lack of college degree, I doubted that my resume would get past the trash basket at Goldrich, but a job wasn't my real goal.

Carrying my attaché, wearing a dowdy black business suit and an ugly three-quarter wool coat found at the thrift store, I entered the glass-walled headquarters of Goldrich Mortgage a little after noon. I'd texted Graham and Tudor to let them know where I was. Both ignored me. I figured they had some heavy crap on their hands and didn't have time.

I'm a loner. I didn't need anyone's approval. But I wanted to have sex again in this lifetime, so I tried to stay alive and somewhat on Graham's good side. I approached Goldrich headquarters warily.

Unlike many city offices, the mortgage company apparently liked to make the public feel welcome to walk in off the street. They apparently owned the building and had no off-putting security sitting at a barren desk in an empty foyer, keeping people out. I entered what appeared to be a busy office, with business suits striding briskly through the foyer and disappearing down corridors.

I introduced myself at the receptionist's desk and requested the head of Human Resources, a fellow I'd found on the internet. She asked if I had an appointment.

"Yes, of course," I lied through my pearly white teeth. It's easy to lie when you know no shame.

She tried to look up the Patty Pasko name I gave her. After studying her computer with some consternation, she made a phone call.

With interest, I observed the suits behind her rushing around more frantically, frowning and talking into their phones, just like the suits on the street.

How fast was the stock market dropping? I knew the possibility of losing all our money was giving *me* failure of the heart, but what did the stock market mean to mortgage companies? Bad vibes were pulsating so loudly through the office that even insensitive me could feel the tension.

The receptionist apparently wasn't getting any answer to her calls. Welcome to my life, I thought wryly. But this time, I applauded the lack of response. She was forced to apologize and step away from her desk to seek higher-ups. She took the corridor on my right.

Ever a proponent of seizing opportunity, I immediately strolled down the opposite hall.

A scream from a back office sent me running—not easily done in pumps and straight skirt.

"My files are gone! All my files are gone!" a blond woman wearing a shiny gold necklace screeched. "I've lost *everything*!"

"That's not possible." An African-American man in an expensive suit pushed her aside and began tapping at her keyboard. "I need that profile to close this deal."

"It was there! I had it all done last night, but they're all gone!" The blonde's decibel levels were reaching hysterical.

Realizing no one was about to die, I shamelessly eavesdropped as curses rang from another cubicle and shouts of fury echoed from down the hall.

This wasn't precisely how I'd intended to meet Goldrich's bigwigs, but as already proven, I'm an opportunist. I calmly walked in and shoved aside the black guy and the blonde and shut down the computer.

"This was what I was trying to warn management about. But would they listen? *Nooooo.* Shut down all your computers, *now*," I ordered in a voice of authority. "The virus attached to the spyhole will destroy everything in your hard drives if you don't."

I was pretty sure I wasn't lying. What I was doing was concealing a boatload of alarm—because the MacroWare beta-spyhole was designed for reading and manipulating files, not destroying them wholesale. After Tudor's mini-disaster, the state department's website had gone back up. I assumed that was a sign that his monster hadn't gone too far. But if all Goldrich's servers were going down...

Something had crawled through that hole bent on destruction. I prayed it wasn't Tudor's monster.

If a destructive virus had corrupted dozens of very busy government computers, and the spyhole allowed it to escape, how long before it actually ate the internet? That possibility savaged a hole right through *my* middle.

I had this horrific vision of our Swiss bank account disappearing in a swirl of crashing computer bytes while our mutual funds sank to the bottom of the sea. Staring at poverty again terrified me, and gave me some understanding of the frantic suits rushing down the halls.

Following my example, the black managerial-sort started down one side of the hall, ordering computers shut down, while I worked the other side. Wide-eyed horror was everywhere, not helping my panic much. The air turned blue with foul language in different accents. I understood and sympathized with their alarm. If I was about to lose all my hard work, I'd be a screaming meemie about now too.

Fortunately, my valuable files were in my attaché case. Even if the cloud collapsed, I had my work intact. I knew how to start over. I just didn't *want* to.

A contingent of Italian suits and loafers emerged from a conference room at the end of the hall. The wearers of said suits looked mean—as in, *I'm going to kill someone* mean. And deservedly so, if my fears were correct. I was thinking this was not a good time to confront the top brass.

I peered around an office door and tried to identify the hornets. To my shock, I was pretty certain one of them was Brian Livingston, the manager of the hotel in the center of our little controversy. He looked as if he was about to be taken out and hanged.

Strangely, instead of the usual conservative American flag pin in his lapel, he wore a tiny rose. Where had I seen a rose pin lately?

That's when I spotted Senator Paul Rose and nearly gagged at the pin's symbolism—a rose for Rose. I wanted to spew on their shiny shoes.

But my luck had run out. I noticed a couple of Rose's dangerous business buddies in the crowd, looking stone-faced, and my gut clenched. I'd run into those guys my first few weeks in D.C. They hadn't reached the top by being nice men. I frantically began hunting a bolt hole.

Power, wealth, and prestige gave Rose and his Top Hat

financiers free rein to do anything they liked. I was pretty certain their minions had killed my well-heeled, well-protected grandfather. They were capable of removing *anyone* who got in their way—like Maggie and my entire family.

Rose had seen me once in full Magda mode. I didn't know if he'd recognize me in dowdy business attire, but I wasn't taking chances.

I darted into a restroom and waited until they'd gone by.

If Paul Rose and his cartel had hotel management *and* Goldrich by the balls—who else did they have? I was spread too thin. I began texting warnings to everyone I could think of.

***

Tudor's Take:

TUDOR SCRUNCHED UP HIS SHOULDERS and stared at the computer screen, aware of all the wankers studying him as they strolled past his cubicle. He didn't care what they thought, but it was hard to work under scrutiny. Besides, the machine didn't have enough RAM to run his software, and after working with Graham's super satellite connections, the internet here was a total shambles.

He thought he had the code to patch the spyhole *and* stop his monster, but he couldn't test it. He was debating going back to the house when he heard a commotion on the other side of the cubicle farm. Had this been school, he could have ignored it. But adults normally didn't create that kind of aggro.

Tudor got up and made his way through the strangely empty newsroom—in the direction of excited voices.

"Russian hackers!" someone was shouting with authority. "It's a terrorist attack on our economy. I've been warning you!"

"The only terrorist involved here is Wall Street," someone else yelled. "Wall Street can turn off the panic-spigot anytime, but they haven't. One bad program won't ruin MacroWare."

"Yeah, but the collapse of the internet will," a woman's voice insisted.

Her warning was almost drowned in a sea of loud theories. Tudor hid outside the break room, trying to work out what had them arguing. These were journalists. They thrived on trouble. But the mention of Russian hackers had his insides churning.

"Someone just reported Goldrich's website down," a louder voice yelled. "So are two more brokerages and three of the major banks. I'd say it's a cyber-attack on our economy."

Just as he'd feared, it had all gone pear-shaped. Gutted, Tudor closed his eyes against panic. *His cookie monster had escaped its cage?* How? It wasn't designed to go anywhere—unless some nutter adulterated the program. A few code changes... and it might attach to documents from an infected site and travel anywhere the document did—and keep traveling and chewing and multiplying.

If Ana was right and someone was spying on banking committees through the beta program...

The Frankenstein monster might really devour the internet.

Swallowing his alarm, he returned to his computer. He needed access to a lot of speed and a lot of servers, really fast.

What better place than the MacroWare office just blocks from here?

Ana paces anxiously

ONCE THE GOLDRICH HALL WAS CLEAR, I slipped out of the restroom, studying my cellphone like everyone else. With the internet on the eve of destruction, I worried that I hadn't heard from any of my family or friends and might not again if communication servers crashed.

Clusters of people stood in the corridors, shouting into their instruments of Satan, so I assumed phone lines were still in place. Whether the mortgage company survived depended on the security of their backup. They had only the spyhole and themselves to blame for this fiasco.

I really liked the idea that Goldrich and Rose had been hoist by their own spying petards and Tudor's nasty little monster. I had no proof, but I had a glorious feeling that Rose's evil empire had just been shot down by its own villains.

If it weren't for my concern over our money, I'd burst into song. Well, maybe not.

Knowing that Goldrich, Top Hat, and hotel management were linked, possessing evidence that they practically owned MacroWare execs, I cheerfully abandoned them to their drama.

Motive was becoming a little clearer—money being the root of all evil and all that. *Opportunity*... not so clear. Paul Rose and his cadre wouldn't be caught dead in a hotel kitchen. Logistics—completely escaped me.

Out on the street, I tried calling Tudor. No luck again. I rang Nick but his greeting wasn't as sunny as usual.

"How bad is it?" I asked.

"Pretty scary," he admitted. "They're calling it a terrorist cyber-attack. Wall Street just cut off trading. The White House has advised shutting off vital websites. The embassy is monitoring the situation for fear the worm will infect British computers next."

"You need to talk to Tudor and Graham. I have no clear understanding of what Tudor's monster is capable of, but it sounds as if it may have mutated. The attack might be real, but if it's just Tudor's program, then it won't go anywhere without that hole in the operating system. Advise your people to remove any beta software, and don't accept any attachments from anyone."

I wanted to go to MacroWare headquarters, but programming really was Tudor's bailiwick, not mine. I'm a researcher, and sometimes a harpy, but I had no real programming training. I regretted my lack of education for many reasons.

After hanging up on Nick, I tried calling Graham again. Protecting the world from itself was a lonely job. I thought he might need human contact occasionally. Or a mosquito buzzing in his ear.

"Tudor isn't answering my messages," was his greeting—but at least he'd answered.

"Not a good sign," I agreed without argument. "I'll try to have Sean check on him, but it's crazy out here. Without a computer, I'm helpless. Any new direction I need to follow?" I asked this out of panicked politeness. I was already aiming for the Metro.

"Tudor's worm is corrupted almost beyond recognition," he reported. "There are IT departments around the globe gleefully accessing any beta hole they can find, and in return, Tudor's malicious worm is attaching itself to everything they copy. If it gives you satisfaction, I'd say that all these amateur spies are downloading infected documents and passing them on to all their buddies."

I whistled happily. "So the villains destroy themselves. Karma rules."

"Except they're taking the rest of the world down with them, and the Russians and Chinese are exploiting the beta problem with vigor. We need Tudor working to close the hole and stop his monster because management at MacroWare is running around placing blame and accomplishing nothing."

He sounded exhausted. It would be nice to lead the kind of life where we comforted each other with hugs. That wasn't happening anytime soon. "I know Tudor's working on it, but I'll talk to him. I want to have a chat with Adolph. We need to get to the bottom of the murders so you can return to your office."

"Miss me?" Graham asked with what almost sounded like real human humor. "Civilization as we know it comes first. Find Tudor."

He hung up, of course. He was a busy man. I got that. But he was also a paranoid robot who'd shut down anything resembling human emotion. Some days, I approved of the robot.

I stood on a street corner, trying to reach Tudor. Or Sean, who might know who to call in the office. I watched as frightened businesspeople rushed by, staring in disbelief at their mobile lifelines. Mostly, the non-business types appeared ignorant of imminent disaster. Mothers walked babies. School kids trooped in and out of buses, chattering.

Bombing the internet in no way resembled bombing buildings. It took a long time before economic carnage became visceral. That didn't make the destruction any less fatal.

I hoped and prayed that hospitals and vital resources like police and fire departments weren't so advanced as to be playing with beta software. The internet affected everything in our lives.

Tudor still wasn't answering his phone or texts. Neither was Sean.

I hadn't worried about my little brother while he was at school. We'd never really talked in years. I shouldn't be concerned now, but I was.

Even as I thought that, my phone rang with the *Jaws* theme I'd designated for Magda, the Hungarian Princess.

I didn't need her asking what Tudor had done now or offering helicopters. I let the call go to voice mail and headed for the Metro.

Once my phone quit thumping, I called Mallard. Unlike the rest of us, he could usually be counted on to be home. "Have the police concluded we're not hiding in the woodwork yet?" I asked.

"They have departed the premises with a warning to alert them as soon as you return," he intoned solemnly.

"Bugged the place, did they? That's not legal. We'll ask Oppenheimer who to sue." Graham had the whole house bugged, so this was just business as usual. "In the meantime, have you seen our resident alien? He isn't answering his calls." If there was any chance of bugs, I wasn't using Tudor's name.

"There is no one here but me. I shall see that the car meets Miss Elizabeth Georgiana at school."

I glanced at my watch. It was well past lunch, and I was running on empty. I liked being there when EG got home, but it didn't look like this would be one of those days. "Thanks, Mallard. We'll owe you big time. Hold the fort."

My bratty little brother had a bad habit of disregarding calls and dropping off the radar. Besides, Sean should be with him, and there wasn't a darned thing I could do to make Tudor work faster. I'd only had an apple and a breakfast bar all day. The hotel was on the way to the newspaper office. I could do double duty, take time for a fast bite of food and make a call on Adolph.

I texted a threat to Tudor and left voice mail with Sean.

It was disconcerting that Graham had actually been the only one to answer my call. He normally ignored us, but he had an eerie ability to know when disaster was about to strike.

I hopped a Metro car just before the doors shut, and for a change, I tried prayer to any god that might be listening. I had a feeling a higher source than little old me was needed to save the day.

Twenty-two

Ana tackles the kitchen

I'D ONLY FORMULATED A HALF-ASSED PLAN for approaching Adolph by the time I arrived at the hotel where presumably Graham was still staying. I didn't know how many security cameras Graham could follow at one time, so I didn't bother waving at them as I entered the hotel restaurant.

I was convinced Adolph was the key piece to my puzzle, but he was elusive. I couldn't think of any way of tricking him into revealing what he knew, and he had no reason to speak to me that I'd been able to dream up.

I'd learned that Maggie worked catering conferences for extra money, but normally she was day shift in the restaurant. I didn't see her as I asked for a table in a corner, where I could keep an eye on everyone in the room. I'd been hoping for her aid, but I'm creative. I'd find another way of reaching Adolph.

Perusing the outrageously expensive and not very comfort-food-friendly menu, I wondered if I could charge the meal to Thomas Alexander's room. Thinking better of it, I ordered tomato soup and a cheese sandwich. They weren't on the menu but the waitress didn't argue.

I had second thoughts about tomato soup as soon as she left. Obviously, I hadn't been thinking. Did botulism have a smell?

Could I end up in the same ward with the MacroWare execs? I'd love to interrogate those guys, but with a murder rap hanging over Graham's head and the feds looking for Tudor, I figured I'd better keep my distance. I certainly preferred not to gain entry to their ward through tomato poisoning.

Like everyone else in the almost empty dining room, I punched my phone. No replies from Tudor or Sean. I texted Patra, just in case. She was supposed to be in Atlanta, but she could be with Sean after they broke the nasty news story about the beta program.

By the time I'd eaten my soup (diced tomatoes, basil, no cream) and sandwich (I wasn't venturing to guess what kind of cheese or herbs), I'd dug into my cloud files and uncovered Adolph's mobile number. If I was going to develop food poisoning, I'd be sure to spill my guts on his shiny shoes.

Maggie had told Adolph about the potentially poisonous salt shaker, and *he hadn't told the cops*. That, in itself, was suspicious.

If Wilhelm was telling the truth, Adolph had made the salsa that could have contained spoiled canned tomatoes.

Our unfriendly hotel chef also appeared to be benefitting from MacroWare's connection to Goldrich—which looked like an insider pay-off to me. He had a spotty reputation with the law and alcohol and no good means of climbing higher than a hotel kitchen unless he pulled strings.

And he'd been in the safe room when Hilda had been shot. I didn't think he had sufficient motive to be suspect Number One, but he looked like a solid accessory. Of course, whoever had crossed the wiring was the real accessory, but that could be any of a few thousand people.

Feeling stupidly safe knowing Graham was a few floors above me, I rang Adolph. He didn't answer. I wouldn't either if I didn't recognize the number.

"I know about the salt shaker," I told his voice mail. "And Goldrich is going down as we speak, so your mortgage is already in jeopardy. If you're prepared to tell what you know, there's nothing anyone can do to stop you. I'm waiting in the dining room for the next ten minutes."

I was giving Adolph the benefit of the doubt because I just didn't think he had sufficient motivation to kill five MacroWare execs.

I ordered coffee and waited.

Tudor's Take:

ALL THE PILLOCKS WERE SO BUSY ARGUING over potential economic collapse that Tudor slouched out of the newspaper office without anyone noticing. He felt as if he carried the weight of the bloody world on his shoulders. Babies might starve if he didn't repair what he'd broken.

Not that he'd *broken* the dodgy betaware. But no one had

expected a worm to crawl in and start burrowing through their files either.

The creepy kid song, *the worms crawl in, the worms crawl out*, dug into his brain cells and couldn't be dislodged.

People had probably been *killed* because he'd found that beastly hole. The internet could still die if his monster wasn't stopped.

If his fix didn't work, he'd have to call his mother and take a helicopter to Africa and hide. Or Thailand, maybe. He heard there were lots of pretty girls in Thailand, and beaches. He needed to research extradition treaties.

The worms play pinochle on your snout...

The D.C. MacroWare office wasn't far from the newspaper office. Accustomed to the London tube, Tudor easily located the Metro he needed to get there.

He'd done his research and knew that even at a low-level sales center, MacroWare had multiple stages of safeguards. He'd dug through Graham's security files until he'd located the emergency back door code, along with multiple warnings from Graham to the office wankers about not changing the code frequently enough. He'd have to hope this latest one hadn't been changed.

Tudor knew not to carry in thumb drives or other bits that security screens would spot. He also knew he was asking for trouble, but Graham and Ana were more interested in catching bad guys than fixing what was wrong. He admired what they did. He couldn't do it, but he was good with other things. His task was clear.

He had the patch to stop his monster. He had to see if it worked, and he couldn't do it without MacroWare's servers.

He repeated that mantra as he donned a plasticized ID card he'd nicked while rummaging inside Graham's console. The photo didn't look like him, but he wore it flipped over as if blown by the wind as he walked through the back door. The guard at the desk didn't notice. The bar code got him past a card check. If they had eye or thumbprint checks, he was screwed.

But this wasn't MacroWare's main operating headquarters, just a small sales office. Apparently the prats didn't realize how easy it was to access the national main frame from the D.C. server or they'd think twice about their security.

Well, Graham had warned them. Tudor had seen it in the files. Someone hadn't wanted to pay the extra expense of securing every employee and door in the D.C. office.

He pondered that as he stalked past offices in shambles and milling, worried twits. *Why hadn't management wanted real security?*

With a shiver of apprehension, he prayed that the passwords he'd copied inside his jacket pocket would get him straight into the company's servers. He had to be able to access his cloud account where he kept the patch code, and he didn't need potential killers breathing down his neck.

First, he needed a computer.

He had no clue where to go once inside. This ground floor had carpeted hallways, real offices, and names on the doors. He knew MacroWare only occupied the first two floors, and he assumed he'd blend in better with cubicle dwellers. Hoping he'd find them on the next level, he took the fire stairs up. He could always pretend he was maintenance if everyone else wore suits and ties.

The predictable cubicle farm on the next floor hummed with unhappiness. Khakis and long-sleeve tees seemed to be appropriate office attire. His grungy sweater and corduroys weren't entirely out of place. He rubbed his shorn head and hoped he wasn't on wanted posters on every cubicle divider and screen saver.

He eased toward a darker corner, away from the water cooler crowd. The wonks in the cubicles he passed looked grim and appeared to be juggling phones and not computers. Sales, right. He bet they were being hit by a butt-load of grievances.

Swallowing his guilt, Tudor chose a cubicle with no photos adorning the dividers and no papers on the desk. The dual monitor was a beaut. He powered up the drive and got the expected password demand.

Biting his bottom lip, he checked the list in his coat pocket and began typing. If none of these were general override passwords...

He was in. Not feeling any relief yet, he started digging into the computer's security.

Before he could get past the first level, he had a yahoo leaning over his shoulder.

***

Ana goes mad

ADOLPH STOOD ME UP.

Well, that was to be expected, after all. Maybe he hadn't checked his voice mail. Maybe he wasn't ordering his hard-working staff around today. Maybe he'd scarpered after I'd tackled Wilhelm.

At least I'd been fed.

The newspaper office wasn't far away. I had time.

I wasn't moving on until I knew the chef wasn't on the premises. I needed better confirmation of my nebulous theories before bearding any lions, and Adolph had been right there, front and center, while the poisoning was happening. He'd also been in the room when Hilda had been shot. I needed face time.

I took the elevator to the lowest level and wandered ugly concrete block corridors until I heard the kitchen.

"She's up there now!" I heard Adolph roar. "I don't know who the hell she thinks she is, but she's dangerous. Get your silly ass out of my kitchen until she disappears."

Oh, were they talking about little ol' me? How exciting! Did I eavesdrop to see what they had to say, or just present myself and grin?

I *sooo* preferred eavesdropping. Old habits were hard to break. I leaned against the cold block wall and listened. At least I wasn't hiding in a closet, my former modus operandi.

"But we are guilty of nothing," Wilhelm whined. "What can she do? My sauce, it is almost done. I cannot leave it."

"She can have you deported," Adolph said nastily. "Now get out. I'll watch the sauce."

That didn't precisely sound like a lover's spat. Curious, I waited for Wilhelm to depart.

He didn't, not through this door. I knew there was more than one.

Well, blast. Now I'd have to enter hell's kitchen, where they kept all the long knives. I rang Adolph's number and parked myself against the door jamb to watch the kitchen. I hoped I had enough distance to get a head start if he came after me with one of those hatchets I'd seen Mallard wield.

From this angle I could see Adolph in his chef's whites on the far side of the kitchen, whisking something on the burners. He pulled out his phone, then shoved it back in his pocket without looking up. So much for the importance of my call.

Since I hadn't come up with a better plan, I leaned against the door jamb, crossed my arms, and whistled. The nearest slavey heard me and glanced over. He poked the person next to him. The din in the kitchen slowly silenced sufficiently for Adolph to notice and look up. I waved.

"You!" he shouted, grabbing one of those knives I feared. "Get out of my kitchen! Get out of my life! You are to leave my people alone!"

I shrugged, pretending insouciance. "I'm not your problem, honey-pie. In case you haven't figured it out by now, the rich honchos you're hanging with are killers. Money doesn't grow on trees without a little bloodshed to fertilize it."

Adolph was not a small man. Nor was he a weak one, like Wilhelm. He had a few extra pounds, but they didn't slow him down. He shoved past kitchen workers, bearing down on me, knife in hand.

I really didn't think he'd gut me in front of witnesses, so I didn't run. But defensive tactics were called for if I wanted to pry information out of him. I dodged to the other side of the complicated maze of tables and burners.

"You want to discuss it here, with everyone listening?" I taunted from behind a massive steel stove and an array of saucepans. "I'm good with that."

Really, I wasn't. I just wanted to hide in my basement and play safely on my computers. But he had information I needed, and I wasn't letting Tudor and Graham down because I was terrified of knives.

What didn't kill me, made me stronger, right?

"I know nothing!" he shouted, edging around an aisle of appliances to get at me. "I told the police all I know!"

The kitchen staff obligingly got out of my way as I ducked under a worktable and came out in a different aisle. There are advantages to being small. Adolph couldn't manage that maneuver without cracking his head or a few ribs.

"You didn't tell them about the salt shaker, did you?" I demanded. "Where is that now? Who dried the fish guts?"

In a moment of brilliant insight, prompted by holy terror, I concluded, "*You did*! You dried all those poison livers that Kita was throwing out! No one else would know how to do that. Did Kita confront you? Is that why he's dead?"

"I wish that I had never heard of Kita!" he cried, waving his knife and bringing down a hanging pan with the force of his swing. It clattered to the stainless worktable with a resounding bang he didn't appear to notice. "Fish soup is disgusting! If those imperialist pigs must eat poisonous fish, they deserve to die!"

"Tell me what you really think," I said dryly, darting around a stove bubbling with lunch specials. "But you'll do what the hot shots ask because they return the favor, right? Tray wants you to serve puffer fish. You need a new restaurant. Quid pro quo... am I getting close?"

"Yes, Tray wanted me to hire the little Kink ferret, but I... did... not... kill... Kita." He whacked his knife against a chopping block to punctuate his words. He was starting to look pretty fiery-eyed. "I did not kill *anybody*! Dried *fugu* is nothing." He swung the knife and decapitated a string of garlic.

"And what did you get in trade for hiring Kita and drying fish guts?" I reached the refrigerator section and decided that wasn't a good direction. I ducked under another table while the kitchen sheep just watched us as if we were a TV movie.

"So, I do a favor for a friend who wants an aphrodisiac!" Adolph shouted. "That is stupid thinking but not poison!" He made as if he was coming at me from one direction, then darted the other when I tried to avoid him.

Trapped by refrigerators, I skidded to a halt and looked for a weapon. A nearly empty giant sack of flour was all I could find. I flung it in Adolph's direction, then ducked behind stacked shelves of dessert trays. "Hogswallow!" I called back.

He stabbed the sack in mid-air, showering himself, lunch, and half the kitchen in a white powdery blizzard. The desserts were deluged in a white film. Shame to waste them. I ran my finger through a particularly sumptuous icing. If I was about to die, I wanted chocolate first.

"Kita's soup wasn't poisoned. He was too honest for that," I declared, making up the scenario as I dodged Adolph. "But you needed imperialist pig mouths numbed so they couldn't taste your rotten tomatoes," I called while Adolph angrily shook out his chef's hat, spraying more flour. "You're not so dumb that you wouldn't have looked up the results of dried puffer fish liver."

"They do not eat anything that tastes good!" he cried, diving for the dessert shelves as if to reach through them and strangle me. He succeeded in knocking a fat carrot cake slice in my direction. I caught it and nibbled as we danced back and forth on either side of the trays.

"One asshole doesn't want gluten," he roared. "Another doesn't eat meat but fish is okay. Another wants no dairy! They don't use their taste buds anyway!"

"Who asked you for the dried guts?" The cake was dry. Dry carrot cake is a sin. I threw the rest of it in a sink and wiped my hands on a towel as I skirted around the frozen dessert chef—as in, the chef seemed paralyzed, not her desserts. She didn't even smack my hand when I swiped a handful of chocolate morsels.

Adolph flung a bowl of draining pasta at me. I ducked, and spaghetti strands stuck to shelves and counters. Perfectly al dente, nice.

"Ask Mr. Livingston," a voice called from behind me. "Euan said she overheard him talking to Adolph about aphrodisiacs."

"Ah, now we're getting somewhere, thank you!" I called to the snitch over my shoulder. The hotel manager who knew Tray and Paul Rose and knew about old wiring that could be shorted with pennies was another nice connection.

My expertise seemed to be in seeing the big cynical picture, then finding the puzzle pieces that fit. The picture was slowly coming together.

"Wonder what happens to all the underwater mortgages you're all holding if Goldrich gets indicted for fraud?" I asked, hitting him where it hurt to see what happened. "Do you worry about that, Adolph? Huh? Will imminent foreclosure persuade you to talk?"

Adolph stabbed his knife into a chopping block with a blow so vicious, I thought the heavy wood would crack. Without a single look back, he stalked out of the kitchen.

Score one to the harpy.

Grimacing, I followed. I borrowed a loose knife, just in case he had more hidden in his coat.

Twenty-three

RELIEVED THAT THE GORMLESS BLOKE who thought Tudor was IT maintenance had only wanted him to fix his computer, Tudor sat in the prat's fancy office, patiently attempting to explain computers.

"Look, all you need to do is clear your caches and run a defrag before you go home tonight," Tudor repeated in frustration. He pushed out of the posh office chair and tried to get around the big wanker in a pin-stripe suit blocking his exit. The guy had dragged him down to the office level, away from the program he'd almost broken into. "I have to update the system before I can leave tonight. If your defrag doesn't work, I'll look at it again tomorrow."

Only in another dimension, he thought, but he had to escape the tosser in the expensive Rolex. Lying seemed expedient. He should never have followed him down to the first floor, but he'd been nervous about refusing someone who had to be management.

"Look, we're in the middle of a crisis here," Rolex argued. "We have to know if there are any security breaches causing the servers to crawl. You guys can check for that kind of thing, can't you?"

"It would be easier for me to go through an unused computer to check that," Tudor assured him, not as comfortable with lying as Ana was. "That's one of the reasons I'm here." He tried to ease toward the office door.

Rolex invaded Tudor's personal space, pushing him back toward the desk. "Start with *this* computer. I'll get out of your way."

This was a plush office, not an anonymous cubicle. Tudor craved anonymity. Contact with authority made his skin crawl. He was probably supposed to know this dork's name and bow to his grandiose title. But the guy wore no badge, and the door label merely read Vice President of Sales.

Why would a sales guy care about security?

"I don't usually work this way," Tudor said, glancing longingly at the door Mr. VP blocked. "I'll have to back-up your entire drive, and I didn't bring any extra externals with me."

"It's all backed up," VP said proudly, patting a dusty older model drive behind a stack of report files.

Tudor bit off a *whatever* that would have given away his age. "Fine," he agreed in a surly tone. "Just don't disturb me. I need focus. Just one missed piece of code could take days to unscramble."

"Right. Make certain that spyhole they're talking about isn't in there." Smiley-face stood in the doorway until Tudor took a seat at the ergonomically incorrect computer console. "I'll stop by a little while later to see if you need anything."

"I can take care of myself," Tudor muttered and opened the screen—no password. This prat really never used this machine, did he? He rolled his eyes and said nothing as the office door shut behind him. Maybe this wouldn't be so bad after all.

That's what he thought until he tried to access the main frame. A red alert message filled the screen, warning an unsecured application was being executed.

The firewall threw up barriers and the screen went dark.

Ana fights another day

AFTER THE KNIFE-STABBING INCIDENT, the kitchen's shocked silence erupted into cacophony. Since no one offered to help me catch their furious head chef, I raced into the corridor after Adolph. I didn't know what he was up to, but I wasn't ready to let him escape until I had answers or he gave them to the police.

Livingston had asked about aphrodisiacs. Bates had said the salt shaker contained aphrodisiacs. Adolph hadn't denied drying fish liver. Had Livingston asked because Bates had asked him? Or was the hotel manager the inspiration for this little tongue numbing experiment? Since Bates was dead, Adolph had some explaining to do.

Once in the block-wall passage, I saw Adolph stalking toward an exit on my left—and Brian Livingston and security approaching from the elevators on my right. They looked grim.

I now knew that the hotel manager was a Rose minion who had hired Adolph on Tray's recommendation. Except for my dislike of Senator Rose, that wasn't suspicious in itself. Livingston had not been in the room where Hilda had been shot—but his staff could easily have shorted the wiring for the real killer. That was pure speculation.

Not knowing how deeply the manager was involved, I went after the devil I knew. I turned left, in pursuit of Adolph.

Security shouted at me. As previously noted, tight skirts are lousy for running. I yanked the hem up my thighs but Adolph had a head start and the security goons had longer legs.

To my relief, Maggie stepped out of a side corridor carrying a heavily loaded tray. I didn't think her appearance was an accident. She looked wide-eyed but determined as she balanced the tray.

Reaching her, I grabbed the weapon she proffered. With ill intent, I flung the tray and all its contents at the security goons. I hoped that was fish soup soaking their black blazers. Calamari appeared to drip from one guy's forehead.

Maggie winked, then screamed dramatically as she dropped to her knees in the middle of the floor to retrieve her broken crockery, blocking the corridor. This returning favors business worked both ways.

I raced after Adolph. Behind me, I heard the goons cursing as they slid in goo, tripped over Maggie, and crunched her dishes.

Adolph had almost made it to the elevator I had taken once with Euon, the one leading to the parking lot. I'd never catch up with him if he got outside. I yanked my skirt higher and picked up speed. "Down, Adolph, or they'll shoot!"

I could have been lying. Hard to say. Security was cursing and mad enough to shoot, at least.

Adolph threw himself to one side of the hall and slumped to make a smaller target—military training, maybe. At least he knew he couldn't outrun bullets.

I swung around, waving my kitchen knife threateningly at the angry security guys. "No closer. Call the cops, if you want, but you don't touch this man."

Since they probably had been after me, that messed with their minds a little. With their shoes still slick from the mess Maggie had created, the guards slid to a halt and quit reaching for their guns. Behind them, Livingston looked panicked.

Now we were getting somewhere. I liked panic on the face of my victims.

My phone rang with the Batman theme. It was a lousy time for my spy in the attic to finally put in an appearance. "Get Adolph before the goons do," I ordered before Graham had a chance to say a word.

"Tudor is at MacroWare. They've just shut down all their servers," Graham countered.

I had no idea what that meant beyond the urgency of his tone. "I'll get on it." Since he was right upstairs in the hotel with all the security monitors, he had to know what was happening down here in the kitchen. "How close are the cops?"

"They're at the back door." He clicked off.

Well, at least he hadn't told me to get my ass out of this mess. That would be stating the obvious, I suppose. At least he'd called the cops for me and given me enough warning to haul my petite derriere out of sight before they dragged me to their torture chambers and forced me to give up Tudor.

"Adolph, if you don't tell the cops what you know, I will," I said, glaring at Livingston and not the defeated chef. "I recommend that all of you start talking while the rest of us try to put Humpty Dumpty back together again. MacroWare is going down and taking a lot of fat cats with it. The fate of the western world really could be on your shoulders. Try that hat on for size, cowboys."

I ran back to the corridor where I'd last seen Maggie just as the elevator door burst open with the boys in blue.

Apparently watching for me, Maggie swore beneath her breath and followed me down the side passage.

"Try that hat on for size?" she asked in incredulity. "Did you just pull out every cliché you know?"

"Obfuscation and smoke clouds make for great escapes. My brother is in trouble," I told her, racing for the unknown. "How do I get out of this maze?"

"This way." She led me through a warren of service tunnels and elevators until we were at the loading dock in back.

"Think positive," I told her, punching the button to open the wide loading doors.

"I positively think you're nuts and I'm going home," she declared, stalking out onto the dock with me. "I'm not working with killers."

I didn't try to rearrange her thinking. Adolph was no master mind, just an angry, needy idiot who would sell his shriveled soul for money. I needed the real killer. I'd been putting two and two together. If I subtracted Adolph from the equation, the result led straight to MacroWare—where Tudor had apparently ensconced himself. I had a real nasty feeling about that.

I gripped my kitchen knife harder. Maybe I ought to learn to use a knife, but for right now, for my purposes, it was useless.

It was dark as we traversed the delivery alley. I offered my weapon to Maggie for her trip home while I peeled off in the direction of MacroWare.

A black sedan waited for me at the end of the alley. The way my life was going, I prayed it hadn't been sent by the ghost of Stephen Stiles. Or his killer.

Tudor's Take:

"BUGGER IT!" Tudor shouted at the abruptly crashing computer. Fighting panic, he shoved back the executive's chair and headed for the door.

It was locked.

He stared in incredulity for much longer than he should have. Ana would have been quicker off the mark. She'd told him he was getting soft. He hadn't understood—until now.

Even as an ankle-biter he'd had enough gray matter to recognize that animals reacted violently and irrationally when trapped. He'd apparently been nattering with a desperado and hadn't caught on. He grokked computers, not people, blast it.

A quick glance around his prison revealed an office where no one actually worked. No filing cabinets. No big desk drawers filled with potential weapons. No souvenir swords on the wall. Just one old computer on some prissy furniture and a stack of paper.

Old trick—he checked the ceiling. Acoustic ceiling tile, probably on an aluminum grid. Tudor climbed onto the desk and shoved up a tile. He wasn't heavy, but even his weight was likely to pull that flimsy grid down. But there had to be supports up there somewhere.

He pushed the desk to the wall. Fancy wood or not, a desk without real drawers weighed nothing. He climbed up again and found what he needed—a steel beam he could haul himself out on.

Once he got himself into the space between floors that housed all the building's wiring and ducts, he had time to think.

Rolex Prat had lured him down here and locked him in deliberately. Had he recognized Tudor and gone for the feds? Or had he just pounced on any stray IT person? Why? To blame him for the crash? That seemed most likely. Rolex Prat had needed a sucker to take the fall—for what? What was the prat doing?

Unwilling to give up this chance to access MacroWare's servers and save the internet, Tudor eased along the beams, listening for activity. Mostly, he heard shouted obscenities. Had all the servers crashed? He cursed the acoustic tile that prevented hearing normal conversation.

Wondering if any of the wires that he was crawling over might be cable he could connect to a computer, he started removing ceiling tiles and peering into offices. One good laptop would be a start.

His phone vibrated. He didn't want to answer it and admit he was in trouble, but he really needed to know what was happening.

He glanced at a message on the screen.

ALL EMERGENCY SERVERS CRASHED. GET OUT NOW.

From Graham. The man was damned spooky. Did he know where Tudor was right now? And what the bloody dickens did he mean about emergency servers? Did they have them at MacroWare?

Or did he mean cops? Ambulances? Almost anything operating on MacroWare could conceivably be shut down—just the same way MacroWare updated its software—invisibly, while people slept. The possibility that computers to the police and fire departments were offline froze his guts.

Brain power worked better than panic—new mantra.

Taking a deep breath, Tudor found a messy but unoccupied office. On the desk below gleamed a really hot new netbook. Score! He swung down from the beams and shoved the little beauty into his shirt before climbing back into his hiding place. Years of video gaming had taught him when to hide if he wanted to win the treasure.

Turning on the pricey little machine, he checked the battery power and admired the speedy processor with enough RAM to fuel the CIA. Satisfied, he closed the tile and crept to a safer surface to see what connections he could make.

Judging from the icons, the office's wireless network had no signal—a very bad sign. Graham hadn't provided a smartphone with cellular access. Without his hacker programs, it would take forever to manually crack any of the other networks.

He really wanted into MacroWare's servers. If they were down, all his plans would go pear-shaped.

Grumbling, he sent Graham an encrypted text with the password to his cloud account where he'd stored the program patch. He didn't know if the patch would work. He'd wanted to test it while everyone else was fighting crime. But if everything blew up in his face, he wanted back-up out there.

Once that was done, he began hacking at the various networks the system was showing.

He smelled smoke just as he finally broke into a secure network named MWSucks.

Twenty-four

Ana freaks out

THE SEDAN ISOLATED ME from the panic in the streets. Looking out the tinted windows, I only saw worker bees hurrying harmlessly down the sidewalk. I couldn't hear the buzz or sense their anxiety as I had earlier.

But the message from Graham about emergency service computers blacking out was sufficient to escalate my adrenalin. How much did the police and fire departments rely on the internet? What about hospitals?

From my luxury seat, I couldn't tell anything was wrong. Riots weren't breaking out in the street. But the further we traveled, the more stoplights seemed to be out. I vaguely remembered reading about a complex network that allowed computers to change signals in emergencies and rush hour. That network was obviously not working. Cops would have to take subways to bypass the traffic tie-ups. Not good.

The internet on my phone wasn't fast enough for me to flip through the necessary websites to understand what was happening. Texting worked best. I messaged Tudor.

He actually texted back. MW GOING UP IN SMOKE was his cryptic reply.

Oh damn. I glanced out the window—the major thoroughfare the limo was traversing had turned into a parking lot. I couldn't take it anymore. I pounded on the driver's window until he opened the glass.

"I'm outta here," I told him. "Keep heading for MacroWare."

He lifted a hand in understanding. I shoved open the door and jumped into the unmoving traffic, dodging between hulking SUVs blaring their horns—as if miles of cars would magically disappear to satisfy the impatience of Type-A morons.

Once I was on the sidewalk, I could feel the pulse of alarm again. Pedestrians pushed and shoved in their hurry to be elsewhere, all of them shouting into their mobiles. Car horns blared.

In the distance, I heard dozens of sirens, but there was nowhere for traffic to retreat. This was not a normal rush hour. This was more like three concerts, a Christmas tree lighting, and the Olympics emptying into the streets at once.

I made a mental note never to isolate myself in limousines again. No wonder the wealthy had no idea how the rest of the world lived. I'd never fully realized how my prized isolation had cut me off from reality. A rich man's pedestal wouldn't be any better than my basement.

Especially if some Unholy Pratman had the power to stop emergency services while he committed who knew what crimes. I smelled big-time cover-up, at the very least. My gut really didn't like the idea of that much power consolidated in one place.

I didn't have time to reach my clothing stash for more suitable attire. Still in my dowdy skirt and ugly black coat, I slipped through crowds gathering on corners, past the business suits consulting their fancy phones. How long before the phones stopped working?

The MacroWare sales office was only a few blocks away. I wondered how Tudor had managed to get through their security but didn't waste time worrying over that detail—not while the entire MacroWare staff appeared to be spilling from the building and milling outside on the sidewalk.

Was there a fire?—which was what I'd expected after Tudor's smoke message. I heard no alarms or loudspeakers indicating a fire drill. I smelled no smoke and saw no leaping flame. That didn't keep me from panicking at the prospect of a hidden fire with my brother in the middle of it.

If there was a fire, the place would burn down. No fire truck could get through this traffic.

Why was Tudor inside a building where my next best suspect worked? He didn't need to be physically inside the building to mess with their servers—which should be sensibly located offsite. My adrenalin was rapidly escalating into berserker mode.

Where the hell was Tudor? Didn't he have the sense to get out with everyone else? I wanted his long red hair back so I could see him in the mob. But in his knit cap and slouchy sweater, he'd look like every other geek in the lot, except the execs. I strained to find him, but I was too short to see through the crowd.

Under the assumption that Tudor would be watching for me if

he was outside, I sauntered past the mob rather than attract attention by gawking. Around the corner from the employee door was the glass front public entrance. It was dark. I glanced at my phone. Not five yet. They shouldn't be closed.

I tried texting Tudor again but this time didn't get a response. *Not liking this.* If he was outside with the rest of the crowd, he'd be able to hear his phone.

I called Graham and got voice mail. "Don't say I didn't warn you," I said into the recording. "MacroWare is dark. Everyone is outside, but I'm not finding Tudor. I'm going in."

That was about the nicest threat I'd ever left him. I pushed open the front door and entered the dark lobby. Apparently no one had told security to lock the doors during an emergency. Eggheads lacked common sense.

I smelled smoke. I didn't feel heat or see flame. I heard no crackling. I've had a lot of experience with fires. This one just seemed to stink, and it wasn't even a fried-electrical smell. Why weren't the smoke alarms going off? They must have done so earlier to send everyone out.

I found a bank of light switches, but they didn't work. I produced my LED from my bag and proceeded onward. "Ratface?" I called into the darkness. Even in my panic I wasn't using his very identifiable name. I was hoping Tudor would recognize my voice or the old insult.

I heard a noise further down the carpeted corridor. Trusting the building code would require a fire exit at the other end, I hurried down the empty hall, shoving open office doors and flashing my light, looking for trapped employees or Tudor.

Nothing but dark monitors everywhere. A computer company with no active computers is a sad affair. No electronic alarms blared at my intrusion. No security guards monitored my progress or stopped me. In a place like this, back-up generators ought to be kicking in to at least keep the servers and security running.

The lack of electronics was pretty damned scary. It presented a sharp image of a world without internet or security cameras, without fire or burglar alarms—a world where people could just walk in off the street. Wow. Hard to wrap the mind around. It was almost like being back in an old cowboy Western. We might as well have swinging doors.

Apparently hysteria provokes my imagination to strange heights.

I shoved at the next door. It didn't open, and I reached freak-out level. "Ratface?" I called again, more urgently.

Tudor dropped through the ceiling in front of me. I nearly had a heart attack until I saw him holding one of those useless little netbooks that cost three fortunes and a harem or two. Then I wanted to smack him. I was still shaky from imagining his crumpled body behind that locked door.

"Some arse is burning something," he whispered, nodding his head toward the back part of the building. "The ventilator quit working when the electricity went out."

"I don't see any reason to stay in here and find out who," I muttered, but I followed him down the hall. So, yeah, our entire family is nuts, including me. "Doesn't look like you've patched the software hole yet. The entire city is crashing to a halt."

"You haven't given me enough time. And my monster isn't crashing anything. It only eats data files. This is a real attack if servers are shutting down."

That shut us both up. We could be hunting a truly dangerous human monster, not just a cookie-eating one. I'd been hunting a killer, without giving much thought to the killer's agenda. MacroWare's operating system ran over half the computers in the world. Shut down MacroWare's servers, corrupt their operating system and browser... and the result would be far worse than the traffic jam outside. If we had a megalomaniac controlling MacroWare...

One big corporation ruling all computers was such a very *bad* idea.

I pulled Tudor into one of the dark offices and shut the door.

"How much can you do with that tiny piece of overpriced junk?" I asked.

He flipped it open to show me the available networks. "There's a strong signal in the building that isn't MacroWare's. I had just hacked their password when I smelled smoke. I was looking for the source when you yelled at me. I don't know even know if MacroWare is still online, but the wireless ought to be strong enough for me to try to tap into their off-site servers if I go outside and find a hiding place."

I wanted him safe and a hundred miles away, but if Tudor was our only hope of getting the world as we knew it back up and running... "There's no one up front. Head that way, sit by the front door so you can escape if necessary. No one on the street should be able to see you. I'll look for the smoke."

He yanked a fire extinguisher off the wall and handed the canister to me. Then he hit the fire alarm for good measure. Nothing happened. "Is that what Graham means when he says emergency services are down?"

"I'm guessing MacroWare's security is shut down," I said. "And for good measure, Pratman may have disconnected police and fire department computers so they won't get here until he's done with whatever he's doing."

Tudor snorted at the epithet I'd created from his slang, but he didn't interrupt while I thought out loud.

"Emergency services ought to have some kind of radio communication," I continued, "but it won't do them much good with the traffic out there, so stay by the door where I can find you. I'll locate other fire exits, then hunt our smoking gun."

He took the *gun* part literally and looked alarmed. I pointed back the way I'd come. "Save the world, minion."

Apparently accepting that we had different goals, he grimaced and loped toward the front. I lofted the heavy fire extinguisher, decided I could handle it, and proceeded down the hall of executive offices. I was hoping to find my objective on this floor. I didn't want to be trapped on the second floor if there really was a fire and not just a smoking rag.

The stench of smoke grew heavier as I progressed down the hall. The titles on the various doors grew increasingly more officious. I'd reached Chief Financial Officer before I heard the muttering.

"I'm not a damned programmer," I heard a man's voice whine. "I'll make it all go away, if you'll just leave me alone. You knew we couldn't do this forever."

I didn't hear anyone reply. Assuming he was on the phone, I eased past the CFO's office and on to a double door suite with no label on it. Conference room was my assumption. I peered in the sidelight window. At a console of monitors against the near wall, I could see a tall man in a high-backed chair. Shades of Graham.

But this wasn't competent, self-assured Graham. Whoever this was, his body language revealed a terrified, weak dude apparently in over his knucklehead. He kept rubbing his brow and practically wringing his phone while slumped over a keyboard.

At this hour in the winter, the floor-to-ceiling windows were mostly dark, except for illumination from a distant street light. So it was only the building electricity that was out. The smoke was stronger here. I didn't find the source until I saw the man feed papers under a desk and watched smoke billow out. Really, who burns papers anymore—unless he was trying to set off the sprinklers. Water would certainly wipe out any evidence in the mainframe servers, if they were in this building. It wouldn't wipe out any off-campus back-up, but this guy didn't look as if he was thinking too clearly.

He set his phone down on the desk and returned to pecking uncertainly at his keyboard.

What should I do now? Given what I could see of his height and shoulders and what I'd put together so far, I was pretty certain this was Wyatt Bates, brother of the aphrodisiac-wielding dead exec, and that he could be a desperate serial killer.

But he'd just talked to someone who apparently knew at least some of what he was up to. He had accomplices.

That scared the crap out of me.

My usual verbal attack wouldn't work with a real killer. I only intimidated the powerless. The possibility of murderers with weapons roaming the hall was frightening. I should have sent Tudor away.

But the moron in the conference room could be destroying the internet for all I knew. He was most certainly destroying evidence. If I was right, he had killed one of the most important men in the world. He could easily have shot Hilda. For what? To spy on banking committees?

To save an all-powerful mortgage company. One partially owned by the family of another MacroWare exec—Bob Stark. For all I knew, Goldrich owned half of MacroWare and half the politicians in D.C. in one manner or another. Money has a way of creating its own influential fiefdom.

But Stark wouldn't poison himself.

Remembering Senator Paul Rose and his tribe of wealthy

investors in Goldrich's halls—there was more than a simple mortgage company involved. I had huge files on the senator and his Top Hat cabal and knew they ran entire mega-banks and brokerages. Legislation controlling their realms could endanger all of them. Could Stiles' death just be about money? That sucked so bad I wished the killers could all die more than once, in painful ways.

Leaning against the wall, fire extinguisher in hand, I worked through a scenario to keep from going off half-cocked. If I was afraid of losing our meager rainy day fund as the stock market slid downward, I could just imagine what guys worth gazillions must fear now that the spyhole had gone public. MacroWare stock was plummeting. Soon, the rest of the market would follow.

Whoever had created the spyhole was about to lose everything because they'd wanted to control banking regulations. They were so arrogant, they had thought the peons would never catch them.

It would take time and a lot of quick thinking to cover their tracks—hence the emergency shutdown.

Hence the mass murder of MacroWare execs? They'd been the first to learn of the spyhole.

If Stiles or his execs had informed the government that someone in his company had been using software to spy on government agencies, all hell would have broken loose. Homeland Security had the manpower to locate the spyholes, the spies, the information leaked, and how it was used. The powerbrokers would have all gone to jail.

Desperate men led to desperate measures, and they could justify it to each other in the end.

I was scared, but I was also majorly ticked as I worked all this out. I snapped a blurry photo through the window and sent it to Graham. I'd sent him one earlier of Rose and company but he hadn't acknowledged it. I assumed he'd identified the cabal by now, but whether he could tell anything from this profile was doubtful. The guy in here was just another peon.

The Top Hat guys never got their hands dirty—but one of these days, I was going to nail a witness who would squeal. This was as good a place as any to start.

With no police to back me up, I didn't have a lot of alternatives. I needed to halt whatever he was doing.

I shoved open one of the double doors, aimed the fire extinguisher, and opened a stream of foam on his trash can. It was very definitely Wyatt Bates who looked up. I needed to run, but working out the cover-up hadn't cooled me off. I was geared for a fight.

The Big Guy bellowed and came after me. I kept spraying, knocking out his computer and the trash can fire, while liberally coating him with foam. I didn't know what was in this stuff, but it couldn't be good for the eyes.

He reached for his coat pocket. Uh oh.

I flung the extinguisher at his head and took to my heels.

I aimed for the nearest fire door but it burst open under the power of several camouflage-jacketed goons carrying very large weapons. I could probably recognize an Uzi if pressed, but guns were guns. They all killed.

I was so outta there. Not taking time to determine if they were good guys or bad, I turned and zig-zagged in the other direction.

As expected, automatic gunfire rang out behind me—but no bullets whizzed by my head. I figured it was just a matter of time.

Tudor's worried face peered around the corner from the lobby. At my gesture, he disappeared.

I hated this skirt. I skidded around the corner just as more gunfire broke loose. This time, bullets hit the wall behind me. That made them bad guys in my book.

Tudor was outside, shouting into his phone as I burst through the glass doors. I didn't hear heavy footsteps following. I figured the gunmen were finding a less obvious line of attack than running into the street spraying cars and pedestrians with lead.

"Outta here!" I shouted, grabbing Tudor's arm and dragging him through the line of traffic inching down the street. We ran into a Starbucks packed with frantic people trying to call home. Our abrupt entrance hardly rated a second glance. They hadn't heard the gunfire and were dealing with their own individual calamities.

I prayed the gunmen wouldn't mow down an entire coffee shop full of innocent people. "Safety in numbers," I told Tudor, pulling out my phone and hitting up Graham's name. "Go look anonymous in some corner and keep on doing whatever you're doing."

"I can't. We're too far out of range," he protested. "I need back in the building. The Wi-Fi in these places suck."

"We need you alive more than we need the internet fixed." I shoved him into a chair and stood in front of him, while watching out the plate glass window. No armed men emerged from MacroWare's front door.

I got Graham's voice mail again. "Goons just shot Wyatt Bates. He was burning papers and sabotaging something from a computer. Tudor can't get in to the network to find out what. Your call now. I'm just sitting here waiting for my limo to roll by."

Okay, so I'd already changed my mind about isolating myself—a limo worked just fine when gunmen were on your tail.

Twenty-five

THE DIN IN THE COFFEE SHOP sounded like Tudor's bunk on a Saturday night. He shut out the noise and tried to access the network he'd found inside MacroWare, but it had gone off line. Ana had probably fragged it.

Muttering all the profanities he knew and inventing a few more, he tried the Starbucks Wi-Fi to reach Graham, but it was overwhelmed by the frantic crowd.

Graham hadn't trusted him with an internet connection not directly under his supervision, but Tudor knew his sister had one. "I need your cell hotspot," he told Ana, who was looking decidedly grim as she talked into her mobile and held up a finger to tell him to hold on.

Knackered, gutted, ready to return to a boring school room, he glanced out the plate glass front windows. People were running away from MacroWare's office. His gut clenched with fear, as if this were a real war zone. He wanted to burrow down under a table and hide but figured that would look pretty dodgy.

The geek squad from MacroWare poured through traffic in this direction, and Ana stiffened. Did she see the gunmen? He strained to look, but she handed him her phone. "Give me yours. Take this and find a place with lots of exits and a good sight line."

"Won't work," he protested. "I need Graham's satellite connections or something way stronger than cellular to finish this job. I just wanted to see what was happening over there." He connected her phone with the netbook, but he was really getting scared. No cops, no emergency services, and gunmen with automatics were the worst kind of cock-up.

"All right," she reluctantly conceded, watching MacroWare's employees stream into the already crowded shop. "Call Mallard, tell him to use his creativity to get you past the cops and in the back door of the house. There's a limo out there somewhere, give it a call, but I doubt it can fly over gridlock. Don't get arrested. Go save the world. I'll take care of the stampeding camels."

That made no sense at all, but confident Ana could do as she said, Tudor headed for the back door. He'd learned bolt holes at his mother's knee.

Ana holds a meeting

THE MACROWARE GEEKS running across the street were frantically shouting into their phones. Even the panicked crowd inside the shop noticed as the first few burst in shouting "Call the cops! We can't reach 911! It's a terrorist attack!"

I sighed. That was bound to lead to logical thought and sensible results.

"Just common ordinary criminals," I shouted back. A woman standing next to me kept yelling into her pricey Peanut phone. Irritated, I snatched it away. "I need a little attention here," I yelled. She smacked at me but I was already climbing on a table—not a pretty sight in the crappy skirt.

"The cyber-attack is coming from inside MacroWare. They've blocked emergency services," I fabricated. The roar of hysteria didn't lessen. "All of you, sit the hell down!"

No one listened. I kicked the shoulder of a big man shouting into his cell. He turned to glare, and I took his phone too. "Pay attention! Shut this crowd down so we can save ourselves."

The clamor reached jet engine decibels. I couldn't possibly yell over it.

When the big man didn't seem interested in helping me, I figured he deserved what came next. I pulled my super-whistle from under my blouse and blew hard enough to puncture eardrums. In a small room like this, the effect echoed off high ceilings and ricocheted like bullets.

That did the trick. People held their ears and turned to glare. Well, I'd tried to make them listen. Every time someone started talking, I shrieked the whistle. Even dogs learn after a while. The crowd started thumping any of their fellows stupid enough to argue.

"Where are the gunmen now?" I asked one of the late arrivals.

"Searching the building," he shouted over the heads of my audience. "Wyatt was supposed to be getting us back online while we waited for the fire department. What's going on?"

Okay, the smoke had been a distraction. That made sense.

"The city is shut down," I told them. "Emergency services can't get through. And my bet is that Wyatt wanted it that way. I'm also betting he's dead and the gunmen aren't."

That got the crowd murmuring again. Only half the people in here knew what I was talking about.

While I waited for the crowd to sort things out and more MW employees squeezed in, I handed the big guy's phone back to him and unwillingly gave up the pricey Peanut-phone. I hated being stuck with Tudor's piece of crap, but at least it had Graham's secret contact number in it.

"You've got two choices," I informed the crowd once I had them listening again. "I can't make them for you. Wyatt sold you out. I don't know how badly he's sabotaged your servers, but all emergency services are currently offline, and that seems to include jamming the street traffic computers. He was killed before he completed whatever he was doing."

Whispers passed through the crowd. People were snapping shots of me, making me nervous. But I had my hair hidden by my knit hat and still wore the bulky coat. I shouldn't be too recognizable. They waited for me to finish, and that was all I could ask.

"The goons who killed Wyatt are still out there, probably looking for me. I didn't interview them and don't know." That produced some nervous giggles. "You could, and probably should, try to find your way home and hide until the dust settles."

"And the alternative?" some smart ass in back asked.

I focused on that guy because he was paying attention and reading between the lines. No geek glasses or knit cap, big build—I pegged him for ex-military, at the very least. Testosterone driven, for certain. Interesting. "You go back in and straighten out whatever Wyatt did and bring the city back to its feet again."

Several people cheered that suggestion. I figured they weren't MacroWare employees who would have to risk their necks.

"Anyone choosing to go back in—find a leader," I suggested. I didn't see any pin-stripe suits in here ready to earn their hefty salaries and lead their employees into the fray. "You're going to need someone to coordinate your efforts."

"What about you?" military guy asked.

"I don't have your knowledge of computers. And I have some bad asses to kick." Just as soon as I figured out how to go where I needed to be to kick them.

I jumped down from the table and left them arguing. I didn't hold out a lot of hope for an office full of sales people, but I'd done the best I could. Sales people knew other people. They could make it work if they put their heads together.

People tried to grab me to ask questions, as if I were the only authority around, but I didn't have any answers. I threatened them with the whistle if they held me up, and stepped on toes until they let me pass—out the back, after Tudor.

I discarded my black coat on an employee coat rack and stole an equally cheap fake-down jacket in bilious green nylon. It had one of those squared-off, billed caps smashed into the pocket. I wasn't squeamish about lice when bullets were more likely, so I left my black knit in trade. Then I eased into the alley, keeping my eye out for goons with guns. In the growing dusk, I was as likely to startle them as vice versa.

I checked Tudor's phone and hit up Graham's fake number. "You might want to meet me at the hospital," I cheerfully told his voice mail. The call would go through as Tudor's, but I didn't think he'd have a problem figuring out the trade-off. "Or maybe not, because I'm going to kick your shins for not answering our calls."

I traipsed down the alley and headed for the nearest Metro. I wasn't hiking out to the hospital in this weather.

Wyatt had been a peon. He may have killed Hilda, but a hired professional had killed Kita. I couldn't see a geek salesmen like Wyatt knowing assassins. And the poison plan... well, he might have come up with some portion of that, but he wasn't high enough up the MacroWare ladder to have been at the head honcho table, and I was betting he wasn't smart enough to be there either. Wyatt was merely the puppet. I was after the puppet master.

There had been only one person at MacroWare with the clout and financial skills to associate mortgage companies, MacroWare, and Top Hat. I didn't have all the connections yet. I couldn't envision Wyatt poisoning his own brother, for instance. And it was hard to see how anyone at the head table thought they'd survive if they poisoned themselves along with everyone else. But time was running out. I had to start asking the really tough questions from men who were surrounded by security.

The Metro was chaos but still operating. I was feeling lonely out here on my own, facing another foray into the impossible. A normal person would have called it a day, gone home and had dinner and let Graham handle his own idiot problems.

Unfortunately, I wasn't bent that way.

Tudor finally texted that he was safely in the carriage house. That didn't mean he hadn't been seen or that the police wouldn't come calling. I just had to hope that the cops or the FBI would be safer than gunmen.

I had no idea how to reach my objective once I arrived at the hospital where the MacroWare execs resided. The poisoned CEOs were out of ICU the last I'd heard, but it wasn't as if anyone was advertising where they'd been moved. I could look for floors with heavy security, I supposed. The hospital had coyly refrained from posting a map of their internal corridors anywhere on-line.

I hit the first restroom I found when I entered the main doors. I needed to stash my bilious green coat but I figured I wouldn't get it back if I left it on a stall hook. Hospital environments are so darned sanitary and uncluttered.

The phone rang, although since it was Tudor's, I didn't recognize the ring. I glanced at the number and it appeared to be an international call. "What floor?" I demanded, hoping it was Graham but figuring I could scare Magda if she was trying to call Tudor.

"Cafeteria, basement, kitchen door. The food tray racks are lined up there."

Graham clicked off before I could tell him that rolling racks couldn't talk and wouldn't help me find anyone.

I found a directory map of the hospital lay-out, located the cafeteria and employee-only areas, and took the elevator down. Maybe I should become a kitchen worker. I could reside in my natural underground habitat all day and theoretically never get shot at.

Given my personality, that probably wasn't a sound theory.

The bilious green coat got stashed in an unlocked locker. In the laundry room, I debated camouflage. I preferred anonymous scrubs. But I didn't want to give up the bag of tricks in my attaché, and I was wearing black pumps. Not too many overworked nursing assistants wore pumps and carried attachés. So white coat it was.

I hoped Graham had eliminated security down here because I had no name tag and no ID and no business in these environs. I sauntered into the kitchen corridor as if I belonged. Hoping my white coat was camouflage, I took a clipboard out of a rack and began flipping through charts, pretending I had a clue what to expect.

"About time you got here," a familiar rich baritone complained.

A tray rack mysteriously emerged from the ranks and rolled toward the elevators. "The top floor patients complain if we're even a minute late," the rack said.

I gaped, strode after the talking metal frame, and tried to process. Graham couldn't have an intercom in here. He had to be right here, speaking to me *in person*. The spy in the attic was out in public!

I assumed he was actually speaking for someone else's benefit, since I didn't care if privileged patients learned how it felt to go hungry. I glanced around and saw a couple of salmon-coated workers heading our direction.

I was having a hard time grappling with the knowledge that Graham had actually emerged from his techno-cocoon to help me. My brain was a little slow from shock, but it caught up.

"Room 1140 will complain when he sees that diet," I said, flipping pages authoritatively for the benefit of our audience. "Let's get this over."

We rolled the tray rack into the freight elevator as soon as the doors opened. They closed without alarms screaming.

"Security could be waiting when we get off," I murmured, trying to see around the rack concealing my nemesis. Graham wasn't exactly invisible in any setting. He needed to stay between the tall rack and wall just to conceal his conspicuous height.

"I *am* security," he murmured back, sending a thrill up my spine. I do love a man with authority who knew how to use it.

"Mrs. Stiles didn't think you were," I reminded him, trying to keep my attitude while my hormones were reacting to his proximity.

"Louisa only knows what she's been told. And she's one of the reasons I don't want my cover blown, so let's try to play this safe. Our patients are due to be dismissed in the morning."

I wasn't lonely anymore. And my hunger wasn't for food.

Graham was the only man who could distract me with just the sound of his voice. Knowing that he came to help me gave me a thrill beyond the physical. I wasn't used to having reliable back-up. Grasping that I wasn't out here on my own would take a while, but I liked the way it felt.

We emerged in a hushed corridor of closed suite doors. Uniformed security watched us pass without question. I didn't dare ask Graham how he had arranged that. As he'd said, he got paid the big bucks because he had the big connections.

Unlike hospitals I was familiar with, no weeping relatives, screaming patients, loud TVs, or chattering nurses broke the smothering seclusion of this private floor. I wanted to rattle aluminum pans and wake everyone up, except our rack contained carefully wrapped and arranged china on heating trays.

"Where's a little fish poison when it's needed?" I muttered, consulting my useless clipboard while Graham located the suite we wanted.

I sure hoped Graham had picked the same suspect I had anyway. It wasn't as if he'd acknowledged any of my messages. But we're both pretty biased against Paul Rose supporters, so I hoped he'd connected the dots.

He knocked politely on a closed door. At a murmur from inside, I opened the double doors and let the rack roll in. I still couldn't see Graham, just his blue scrubs through the shelves. If anyone noticed, they ought to be suspicious about the rolling frame in a private room, but no one appeared to complain. Security had to be watching... but if Graham was actually working undercover security... Wow, just wow.

Feeling truly empowered for a change, I turned my attention to the patient in the bed. This wasn't a simple cot but a large, adjustable mattress. It sat up like any hospital bed except it had a lovely desk that could be rolled across the patient's lap.

The last picture of Bob Stark, Macro's financial officer, I'd seen had shown a short, balding, rotund man. I couldn't tell his height from his sitting position. He was still hair-challenged. But judging by the space between his desk and his belly, he'd lost a few pounds. He glanced eagerly at the food tray, so I assumed he was still a good eater despite the poisoning incident.

Graham remained ominously silent. Despite his prior

diplomatic life, he wasn't precisely a people person these days. That made this my show. How the hell did I get this guy to talk?

"Hello, Mr. Stark. How are you feeling today?" I casually walked to the side of the bed and removed the bell pull from his reach. I took his laptop off his desk as if I, indeed, intended to feed him. "We need to talk, if you'd like to put your phone down for just a minute." I snatched his very nice smart phone from his hand.

While he shouted a protest, I glanced at the phone screen. A line of calls to several local numbers without names. I switched on *record* and handed it off to Graham behind my back. I was hoping the phone numbers were evidence and the recording legal, but mostly, I wanted answers.

"Those aren't very nice words," I told him when he stopped cursing and started to climb out of the bed after his precious phone. He was wearing starched blue pajamas. How cute.

He grabbed for me. I caught his arm, twisted it, and pinched my fingers into the pressure point at his elbow, nearly bringing him to his knees. Then I shoved him back in the bed. I'd brought down bigger men. This one was still too weak to put up a fight. "Talk is all I want to do. Unfortunately, that isn't all you did to Wyatt Bates, is it?"

"I don't know what the hell you're talking about." He rubbed his arm and glared but he wasn't stupid enough to think he could overpower me. This was a man accustomed to paying others to do his dirty work for him. He yanked his covers back over his designer pajamas. "Who are you?"

"I'm usually just an observer, but mostly, I seek the truth. Wyatt Bates had a creative mind, but he wasn't particularly smart, was he?" I liked to lead my victims down the garden path until they were so lost in the maze, they panicked.

"Why are you asking me? He didn't get poisoned. I did. Are you saying he was the one who poisoned us?" His gaze shifted from the window to the door, as if hoping Superman would rush to the rescue. The tray rack nicely blocked the doors and this was the top floor. No one was entering without heavy weapons or a helicopter.

"I'm thinking initially, Henry Bates poisoned everyone." *Unwittingly* went unsaid. I just liked seeing the shock on his face.

He looked upset enough not to have known. "You're kidding me! Henry was a straight arrow. Why the hell would he do that?"

"Because Wyatt tricked him into it. You didn't know that?" I really wanted the timeline here, but I didn't have a lot of experience at interrogation.

"Wyatt was Henry's brother! Why would he poison him?" He was shocked, all right, but he was frowning in thought and still not looking me in the face. Starks was not a stupid man. He knew more than he was saying.

"I'm waiting for you to tell me," I said casually, "Or I'll have to call the cops and let them ask the questions."

"Don't be ridiculous. Get out of here or I'll yell for the nurse." He crossed his arms over his plump chest and looked like an angry bald elf.

"You do realize that Wyatt is lying in a pool of blood back in MacroWare's conference room, don't you?" I asked, watching his reaction with interest.

He flinched. "Wyatt? Why would anyone kill that overgrown puppy?"

He was a very bad liar. And he'd quit threatening to yell for the nurse as proof. "You know why, don't you? I'm guessing the police won't let you go too far." I sat at the foot of his bed and tried to look helpful. "If you'll just give me the bare details, I'll arrange to have your accomplices rounded up before you get out of here. Less retaliation that way, don't you think?"

He turned on his side to reach beneath his pillow.

Graham broke cover and probably broke Stark's arm in the process.

Twenty-six

STARK SCREAMED as if he'd been stabbed and struggled to escape Graham's grip. Undeterred, Graham strong-armed the patient off the bed, letting Stark dangle in the air while I removed a pistol from under the pillow. Nothing said paranoid like a gun in a hospital bed.

Despite the screams, no one came running. Nice soundproofing or Graham had paid everyone to disappear. Given that I'm not in favor of violence, that last possibility was a little discomfiting.

"Shame on you. Weapons aren't allowed in here!" I said in a tone reserved for naughty schoolboys as I snatched the gun.

I hated guns, but I knew how they worked. This was just a small semi-automatic. I removed the bullets and flushed them down the toilet. I stuck the empty pistol in the back of my skirt, beneath my jacket.

Graham growled unhappily at my disarmament—he would have liked me to hold a gun on Stark, but I'd seen too much blood in my lifetime to consider spilling more.

Reluctantly, my personal bodyguard played nice and dropped our patient back to the bed. Graham's Hulk performance was almost as erotic as his James Bond diamond-cufflink routine. He needed to go back to hiding behind the rack so I could keep my head focused.

Stark yanked the covers around him and glared at the towering, broad-shouldered "kitchen worker" who'd so easily manhandled him. Graham wore a cute paper hat over his distinctive thick black hair. He had it pulled half way down his forehead to hide the burn scars. His blue smock couldn't conceal the muscular build he worked hard to maintain.

"Don't mind Tommy," I said cheerfully, warmed by Graham's scowl. "He's just here to make certain I don't hurt anyone."

I thought I heard Graham snort, but maybe I imagined it. "Now, back to the subject—why don't you just tell us what you know and let us take it from there?"

Graham crossed his bare arms over his massive chest and glowered more fiercely. Stark shrank back against his pillows.

Amazing how cowardly the Wizard of Oz was once he was exposed.

"I'm only the numbers guy," Stark protested weakly.

"Who sold all his MacroWare stock right after the hole in the beta program was reported," I added, so he knew we weren't bluffing. Much. "Insider trading."

My knowledge deflated his arrogance, and he sighed in defeat. "They were supposed to patch the breach at the first hint of discovery, but no one expected *Stiles* to find out first! In just one day, he'd dug out a list of people involved and wanted canned. The stupid ass didn't care that mass firings almost guarantees the media would pounce. Stiles wouldn't listen to reason."

Looking overwhelmed and gray—my guess was that Stark really hadn't recovered his health—he glanced longingly at the phone Graham had shoved in his smock pocket. Graham faded back behind the tray rack again, out of reach.

If I knew him at all, he was performing magic with the phone's insides. I hoped he didn't mess with the recording. Just in case, I set Tudor's to record. I held it up and said "Record" aloud so I could say he'd been warned. I didn't think Stark was really connecting to reality, but that was his problem.

At my steely glare, Stark sighed. "After Stephen learned about the leak in the beta program, Henry admitted that he'd had it created to measure how the program was being used," Stark said. "The company was anxious to get the new release right. The government was threatening to take bids on Peanut machines instead of ours if we screwed up the new system. We'd lose half our customers and most of our profit if they switched to Peanut instead of MacroWare. We couldn't afford to take the hit."

"Right," I said, wanting to get past the obvious. "And since the government that you love to hate started getting cranky about mortgage and banking fraud as well, your personal stress levels had already skyrocketed and you couldn't take more, right? So you thought you'd use that handy hole for more than market analysis." Brick by brick, I built my cynical case. I hope the cops appreciated this when we handed the phones over.

He shrugged and looked unrepentant. "My family's mortgage firm hasn't done anything illegal. The financial committee's legislation is simply government harassment. We just wanted to know which way the wind blew so we could act accordingly. If Henry was helping Wyatt make government contacts, why shouldn't my family get a little benefit?"

Ha, he'd just admitted what I'd suspected. This was no criminal mastermind, just a greedy man who protected his own—even if it meant screwing everyone else. Had to love that attitude.

"To clarify—" I said with only a touch of sarcasm. "You needed to know when to sell off all your underwater loans to government entities before they went bad, got that. The spyhole into the banking committee was just a security measure."

"My family doesn't make bad loans," he said stiffly. "It would be bad business."

"No, you just offer loans as favors to good buddies; I totally understand. So instead of just sending the holy software—" Sarcasm laced my tone. "—to beta testers, you arranged for the beta program to go to banking committees, the *NSA*, and who knows who else."

"I did not authorize giving the program to anyone in the NSA," he said stiffly.

Interesting. More fingers in the pie, but I'd already known that. Rose's cabal wouldn't miss a lucrative opportunity like a spyhole. "How did Wyatt Bates fit into the picture? He's little more than a software distributor, but the mortgage your family gave him is seriously underwater."

Stark put on his stubborn face. "He's a good company man with a good salary who needed a mortgage, and he was Henry's brother. Henry simply suggested that Wyatt use Goldrich like everyone else in the company. My family gives favorable terms to MacroWare employees because they know we pay well."

I tried not to roll my eyes. "I've seen the numbers. You loaned more than they could possibly pay, collecting *interest* in the form of favors. Again, I understand, so let's not be coy. Spell it out for me in simple words. Did Stiles know that you asked Wyatt to give *government entities* beta programs containing a spyhole?"

"It wasn't a spyhole!" Stark insisted heatedly. "They were *test* programs. Everyone knows that."

"Sure they were. And if even the NSA couldn't detect the flaw, you and your buddies could have installed those corrupted programs anywhere and everywhere. Oh what fun that would be, reading and uploading private data from the entire internet! I can just imagine the applications and profits," I said, patting his feet sympathetically through the covers. "I bet you found lots of nice people who were interested. What a lucrative sideline!"

I was thinking of Senator Paul Rose's rich and powerful friends, but I didn't want to lead the witness.

"Government regulations are destroying the free market," Stark agreed, without seeing the irony. "We were performing a patriotic service. But then some idiot hacker, probably a pimple-faced Russian troll with nothing better to do—" I winced at this description of Tudor. "—hacked a government website through the hole and all hell broke loose."

"And Stiles went ballistic," I simplified pleasantly, as if we were all in this together.

Of course, the minute his dead boss's name came up, so did Stark's defenses. "We could have fixed the problem internally," he insisted. "But Stiles got all huffy about ethics and called outside security, which was when Wyatt panicked. He said he needed time to change out the programs. I figured there wasn't time to exchange or repair all those systems before the press got hold of the news. That's when I bailed. So, I sold out. Sue me."

"You didn't know Wyatt was stupid enough to delay or try to stop the program exchange entirely with fish poison?" I asked, not hiding my incredulity. It made total, rational sense that Bob Starks and Henry Bates would hate to give up their lovely little spyhole— and so would Top Hat and Goldrich. And he was telling me he didn't know about Wyatt's plan to stop Stiles?

"Did you think I'd have eaten the damned soup if I'd known?" Stark asked in genuine umbrage. "Wyatt was a fruitcake. If I'd known that, I would never have involved him."

"So you had him eliminated, nice." I sat back and tried that version on for size.

"I didn't have anyone *eliminated*," Stark said in disgust. "I wouldn't even know how to begin."

"But your family does," Graham said, emerging from his hiding place to hold up the phone. "I just sent your phone records to the police. Want to place any wagers on which of the people you called will spill first?"

I watched an aghast expression cross our patient's face, then fear. Gotcha. He'd warned his family that Wyatt was in panic mode, shutting down MacroWare while trying to glom up emergency services until he'd saved his nasty little hide. I could see where people who knew assassins might cut off their losses by snuffing a wild card who'd lost his usefulness.

"I want a lawyer," Stark replied intelligently, leaning into his pillow and crossing his arms in defiance.

Predictable. People quit talking when attacked. I shot Graham a scowl for his interference, then returned to my interrogation. "Will we find Adolph and Wilhelm alive when the police arrive to pick them up?" I asked, just because I wanted the chain of command spelled out.

He raised his graying eyebrows. "Why would anyone kill Wilhelm? He's a special snowflake who did whatever Hilda told him. I have no idea what he was told."

"I'm pretty sure *Hilda* didn't tell Wilhelm to poison you. She was outraged, she knew about the spyhole, and she suspected someone in the company—probably one of your friends," I explained cheerfully, although I had no evidence other than opportunity and the feeling Goatee Boy had been lying. "Asking for puffer fish soup was probably the inspiration for Wyatt's murderous plot to cover his rear. Who asked for the soup?"

"Stiles was bored easily. He had exotic tastes," Stark said with a shrug. "Tray had a pet cook who fixed the soup and who needed a job. Adolph needed a restaurant. We worked it all out to make Stephen happy. People think we're nerds, but we can brag that we get high on poison fish. We've done it before. It's never made us sick. What does this have to do with anything?"

He really didn't get it, did he? I tried not to sigh too loudly at the testosterone-driven stupidity. "Except Stiles' gourmet requests and your need to get high gave Wyatt ideas. He or one of his compadres took the poisoned fish guts and had Adolph dry them, then called them an aphrodisiac. Do you remember the salt shaker?"

Stark actually seemed to be considering. "The salt shaker Henry passed around telling us he had babes lined up in the hotel, and we'd all get lucky? The shaker was poisoned? That makes no sense."

But I could see that he was mulling over the possibility and accepting it. He looked ready to murder, if he hadn't already.

"Henry trusted his little brother, didn't he? If Wyatt told him the shaker contained an aphrodisiacal drug, he'd take him at his word," I suggested.

Stark shrugged. "Henry had a few problems in the bedroom. We just played along. It's not as if the soup really helps much, and it certainly needed salt."

"Dried and in enough quantity, the fish guts might have put you out of commission for a day or two," I explained. "Wyatt needed time to keep Stiles from following up on the spyware problem and canning everyone concerned."

Stark grimaced. "Wyatt demanded time before we patched all the holes. Stiles was refusing."

Or Top Hat had demanded time. I had no proof. "Stiles would have had entire departments producing patches and updating software immediately," I suggested, "but Wyatt wouldn't want them all patched. He was probably paid well to keep his more vital spyware open. That was a little tricky."

"So Wyatt got Henry to poison us?" he asked, obviously confused.

From his expression, it looked like Stark hadn't done any actual poisoning. He'd just helped create the situation that ended in murder—especially if he'd had a hand in telling fruitcake Wyatt to stall. He didn't seem ready to admit that to me. I'd leave it for the judge. All I wanted was to get Graham and Tudor off the hook.

"Adolph probably dried the fish guts," I told him. "He thought that's all Wyatt wanted, a harmless drug that would at most kill your taste buds, and if he was lucky, make all of you a little ill. He's not fond of any of you."

"So the soup wasn't poison but Henry's damned drug was?" Stark asked, finally catching on.

"Just as poor Kita told the cops, the soup was fine," I said shrugging. "And as I said, the dried fish guts would have done little more than numb your mouths so you couldn't taste the *pièce de résistance*. That's where the real poison comes in. And why someone killed Kita. He knew too much and wasn't loyal to the cause."

Stark looked bleak. "We were drinking that night. Stiles was furious and taking it out on us and we feared for our jobs. We wouldn't have noticed if they'd served cactus needles."

"Exactly. But it was adulterated tomatoes in the risotto and salsa, not cactus needles. You might have all shoved the veggies aside if they tasted off, but you weren't tasting anything."

"Wyatt gave us spoiled tomatoes? That's where the botulism

comes in? I'm glad the bastard's dead," he muttered viciously. "He could have killed us all!"

"Probably not a bad idea in his wasted head, but Wyatt wasn't in the kitchen," I reminded him. "Wilhelm, your aunt's stooge, was. Someone gave Wilhelm spoiled tomatoes to make good and certain the program problem was covered up—which means someone really wanted you dead. Maybe Wilhelm didn't know what was in the tomatoes, maybe he did, but he used them in his vegetable dish and lied about it. With Wyatt's fish toxin weakening your systems and concealing the botulism, the tomatoes could have killed all of you. Kita knew his soup was good, so he may have guessed about the tomatoes and threatened to tell the cops to prove his innocence."

"You have no proof of any of this," Stark argued, frowning in puzzlement. "It makes no sense. We were all helping Wilhelm."

"By telling stupid Wilhelm to listen to crazy Wyatt. Very helpful, indeed," I agreed with sarcasm. "Whose idea was that?"

"Hilda wanted us to find him a job," he said with a shrug, still frowning. "Adolph was eager to do anything to get his restaurant, so he took him on, even without papers. Wyatt was supposed to know people in D.C. who could help him become legal."

"And there it is," I said with disgust, seeing most of my Top Hat conspiracy theories go up in flame. "Wilhelm did whatever Wyatt said so he could be legal. Wilhelm had no way of knowing that Wyatt wasn't your friend. He was brought in at the last minute, not given what he needed for the recipe, and took anything anyone offered. Wonder how Wyatt delivered those tomatoes?"

"But why?" he asked. "Why would he want to kill us?"

Since it was obvious Stark couldn't provide answers, I spun my ideas further. I didn't want to give up on the banking conspiracy.

"Wyatt didn't need you anymore. You and Hilda had thoughtfully provided his big house, and he'd met some influential new friends who really liked the spyholes and didn't want them closed and were willing to pay well to keep them open. Have you no understanding of human nature at all?" I shook my head in despair. "Some men prefer to skip out rather than pay back what they owe."

Stark was a finance man. He got the reference, if not the analogy. "Someone else offered to pay off Wyatt's loan," he suggested wearily. "Someone else bought Wyatt, and he didn't need MacroWare anymore."

"Probably. Kill two birds with one stone," I added cruelly. "Wyatt could get rid of all the high muckety-mucks to whom he owed favors, the brother who got all the accolades, dump his debt, and gain the favor of some rather nasty folks who shoot fish chefs— although he was too dim to figure that out."

"Who?" Stark demanded. "Who helped Wyatt?"

Pity I didn't have the evidence to convict Paul Rose and Friends so Stark could send his loan sharks after them. I had to confess my ignorance. "Besides you? I assume the same people who wanted the beta spyhole installed in the first place. Have any good ideas?"

His eyes widened ever so slightly. He had a good idea. He shook his head negatively, but I could tell he was making mental notes.

He wouldn't tell me. Okay, we'd let that one play out. Judgment day was coming. One of these days, I hoped to be on the jury.

"Make a list of suspects to hand to the police," I suggested. "Maybe they'll give you a commendation for your helpfulness." Probably not. The police wouldn't touch any execs in the Top Hat cabal with whips, chains, and Uzis. They'd call Wyatt a serial killer, Wilhelm an accomplice, and end it there. Poor Kita's assassin would never be found.

Graham tapped his earbud and shoved the rack out of way of the door. "Time to go."

I trusted his early warning system and got up off the bed.

"Have a nice day," I told Stark, who appeared as if he would weep. "I'm sure you can afford a good lawyer. After all, all you did was have your family kill a killer. Convenient that shooting Wyatt wiped out the evidence of the rest of the conspiracy, but what the heck. After that, a little insider trading is nothing."

I knew in my heart and soul that the buck didn't stop at Stark. But Wyatt had been the key to the plot, and he was gone. I'd read the police files later, but I was pretty certain they didn't have the manpower to find hired assassins.

Unless I called in Magda, I simply didn't have the resources to go after whoever had paid Wyatt—without endangering everyone in my family. I could hope someone got stupid and spilled. In the meantime, I kept copious files and held grudges.

I skedaddled after Graham, hiding behind the huge cart as best as I could so anyone approaching wouldn't see me. We used the racks at the elevator as a wall between us and the corridor.

The elevator doors opened, and the police captain who had come to our door looking for Graham stepped out. I nearly had a heart attack. The cop looked grim and had a few rather determined men in blue with him.

Why did I think they were hoping to catch Graham and not our guilty patient?

The cops brushed right past us without looking our way.

With more nerve than sense, we rolled the cart past them and closed the elevator doors.

Once the door was shut, I held out my hand and pretended my heart wasn't jumping out of my chest. "You can have the SIM card, but I want that pretty phone."

"Buy your own," he said grimly. "You're worth millions."

I glared at him in incredulity. "I just got you out of a murder rap, and this is how you treat me?" I couldn't smack him. He'd got me into the hospital so I could interrogate my best witness. Without his aid, I'd not have been able to confirm my suspicions. He was still an arrogant ass.

"You scared Wyatt into stopping the entire city," he countered. "I couldn't do anything with emergency services shut down. What if Wyatt really had set fire to MacroWare?" He leaned against the elevator wall and looked more weary than angry. Beard stubble looked good on him.

"I didn't stop the city!" I protested the unfairness of his assessment. "I just stopped Adolph. How was I supposed to know Wyatt had flipped over the edge? As far as I'm concerned, anyone who takes a human life is subhuman and wasn't rational to start with."

"The gun used to kill Hilda and Kita will be traced to Wyatt," Graham informed me as we got off the elevator on the ground floor.

"The chances are pretty good that Wyatt did kill Hilda," I pointed out, hurrying after him as he headed for transportation—I hoped. I needed an express ride home. "Wyatt could have texted the hotel manager to mess with the wiring and black out the room, and Livingston wouldn't have questioned why with chaos breaking loose. All these guys knew each other through MacroWare, one way or another. The police can talk to Tray and Adolph and Livingston and confirm everything. Wyatt was the only one in that room who knew enough to want Hilda to shut up, except Mrs. Stiles, of course."

"Of course," Graham said stonily, with heavy emphasis.

"Oh crap." I got his message. I didn't like it. I tried picturing that small room packed with people and shook my head. "I don't believe she'd dirty her hands like that."

"Probably not," he agreed, heading out a back door near the Metro. "But who do you think had more power to order someone to black out the safe room, Wyatt or Louisa?"

I'd been thinking Wyatt had texted Livingston, but Louisa probably had bodyguards who could have crossed the wires without even involving Livingston. Crap, and double crap. I wanted to go home to my relatively sane family.

"*Louisa* wanted to keep the spyholes?" I asked incredulously.

But now I remembered where I'd see the rose pin similar to one Livingston had been wearing. Louisa Stiles—a Rose supporter?

Graham didn't answer. He just kept stalking across the parking lot, his long legs outstripping mine.

Surely he wasn't taking me to the damned Metro? "What, no helicopter to whisk us to safety?" I asked, seeing nothing that would take us anywhere.

I was agog with curiosity. Graham never showed himself in public, and the Metro was as public as it could get. Besides, I hadn't had time to rescue my ghastly green coat. I was about to freeze my buns off.

He flung his scrubs in the nearest trash can. Underneath, he wore dark trousers and a long-sleeved knit black sweater pushed up to his elbows. "Go home," he said. "I've got clean-up to do."

"I hate you. I really hate you," I told him, tagging on his heels. "You can't hint at Louisa's involvement and walk away."

"Stephen told me she's a closet Rose supporter. He was afraid she was involved in the program cover-up, which was why he was so furious. If even Stark doesn't know that, we can't prove anything."

Before I could formulate a retort, Graham hauled me off my feet and kissed away any form of thought. All my frost melted.

He dropped me as abruptly as he'd kissed me. "Go home, Ana. You've done what I paid you to do. I'll take it from here." He walked faster and slipped into the shadows before we reached the Metro.

I ran to the place where he'd disappeared—a dark alley I didn't want to enter. A motorcycle roared out the other end, in the opposite direction.

Damn the man, I should have kicked his shins when I had the chance.

But the kiss had been infinitely more satisfying in ways I wasn't prepared to consider.

Twenty-seven

TUDOR APPLIED THE FINAL CODE to the O/S patch, backed it up, and shot it off to his cracking new friend in MacroWare's programming department. The swot had caught him cyber-digging in the files, only because he'd been doing the same. Ana had apparently sent the MW employees back to work with fire blazing in their eyes. After these last few hours, Tudor was confident the crew he'd been working with intended to memorialize Stiles by updating all the beta programs overnight.

Once the holes were closed, his wonky cookie monster would be blocked. And the blokes would go looking for whomever or whatever had warped it. For now, they'd taken his code apart and created an anti-virus. And they had servers back online so emergency services should be up and running shortly.

He slumped over the desk and tried to summon his next move.

"Dinner, *now*," the intercom on the desk spluttered.

He snarled, but that was Ana's voice. She was home.

The rush of relief felt weird. Needing to verify that no harm had come to his nutter half-sister, he glanced at the computer clock. It was late for dinner. Mallard must have held it off until she arrived.

With a gut-load of trepidation, Tudor jogged down the stairs, lured by the aroma of pizza well laden with pepperoni.

The whole bloody family had gathered in the dining room—even *Patra*. He couldn't remember how long it had been since he'd seen this many of his family in one place. Patra was actually looking all grown up in a business suit, with her hair done up fancy—a lot like their mother. Tudor tried not to stare. Head down, he headed for the only empty place setting at the bottom of the table.

"We can't talk with a reporter at the table," Ana warned as he sat down. She helped herself to the salad bowl while EG grabbed pizza slices.

"I can keep secrets," Patra insisted. "I helped, didn't I? I get to know what's going on and won't send in anything until you tell me it's okay. Provided you agree to tell me it's okay."

Tudor tried to ignore the give-and-take. He grabbed two slices of pizza.

"Will the news get you the D.C. post?" Nick asked.

Looking particularly daft in his open-necked shirt and scarf, Tudor's half-brother lifted a glass of wine to admire it. Nick was a useless twit most of the time, but Tudor sensed he knew more than he said. The talk about jobs flew right over his head though.

"It might," Patra answered him in satisfaction. "I just sent in a story interviewing the hotel's kitchen staff about the many ways poison could be introduced to food. It blew my boss's lid off. The station is sending their top reporters to steal my MacroWare story, but if I could get a scoop on who saved the day..." She waited hopefully.

No one replied. Feeling the silence, Tudor glanced up from his pizza to see all eyes turned expectantly in his direction. He scrunched his shoulders and tried to disappear, but that wasn't happening.

He glared. "I just sent a working patch for the spyhole to MacroWare's office, if that's what you're asking. They're pretty rattled and still trying to route around the sabotaged servers, but they're installing the patch tonight. That should stop my monster." He dug his teeth into the pizza so he didn't have to say more.

Ana picked up a breadstick and threw it down the table at him. Her aim was blamed accurate. It bounced off his nose. He grabbed it and set it on his plate and scowled, waiting for the usual interrogation.

"Good job, sport," she said. "No more hacking contests for you, right? The cookie monster dies here?"

Just a little chuffed, Tudor nodded and felt the weight of the world lift from his shoulders.

"And MIT in your future?" EG asked with delight. "You'll be over here next year?"

Tudor looked to Ana, who smiled as if she actually anticipated that moment. And maybe she did. Maybe he actually was part of the family, however crazed.

And maybe he was even all right with not being a lone wolf *all* the time. The pizza was better here, anyway.

***

Ana Does Supper

"IF YOU GET THE D.C. JOB with our story, you have to start taking responsibility for some of the family," I said, pointing at Patra.

She looked a little confused. "What can I do? Tudor will be heading back to London, won't he?"

"This is a generic, all-purpose promise to cover whatever happens next." I was damned if I would be the family doormat forever. We all had to be responsible for each other, and we had to make that promise even before I discovered if we could buy mansions.

"I'll try," she agreed dubiously. "Just don't ask me to be a Girl Scout leader."

"You'll do it if EG asks," I said, even though EG looked horrified at the thought.

"And where is our glorious leader?" Nick inquired, filling his salad bowl again.

Mallard had thoughtfully waited until I had reported my arrival time before putting the pizzas in the oven. Out of respect for his efforts, I helped myself to a large slice. I wasn't fond of pepperoni but the marinara smelled wonderful.

"If you're talking about asshat Graham, I assume he's on his way to anonymously feed his police source everything we know, including a recorded confession and a lot of damning phone numbers. If he doesn't, I've got my backup." I held up Tudor's old phone. "Copy this and give me mine back, please." I shoved the phone down the table toward my hacker genius brother.

Patra grabbed the phone mid-table and hit the play button. Tudor tried to snatch it away but once the unfamiliar male voice emerged from the gadget, they quit squabbling and listened.

I was uncomfortable with sharing, but they'd all played a part in unraveling this mystery and deserved answers. There were a lot of questions, but I wasn't the FBI or the cops. Kita and Wyatt had died at the hands of men with enough arrogance and power to hire goons with guns. We had enough evidence to show that Wyatt had killed Hilda, Stiles, and his brother. That didn't mean the buck stopped there. It just meant I'd done my job—for now.

Authorities bigger than I was needed to bring down the brains behind the brawn. With corporations and top execs and untouchables like Louisa Stiles involved, I just didn't see it happening anytime soon.

Maybe, once we had our millions...

No, I could only use *my* share of the money for mayhem. The rest of my half-siblings were entitled to their own choice of rewards—once they reached an age of responsibility, of course. I'd have to work that out if the money was ever ours, but we'd never be in the same tax bracket as Senator Rose and Louisa Stiles—maybe not even the same universe.

"We need Wilhelm and Adolph's confessions," Patra decided once the recording had played. "Wyatt's dead and can't give us any answers. What about the gunmen who killed Kita and Wyatt? Can we track them?"

"I think Euan, Kita's friend, will give the police what Kita knew once she feels safe. That should nail Wilhelm and Adolph," I said, knowing I'd saved this witness for a reason. We'd finally found her a job at an embassy that preferred vegetarian dinners.

"The police should be able to find Wyatt's killers from Stark's phone records," I continued, "but the goons will be long gone underground if they're any good at all. The gunmen won't know a thing about Stiles or who hired them. Murder on this level isn't a quiet little affair of wife shooting hubby. There are multiple levels of cover-up, and the cops only look at the first—and that's Wyatt. They won't go for the root of the evil. Those people will have to be dug out just as if they're terrorists, which they are, in their own way."

Patra brightened. "Now *there's* a story. Money is the root of all evil. I'll start digging into Goldrich."

I tried not to roll my eyes. "This is why Graham doesn't want us here. Someone at Goldrich quite possibly hired assassins. Does this not ring any warning alarms?"

Since Patra's father had been murdered by the clique of wealthy politicians affiliated with Senator Paul Rose and Top Hat, she at least had the sense to hesitate.

"Pick another firm," Nick suggested. "They all play the same games."

"But Goldrich was essentially responsible for the death of good people," Patra protested. "Wyatt may have been the trigger, but Goldrich was his motive."

"I'll take care of Goldrich," I said with satisfaction. "I have a plan that won't involve guns and poison. You just find a nice safe bank to investigate. And should you turn up an honest investment firm, let me know."

All except Tudor waited expectantly for explanations. I took a bite of pizza and chewed contentedly.

The silence grew long enough that even Tudor finally looked up from grazing his way through an entire plate of pizza, including the crust. He apparently processed the last part of our conversation through his formidable computer of a brain, glanced at me, and shrugged.

"She's going to launder money," was all he said—because really, what else do you do with a filthy rich mortgage banking system that kills good people?

"We're going to MIT as soon as you book the train," I told him proudly.

I DIDN'T ACTUALLY INTEND TO LAUNDER MONEY, although I had taken a few courses. I knew how world-class crooks transferred funds to terrorists and into their own pockets without anyone realizing what they were up to. In this digital age, the ways are countless and really don't require a lot of imagination.

But according to my research, the Swiss bank account that Graham had aimed me at contained our grandfather's money and was thus legitimately ours. Our millions were being held hostage by an antiquated banking system that needed a wake-up call.

It was closing in on midnight. I was totally wiped after an entire day of pretending I was an extrovert. I probably should have gone to bed. But isolation restores my energy, and mischief makes me happy. I sat in my basement office, humming, as I delved through the as-yet-unpatched beta system of Goldrich's favorite banking committee. While my Whiz worked its way through boring financial files, I opened the nifty little netbook Tudor had hijacked from the MacroWare offices.

Huh, the netbook operating system had the spyhole, too. Who had been spying on whom? I'd look a little later but figured it was interoffice politics and one asshat snooping on the other.

It was too damned easy for technology to *spy* these days. We had absolutely no privacy. The Whiz was protected by Graham's tech, but it wasn't protected from Graham.

The hole in the banking committee's firewall made it easy to find a file that would auto-send to Goldrich with my remote access attachment. Remote access sounds really cool when we talk about accessing a home computer from work or watching a puppy from a smart phone. Computer technicians use the program to remotely clean computers—normally with permission from the computer's owners. Graham had made a few adjustments.

As I said, nothing is private anymore.

Once I had my little worm past Goldrich's firewalls, I could roam their data mechanically, reading through the files on the Whiz as if they were my own. See? Technology just makes it too damned easy. Who needs drones? If the government would just learn how to manipulate computers distantly, they could wipe out entire countries with the push of a button. Heck, hackers do it all the time, except they stick to small potatoes like identity theft and credit cards.

It took a lot of digging, admittedly. I'm not a finance or security expert. But I knew how to run searches, and I knew the types of documents I needed. I located Goldrich's banking transfer system, fed in the account numbers on my grandfather's Swiss bank account, and pushed a few more buttons. Bank computers talk to each other better than people do.

Numbers began to roll across the screen—nice big fat numbers that made my eyes roll and my head ache. In the morning, the headaches would be someone else's problem.

I set up several dummy investment accounts and let the numbers from the Swiss banks roll into them in increments small enough and spaced out enough to get lost in the crowd of complex transfers flowing in and out of both banks. A fat amount would trigger alarms, but normal buying and selling and cash flow stayed under the safeguards—as long as I didn't do this every night.

I began another automatic transfer that spirited the funds from Goldrich into the Caribbean bank account where our wicked lawyer had concealed his ill-gotten gains until I'd found them. Dollars weren't just pieces of paper anymore. They're numbers on computers all over the world.

In the morning, the Swiss bank would be immensely poorer and would hunt down the culprit—and blame Goldrich. By the time Goldrich located my ghost accounts, they'd be gone. And so would the cash in the Caribbean account. And there wasn't a country in the world with the power to force the Caribbean drug lords to open their books for investigation.

And once I was feeling good and secure with our grandfather's millions tucked away, I set about relieving Goldrich of a lot more dollars. A few deserving people ought to be rewarded. Goldrich needed to pay for some of their bad karma.

"ANA, WHAT THE HELL are you *doing* down there?" a familiar voice roared through the intercom after noon the next day.

I'd collapsed into bed in the wee hours and had just dragged myself into my office a little while ago. I had only had time to take a bite of the egg muffin I'd prepared for myself. I'd wasted valuable minutes carefully cleaning the kitchen so Mallard wouldn't complain.

"You're back," I responded, mouth full of egg. "No one killed you. What a pity." I called up the overnight news on the Whiz as I talked.

Stark and three employees of Goldrich had been arrested on accessory to murder charges—just for hiring assassins to kill Wyatt, mind you. Hilda and Kita were already old news, but the wheels of justice ground slowly. A good D.A. would get there eventually. Stiles and Henry Bates were mentioned as Wyatt's possible victims with much speculation attached.

Patra had a nice byline on the story.

"I'm back," Graham growled. "I'm not blind. What the devil are these Goldrich transactions?"

So many tales to tell... Let me count the ways I could tell them. He really shouldn't be spying on what I was doing with my computers, so I wasn't telling tales any time soon.

"Has Mallard fed you yet?" I asked sweetly. "You sound cranky. Hypoglycemia kicking in?" I opened email from Tudor. He'd bought tickets to Boston on tomorrow's train. I smiled contentedly. We could afford it.

"I'm still setting up the servers," he acknowledged. "I'll eat later. Or come down and strangle you now."

There was the spy in the attic I knew. It warmed my cockles to have him back.

"Check Michael O'Ryan's Facebook page," I suggested. "Then do a search on Euan Yung. I think she and a few of Kita's friends are starting their own restaurant and naming it in his honor. Be right back."

Still munching my muffin, I shut off the intercom and went down the hall to the kitchen. I threw together another sandwich, made an entire pot of coffee, and added it to a tray. Mallard came in to see what I was doing. I grinned and sent the tray up on the dumbwaiter.

"Your mother called yesterday," he said with disapproval and just a little pleasure, because he worships Magda. "She was concerned that no one answered her calls."

"Tudor is telling her about MIT as we speak. She will not be flying in to chastise her little cuckoos this time." Because we were learning to take care of ourselves. I was proud of our accomplishment.

Mallard blinked but didn't question. I left him the dirty frying pan.

Done eating my muffin, I took the hidden staircase up to Graham's office. I was back in my grubbies today, but I'd chosen black leggings that showed off my legs, and my loose fisherman's sweater—with nothing under it.

Wearing his ubiquitous dark trousers and long-sleeved t-shirt, Graham was in his office, plugging in wires and jacks and cables to Uzbekistan for all I knew. He rolled out from beneath his counter, looking like a hunky cat burglar, and glared at my appearance. Okay, he hadn't heard the dumbwaiter arrive with my peace offering.

I went out in the hall and fetched the tray and carried it back to his darkened den. I switched on the overhead lights now that I knew they existed.

Tudor wasn't here. I'd dropped the stolen netbook in his hands as a reward for his heroism. He knew to wipe the contents so all trace of last night's activity would vanish. I'd left him contentedly chatting up his pals from his room.

I locked Graham's door in case anyone got any ideas of coming upstairs to play.

The sports paintings had vanished, probably behind the

monitors dotting the wall again. Unshaven and actually looking disheveled for a change, Graham sipped my coffee offering, and keyed up the one operating screen.

It opened on Michael O'Ryan's Facebook page. The kid was crowing about looking for a real house instead of a rental. It seemed the house they'd previously owned hadn't been foreclosed on after all but sold for a nice profit.

"Sweet," I said with a straight face, pouring myself a cup of coffee, even though I preferred tea. I wanted to savor the moment before we returned to fighting. "Glad someone's getting a new house out of this. I suspect a few MacroWare execs and their minions will be losing theirs in a few months."

I could almost promise they would. I'd shared their underwater mortgage files with all sorts of banking regulators. Some of them were bound to be interested.

The excited announcement on Euan's social media about a foreclosed restaurant falling into her hands scrolled across the monitor next. I shrugged at the old news, took away Graham's keyboard, and called up the local talking heads. A news video showed Adolph and Wilhelm being led handcuffed into a police station.

"I want to know the rest of the story." I crawled under his console and began hooking servers to cable so he could eat, and we could get back to business as usual. Sort of. That we were both in the same space at the same time and not trying to punch the tar out of each other was a significant improvement. With no bed immediately available, I was content with that. For a while.

"The police interview is in your mailbox. Your suspicions were correct. Adolph dried the fish guts for an aphrodisiac at Wyatt's request, in return for a promise that he could have the MacroWare dining franchise in D.C."

"And poor stupid Wilhelm?" I peered out from beneath the console.

Graham had nearly inhaled his muffin. He had two more monitors up and rolling—just like old times.

"Wyatt gave Wilhelm a pint of homemade salsa, said it came from Stiles' wife. It may have, for all we know," Graham said. "Wilhelm wasn't even smart enough to get anything in exchange for using her salsa instead of the one Adolph prepared."

"Except satisfaction in spiting Adolph. I don't think those two are a match made in heaven, but neither of them are murderers, just the vehicle of distribution," I acknowledged.

With all the cables hooked, I crawled out to sit cross-legged on the uncarpeted hard floor. I mentally did an inventory of chairs that could be moved in here. "Where is Louisa now?"

Graham punched a key to show a grainy security video of the elegant Louisa Stiles—still wearing that ostentatious rose pin—climbing into a limo in front of a sprawling mansion. Judging by the rain, I'd say she was back in Seattle. It was a crisp sunny day here in D.C.

And the rose pin had taken on more meaning—had Senator Paul Rose given it to her?

"She's taking a vacation to the Riviera?" I suggested. "Not very satisfying if she was accessory to her husband's death, and maybe even called for Hilda's."

"We don't know any of that," Graham pointed out, bringing up another screen. "But the dead can sometimes speak for themselves. I had this filed this morning."

A last will and testament displayed on the monitor. I took a keyboard, zoomed up, and read the courthouse stamp, proving it had been filed and was public information. I whistled happily as I scanned the verbiage. I'd done enough legal research to recognize the terms.

"You did this yourself? Or did Stiles actually leave everything to his charitable foundation?" I asked with a purr of delight.

"I just made certain that the most recent will got filed," he said enigmatically.

I wasn't about to question. I liked this pretty picture. "Cancer research and poor people in Africa benefit from MacroWare's monopoly instead of Louisa. That's... generous." It wouldn't seem so to Louisa, but I got a vicarious thrill. Justice came in many different forms. Louisa might not go to jail, but she'd suffer in her own way without wealth.

Graham shrugged and sipped his coffee. "She'll have funds stashed away. She won't starve."

"And so we let karma be her judge. I can handle that. My turn." I occupied another screen and smiled proudly as a large MacroWare Alert appeared advising all users of the new beta program to update their software for a security patch.

They'd apparently released the patch while we slept. Good boys and girls.

"That announcement is an admission that the new operating system is already known to be wonky and will seriously mess with stock prices," Graham said dryly.

"I'll buy a bunch of shares when the price plummets," I said with triumph. "MacroWare owes Tudor for fixing their problem."

Graham snorted. "And for getting their executive board murdered and killing their profits for the next year. Your family is dangerous."

"Glad you realize that." I stood and removed the cup from his hand, setting it aside.

My head barely reached his chin. I grabbed his shoulders. He caught my waist. We made it work. Our mouths clung hungrily. His tasted of coffee. I drank him in with more triumph than desperation this time.

Whether he knew it or not, we were equals now.

I had the funds to buy our family mansion back—finally.

Acknowledgments

I cannot begin to thank everyone who has had a hand in keeping this story on the straight and narrow highway instead of the curvy tunnels I sent it through. And if you still think Ana's tale is twisted, then you need to thank those people too. I might have blown your mind otherwise.

My immense gratitude to Mindy Klasky and Jennifer Stevenson, my early beta readers, who jumped up and down and screamed—*where's the motive*? Okay, so I kind of forgot that essential. I'm sure it was in my head when I started! They contributed a great deal more than that as well, but let's face it, it wouldn't have been a book without motive!

And I have to thank my brainstorming buddies way back in Charlotte NC when I conceived the original concept for this series. They not only encouraged me, but aided and abetted its dangerous insanity. Waving at you Nancy Northcott and Harold Lowry!

As always, my sincere gratitude to the entire Book View Café membership. Without their help, support, and encouragement, this series would never have seen the light of day.

Author Bio

With several million books in print and *New York Times* and *USA Today's* bestseller lists under her belt, former CPA Patricia Rice is one of romance's hottest authors. Her emotionally-charged contemporary and historical romances have won numerous awards, including the *RT Book Reviews* Reviewers Choice and Career Achievement Awards. Her books have been honored as Romance Writers of America RITA® finalists in the historical, regency and contemporary categories.

A firm believer in happily-ever-after, Patricia Rice is married to her high school sweetheart and has two children. A native of Kentucky and New York, a past resident of North Carolina and Missouri, she currently resides in Southern California, and now does accounting only for herself. She is a member of Romance Writers of America, the Authors Guild, and Novelists, Inc.

For further information, visit Patricia's network:
http://www.patriciarice.com
http://www.facebook.com/OfficialPatriciaRice
https://twitter.com/Patricia_Rice
http://patriciarice.blogspot.com/
http://www.wordwenches.com

Manufactured by Amazon.ca
Bolton, ON

33900154R00138